Fox River Valley PLD
555 Barrington Ave., Dundee, IL 60118
www.frvpld.info
Renew online or call 847-590-8706

The
FACE *of the*
EARTH

Center Point
Large Print

Also by Deborah Raney and available from Center Point Large Print:

After All

**This Large Print Book carries the
Seal of Approval of N.A.V.H.**

The
FACE *of the*
EARTH

DEBORAH
RANEY

CENTER POINT LARGE PRINT
THORNDIKE, MAINE

This Center Point Large Print edition is published in the
year 2013 by arrangement with Howard Books,
a division of Simon & Schuster, Inc.

Scripture quotations are taken from the Holy Bible, New
King James version. Copyright © 1982 by Thomas
Nelson, Inc. Used by permission. All rights reserved.

This book is a work of fiction. Any references
to historical events, real people, or real places are used
fictitiously. Other names, characters, places, and events
are products of the author's imagination, and any
resemblance to actual events or places or persons,
living or dead, is entirely coincidental.

The text of this Large Print edition is unabridged.
In other aspects, this book may
vary from the original edition.
Printed in the United States of America
on permanent paper.
Set in 16-point Times New Roman type.

ISBN: 978-1-61173-759-2

Library of Congress Cataloging-in-Publication Data

Raney, Deborah.
The face of the Earth / Deborah Raney.
pages ; cm.
ISBN 978-1-61173-759-2 (library binding : alk. paper)
1. Large type books. I. Title.
PS3568.A562F33 2013b
813′.54—dc23

2012051791

For the Raney brothers: Ty, Steve & Phillip,
who practically wrote this book for me

God, who made the world and everything in it,
since He is Lord of heaven and earth,
does not dwell in temples made with hands.
Nor is He worshiped with men's hands, as
though He needed anything,
since He gives to all life, breath, and all things.
And He has made from one blood every nation
of men
to dwell on all the face of the earth, and has
determined their preappointed times
and the boundaries of their dwellings, so that
they should seek the Lord,
in the hope that they might grope for Him and
find Him,
though He is not far from each one of us;
for in Him we live and move and have our
being . . .

—Acts 17:24–28a

Acknowledgments

I had a host of friends help me with brainstorming this novel, starting with my three imaginative brothers-in-law who enthusiastically gave their input one afternoon at a Raney family reunion. What fun that was! Thank you, Ty, Steve, and Phillip. All those childhood escapades on the river, the railroad bridge, and at the lake sure paid off for me!

As always, the Kansas 8 in Kansas City, and the Stark, Kansas, retreat crew added their insights and encouragement, as did my critique partner and dear friend, Tamera Alexander; my longtime friend and first reader, Terry Stucky; fellow author and encourager, Courtney Walsh; my sweet Club Deb friends; and my beloved sisters and brother. I have been blessed to overflowing in the friend department!

My agent, Steve Laube, remains the best! As do my talented editors at Howard/Simon & Schuster, especially Beth Adams, whose insights and ideas added so much to this story.

To my wonderful parents and my mother-in-law, our four incredible children and their spouses, our growing "quiver" of grandchildren, and the amazing extended family God has given us: God bless you! You all are the absolute joys of my life.

To my husband, Ken: Who would ever have dreamed this winding road we've traveled would land us at such a sweet, sweet destination? I can't wait to see what the Lord has in store for the years still to come. I couldn't love you more.

SEPTEMBER

1

Friday, September 3

Mitchell Brannon fastened his seatbelt and navigated his Saturn through the Sylvia High School parking lot. "Good riddance," he muttered, tossing a look over his shoulder at the run-down brick school building. Most of the time he loved his job, but this school year had gotten off to a rocky start and—today anyway—he would hand over his principal's "badge" in a heartbeat.

Too bad the weather had taken a turn that felt more like the advent of winter than Labor Day. He flipped on the wipers and waited for them to whisk away the raindrops collecting on the windshield. At least it wasn't freezing.

He hoped Jill hadn't hit any weather on her way home from Kansas City today. But as much as his wife hated driving in the rain, from their phone call last night he knew she was ready to be home. He stopped at the entrance to the street, dug his cell phone from his pocket, and punched in her number.

It went straight to voice mail. She was probably in that dead zone around Oak Ridge. That or she forgot to charge her phone. "Hey, you," he said, when the beep sounded. "Just wondering where you are. Give me a call so I know when to start the steaks."

He'd had to do some fast talking to convince his wife to take a couple of days away from a classroom of third graders who adored her and to make time for this professional development conference. But he knew it would be a good distraction for Jill. Their last little bird had flown the nest last weekend, and Jill had been in mourning ever since.

They'd delivered Katie to the University of Kansas on Sunday, and from the gallon of tears Jill had shed since, you'd have thought they'd buried the girl instead of merely transporting her over the Missouri state line. Even though it was nice having Evan and Katie at the same college, their kids were almost six hours from home, and it had hit Jill hard.

They'd contemplated heading to their lake cabin to celebrate their first weekend as empty nesters, but because Jill had been at the conference since Wednesday, she'd talked him into a "stay-cation"—something she'd read about in her latest women's magazine.

"Besides," she'd told him, "it would be silly to go somewhere and spend money we can't afford when we finally have the whole house to ourselves."

The house-to-themselves aspect sounded promising. She agreed not to mope and tried to wheedle a promise out of him to not do any yard work or watch any football.

Now *that* was pushing it. "How about I'll help you grade papers if I can watch football?"

She'd cocked her head, a spark lighting her eyes. "I'll see your football and raise you steaks on the grill."

"Deal," he'd said, before she could change her mind.

Turning onto their street, he touched the garage door opener and smiled. He would never voice it while she was still missing the kids so much, but he was beyond happy they'd finally reached this milestone. He'd loved every minute of raising Evan and Katie, but he was ready for it to be just the two of them again.

He tapped the brakes, waiting for the garage door to open. *Hmm* . . . Jill's car wasn't in its bay beside his. It was after five thirty. Her conference in Kansas City had dismissed at noon, and it was barely a five-hour drive back to Sylvia. Maybe she'd decided to pick up a few groceries on her way home. Probably got stuck in a slow checkout line at Schnucks. But she usually called if she was running late. She knew he worried about her when she was on the road.

He pushed the remote, savoring the satisfying grind of the garage door going down on another workweek. Before he even opened the door, he heard TP's toenails clicking on the kitchen tile.

The dog pranced a circle around him, tongue and tail wagging in unison, proving that three-year-old, fifty-pound chocolate Labs were still puppies at heart. Mitch deposited his briefcase on the island and bent to administer his daily dose of affection. "Hey, boy, where's Mama?"

He refilled the dog's water bowl and checked his cell phone for messages again. Nothing. But the answering machine on the kitchen phone was blinking. Odd. They rarely used the landline. Jill usually just texted. Maybe she'd remembered he had a meeting this afternoon and didn't want to bother him at work.

He grabbed the thawed steaks from the fridge and played back the message while he mixed up his famous steak marinade.

"Hey, babe . . ." Jill's voice filled the kitchen, easing the tension he hadn't realized was forming behind his temples. "I'm rushing to get packed and checked out of the hotel, but I should still be home by five—six at the latest. Tell TP I'm bringing him home a little treat." Her voice turned sultry. "I might have a treat for you, too, Mitchell Brannon."

TP sat at Mitch's feet, his head cocked as if he understood every word. The Lab was Jill's dog. TP stood for Teacher's Pet, although after a certain Halloween when Principal Brannon had been a target of trick-or-treaters, she'd started telling their friends that it stood for Toilet Paper.

Mitch chuckled at the thought, while Jill's cheery voice continued on the answering machine. "If you don't mind getting the steaks started, I'll stop off and pick up some salad stuff. Maybe a loaf of that French bread you like from Panera. Love you. I can't wait to tell you about the conference. And other stuff. It was—" She giggled, and Mitch could almost read her thoughts. She was thinking about how much grief he always gave her for leaving "soliloquies" when she used voice mail.

"Never mind," she said—he could almost see her rolling her eyes—"It was just a really good experience. I'll tell you all about it when I get home."

She sounded good. Really good. He'd worried a little that Jill was taking Katie's leaving harder than she should, moping around the house like a mama cat looking for her kittens.

He checked the display on the answering machine. She'd left her message at one fifteen. Even allowing for a stop at the grocery, she should be home any minute.

It was plenty chilly for a fire. Perfect. He went out to the back deck to bring in some of the wood he and Evan had cut last time they were at the lake cabin. He got a fire started and lit some candles on the mantel. He wished he'd thought to pick up flowers on the way home. Candlelight and roses were usually just the ticket to a romantic evening. Though recently, with the pressure of getting Katie off to college and getting her own classroom ready for the school year, Jill seemed ticked off by his overtures more often than not. But he would take the risk tonight. Surely she guessed what his hopes were for their first weekend in a wonderfully empty nest.

When she still wasn't home at six o'clock, he called her cell phone. Voice mail again. "Hey, babe . . ." He cradled the phone between his ear and one shoulder while he turned the steaks in the marinade. "Where *are* you? I'm going to fire up the grill. Let me know when I should put the steaks on. For what it's worth, I'm starving."

He set the dining room table with the good dishes—the ones they'd gotten as wedding gifts—and lit the tall candles that decorated the center of the table.

At seven thirty, he turned off the grill and put the steaks back in the fridge. At this rate it'd be dark before they ate. He scratched TP behind the ears. "Sorry, boy. Guess you'll have to wait till tomorrow night for scraps." The dog whined, looking disappointed.

The sky was clear and the rain hadn't amounted to anything. But maybe it was worse up near Kansas City. Mitch went into the den and checked area weather on his computer. It didn't look like anything to be concerned about anywhere along the route Jill would have taken. Surely the

16

Labor Day holiday didn't generate enough traffic to make her this late.

By eight o'clock the candles were puddled on the table runner and the sun sank below the rooftops of their cul-de-sac. Still no phone call. No text. He stood at the open front door, staring down the street. The trees cast long shadows across the pavement. It would be dark in a couple of hours. He'd left three messages on her voice mail and called the hotel to confirm she'd checked out. She had. But they had no record of when she'd left the hotel, since she hadn't turned the key in. There were no incidentals charged to the room, and the bill had been paid by the Sylvia school district.

He paced the length of the kitchen, debating who to call next. He didn't have a clue which other teachers had gone to the conference, and he didn't want to bother Jill's principal if it turned out to be nothing. The last time he'd worried over her whereabouts, she'd been home all along, yakking over the backyard fence with Shelley next door.

Maybe she'd called Shelley. Those two were like sisters. He went back to Katie's room and parted the curtains to see if the lights were on next door. Not that he could tell if anyone was home by that. He hated to guess what the electric bills were over there. Shelley Austin kept a lamp burning in almost every room of the rambling ranch. Jill swore her friend simply liked the ambience the lamps created, but he suspected it had more to do with the fact that Shelley lived alone now that her own daughter was off at college.

The kitchen window cast a patch of light onto the back deck of the Austin home and Mitch keyed in the number Jill had set on speed-dial for Shelley.

"Austins'."

"Hey, Shelley, it's Mitch. You haven't talked to Jill, have you?"

"Today?"

"Well, since noon or so. She had that conference in Kansas City, you know, but I expected her home by now. I just thought she might have said something to you . . ."

"No, sorry. I haven't talked to her since the night before she left . . . Wednesday, wasn't it?"

"Yeah. She left on Wednesday."

"Did she ride with somebody? Or maybe had to drop somebody off?"

"I don't think so." He walked through the house and went out onto the back deck. "She drove up by herself anyway. I don't think they were carpooling."

"Oh. Well . . . Sorry. Wish I could help. I'll let you know if I hear from her."

"Thanks, Shelley." He clicked off and dialed Jill's cell again, hanging up as soon as he heard her voice mail. She was going to think something was wrong when she finally checked her messages. Served her right for making him worry. He checked the clock on his phone. If she still wasn't home by eight thirty, he'd call her principal. Maybe she'd stopped by her classroom to pick up papers to grade or something.

He poured a Coke and ate some chips and salsa. A poor substitute for a steak. At eight forty-five, he called Carol Dorchester, Jill's principal at the elementary school. "I'm sorry to bother you on the weekend, Carol, but Jill isn't back from that conference yet, and I just wondered if you knew whether the conference ran late or something . . ."

"Oh? I'm not aware that it ran over, but Jeannie Brent is the only other teacher who went from Sylvia. I heard her tell someone that Bill was meeting her in Kansas City for the weekend."

"Oh, that's right. I think Jill said something about that. Okay, well, thanks . . . I'm sure she'll be home soon. Again, I apologize for calling on the weekend."

"Oh, heavens, don't mention it. Let me know if she's not home in an hour or so."

Mitch hung up feeling a little foolish. He'd completely forgotten about Jill telling him Bill and Jeannie were staying in Kansas City for the weekend. She often accused him of not really listening to her. And too often he was guilty as charged. Maybe she'd told him something about where she was tonight and he'd forgotten that, too. But if that was true, she wouldn't have left a message on the answering machine saying she'd be home by five or six and then not call to let him know she was going to be three hours late. And they did have a date planned.

Maybe she'd called one of the kids on the way home and pulled over to talk. He dialed Katie's cell phone.

"Papacito! What's up?"

Hearing her chipper voice made him realize how much he missed his little girl already. "Hey, kiddo. You haven't talked to Mom tonight, have you?"

"No. Why?" His daughter's voice turned wary. "What's going on?"

"Nothing's going on. I just wondered if you'd heard from her. She's on her way home from that conference in Kansas City and I keep getting her voice mail when I call."

"She probably forgot to charge her stupid phone again."

"That's what I figured. So how's everything going with you?" He changed the subject quickly, relieved Katie had assumed the same as he. "Did you get all your textbooks bought?"

"Oh. My. Gosh. Dad, do you know how much they charge for those things? My psychology book was almost a hundred bucks. I'm talking for one book!"

He chuckled. "Why do you think we made *you* pay for books?"

"Yeah, well, next time I'll trade you, and I'll pay tuition. It'd be cheaper!"

"Not hardly. You talk to your brother lately?"

"Ha!" He could picture the familiar drama queen eye roll. "I try to avoid Big Brother at all costs."

"Unless you need wheels, of course."

She laughed, sounding caught.

"So everything's going good? You've had a good week?"

"Yeah. It's going real good. Calculus is gonna stink, but I like my other classes so far. And my roommate is cool. Hey, Dad, let me talk to TP."

"What is it with you Brannon women? If I didn't know better, I'd think you and Mom like that dog better than you like me."

"Come on, Daddy. Please? He misses me."

"No. I am not putting a *dog* on the phone."

"Come on, Dad . . ."

He looked over to see TP staring up at him with sad eyes, ears drooping. "Sorry, he's on the other line. I'll have him call you back later." He laughed at his own joke.

"You're mean." But he heard the smile in her voice.

"Sorry, but no go. You—" He stopped to listen, thinking he heard the garage door. "Hey, Katiebug, I think Mom's home. I'll let you go, but glad everything's going good. Mom will probably want to call you later this weekend, so we'll talk more then, okay?"

"Okay. 'Bye, Daddy. Love you."

The lump that came to his throat at her endearment took him by surprise—and made him a little more sympathetic to all the moping Jill had done lately.

He hung up and went to open the door that led from the kitchen to the garage. He flipped on the lights. But the garage door was closed and Jill's side was still empty. Apparently it had been wishful thinking. It was pitch black outside now, and the garage windows formed dark rectangles between the tools and lawn chairs hanging on the walls.

It was after nine o'clock. Jill should have been home four hours ago. Where on earth *was* she?

2

Autumn-like air gusted through the screened door, raising goose bumps on Shelley Austin's arms as she padded barefoot across the kitchen in her nightgown. She started to flip off the porch light when she noticed lights still on over at the Brannons'. It was almost eleven, and Mitch and Jill weren't usually night owls. It was the week-end though, and Jill had been out of town. She hoped her friend was home safe. Mitch had sounded genuinely worried when he called earlier this evening.

She unlocked the French doors and went out onto the deck. There were lights on in the back of the Brannons' house too. They must have company. But Mitch hadn't mentioned that, and she didn't remember seeing cars on the driveway. Mitch had said they were going to cook out when Jill got home. But—Shelley glanced back at the doors, remembering they'd been open all evening and she hadn't heard any noises next door. Nor had she smelled anything cooking. And she would have. Mitch was famous for his steaks and grilled pork tenderloin. She'd always accused him of fanning the delicious smells over the fence on purpose, just to make the neighborhood jealous.

She picked up her cell phone from the charger as she went back through the kitchen. Jill's photo popped up in her Favorites app—so pretty with her fair skin sprinkled with freckles, and those big blue eyes Shelley wished *she'd* been born with. She tapped out a quick text message: *Home safe? Your man was worried about u!*

She pressed Send, smiling, anticipating the reply Jill was sure to fire back. It still put a lump in her throat to think of the way God had put her in this house with a built-in best friend right next door at the toughest time in her life. Audrey was barely three when Tom left them, and his leaving had stolen so much. Not only the innocence of their family, but the example of a strong marriage she'd so wanted for Audrey. Thankfully, Mitch and Jill had patterned that beautifully.

Audrey even dated Evan Brannon for a while during high school. Shelley and Jill dared to daydream about sharing grandchildren someday, and they'd both been deeply disappointed when the kids broke up after eight and a half months. It had tested their fifteen-year friendship, each of them feeling defensive for their own child's culpability in the breakup. But once Evan and Audrey went off to college—in two different directions—tensions eased, and Shelley and Jill were able to rekindle the close friendship they'd shared.

Shelley brushed her teeth and checked her phone one more time. Jill usually replied to a text almost instantly. But this being their first week-end as empty nesters, maybe they were already busy "nesting." She smiled at the thought, happy for her friend, even as she pushed away a twinge of envy. Okay, more than a twinge.

She turned off the lamp on her nightstand and climbed into bed, but sleep wouldn't come. She kept thinking about Jill and how worried Mitch had sounded.

She flipped on the lamp and texted Jill again. *You okay? Just checking.*

When she didn't have an answer in a few minutes, she logged on to Facebook from her phone. Jill didn't post there much, but it was worth a try. But her last status update was from two weeks earlier—a request for something she needed for a bulletin board she was making for her classroom—and half a dozen replies that followed.

Shelley turned out the light again. She drifted off, but started awake only thirty minutes later. Something seemed . . . urgent. She'd never put much stock in premonitions until Audrey went off to college five hours away in Springfield. Since then, at the oddest times, often in the middle of the night, she'd awaken feeling compelled to pray for her daughter or a customer who'd come into the gift shop. But tonight it was Jill who pressed firmly on her heart.

She crawled out of bed and went to look out the window again. The lights were still on at the Brannons'. They were up anyway. It wouldn't hurt to call. She could put her mind at ease and finally get some sleep.

Mitch answered, sounding a little breathless, she thought.

Oh dear. She hoped she hadn't interrupted a romantic homecoming. She felt her face grow warm. She missed that part of marriage. "Um . . . hey, Mitch. Sorry to call so late. I just wanted to make sure Jill got home okay."

"No—she's still not home."

She glanced at the clock. "What? It's almost midnight." She regretted it as soon as she said it. Of course he *knew* what time it was.

"I've called everyone I can think of. Nobody at the school seems to know why she wouldn't have gotten home on time. And she's not answering her phone."

She could hear his apprehension escalating. As was hers. "Maybe she had car trouble or . . ." Try as she might, she couldn't think of another good reason why Jill wasn't home when she said she'd be, wasn't answering her phone. "Where else *could* she be?"

"I have no idea, and the police didn't sound like they would—"

"You called the police?"

"I called to see if there'd been any accidents reported. There haven't, but when I asked about what to do if she's not home soon they said they could enter Jill's name and description into a national crime center—NCIC, I think they called it. And report it to some other system . . . MULES, I think it was. I forget what the acronym stands for."

She nodded against the phone. "I've heard of that. That's good then, right? They're looking for her?"

"Maybe. But I got the impression they aren't going to make this a high priority until they're

26

convinced Jill didn't leave of her own accord. Or that it wasn't just a misunderstanding or miscommunication. That's what the dispatcher in Sylvia tried to tell me."

"That's ridiculous. Jill wouldn't do this on purpose! Who else have you called?" Mitch went through a list that included his daughter, Jill's other girlfriends, fellow teachers, everyone Shelley would have suggested.

"There is no way Jill wouldn't call you if she was running this late, Mitch. Or if she decided to stop somewhere. Something just doesn't feel right." She worked to keep the alarm from her voice.

"I know. I'm about to go out of my mind over here. I—I don't know what to do next."

"Call the police back, Mitch. They need to take this seriously! Jill wouldn't just not call. Something's wrong." She tried to conjure up some plausible explanation. "She wouldn't have driven on to Lawrence to see the kids, would she? I know she's really dreaded Katie leaving. Maybe she decided since she was that close to the college . . . ?"

"No, she wouldn't do that without telling me. And it was almost nine when I talked to Katie. If Jill had driven straight there from Kansas City she would have been there by three, or earlier. Katie hadn't talked to Evan, but I know Jill would have called Katie before him. And I just don't think she would have horned in on Katie's first weekend away at school."

"No," Shelley agreed. "I don't either."

"I haven't talked to Evan . . . Or called Katie back. I didn't want to scare them. Not this time of night."

"No, of course not. But . . ." Alarm crept into her tone, despite her attempt to keep her voice steady. "It's not like Jill not to call. And . . . I didn't want to say anything, but I texted her a couple of times earlier and she never answered. That's not like her either."

"No. It's not." His sigh sounded like one of desperation. "I don't know what else to do besides get in the car and go searching for her."

"But what if she comes home while you're gone? Then she'll be the one worrying."

"I know, but . . . what else am I supposed to do?"

"I'm coming over, Mitch. I'll help you make some calls. Or I'll stay there while you go out looking for her. I can't just sit over here wondering what's happening." She hung up before he could argue with her.

As she threw on jeans and a sweater, she entertained second thoughts about going next door. She'd set careful boundaries with her best friend's husband—for reasons she didn't like to admit even to herself.

It hadn't taken too many months of counseling after Tom left her to discover how vulnerable

28

she was to a nice man who treated her with the respect and genuine affection that Mitchell Brannon did. And Mitch wasn't flirting when he complimented a new haircut or teased her about losing her car keys. He treated her the same whether Jill was around or not.

And that was exactly the appeal. He was the real deal. Mitch Brannon got to her in a way that . . . well, it wasn't appropriate to even think about. She wasn't about to ruin the precious friendship she and Jill enjoyed by ever admitting her feelings—to anyone. But she'd spent a lot of hours on her knees, praying those feelings would just go away. When they didn't, she prayed instead that she would never do or say anything that would betray her. And she begged Heaven to someday—*sooner rather than later would be nice, God*—place her in a marriage as loving and secure as Mitch and Jill's was.

Disturbingly, that longing seemed to have deepened over the last year, now that her time wasn't consumed with Audrey's activities. She didn't really miss the ball games and choir concerts and academic bowls that had taken up so much time. But she needed something to fill those empty hours now.

What she needed was a second job. Tom was footing the bill for Audrey's tuition, but Shelley's job managing Serendipity barely paid the bills. Thankfully, she'd been able to pay off the mortgage with the small inheritance she received after her father's death three years ago. And Aunt Mona, her dad's sister who lived in Poplar Bluff, mailed her a nice check every so often—always at just the right time, it seemed. But even though she'd trimmed her monthly expenses to the bone, she lived in constant fear that Jaclyn would decide to close the gift shop.

Serendipity was the only source for gifts in Sylvia, and the little shop did pretty well. Jaclyn had been generous with raises, but every raise only seemed to match a hike in the utility bills or the price of gas. If she was lucky, her savings account might pay for Audrey's wedding in a few years. Although talking to a coworker who'd married off daughters recently, she wasn't so sure. Thousands of dollars for one day? It was enough to make her wish Audrey would meet someone who'd want to elope.

She grabbed her cell phone and went out through the back door. The air was brisk, and she forced away thoughts of Jill stranded somewhere in the cold. The night had taken on an eerie quality, and she jogged the rest of the way to the Brannons' backyard and up the deck stairs. She tapped on the French doors.

Inside, TP started barking, and a few seconds later, Mitch opened the door.

"Hey, thanks for coming over, Shelley. You didn't have to do that."

30

"Yes, I did. Still no word?"

He shook his head. "I checked back with Carol, her principal . . . Nothing. And I called the Highway Patrol. There haven't been any accidents between here and Kansas City."

"This is a little too familiar, isn't it?"

He nodded, and she knew he was remembering another middle-of-the-night meeting. The night Evan and Audrey broke up, the two clueless teens had stayed out until almost three a.m. Not answering their phones, not calling to let anyone know where they were. That night it had been Shelley's house serving as command central. Mitch and Jill had come over around twelve thirty, frantic, and for more than two hours they'd paced and railed and made if-they're-not-dead-I'm-going-to-kill-them jokes. They'd awakened all of Evan's and Audrey's friends, trying to track down the star-crossed lovers, and eventually called the Highway Patrol.

But they'd only had to wait two hours before they'd heard the blessed grind of the garage door, the back door open, and Audrey tiptoe in, her tearstained face telling a story that wasn't nearly as sad as the one Shelley and Jill and Mitch had been writing in their imaginations. Shelley sighed. Oh, how she wanted Jill to walk through this back door. Right now. *Please, God. Let this end the same way. Please . . .*

"Do you think you should call Evan and Katie?"

But he shook his head. "I'd rather not. Not until we just have to."

She looked at the clock above the breakfast nook table. The one Mitch had given Jill for her last birthday. Fifteen minutes after midnight. "They're probably still up, Mitch. It's Friday night. Better now than waking them up at two in the morning."

He rubbed his temples, staring past her. She hated the terror her words had put in his eyes. As if he'd just realized that this truly may not end well.

"Maybe they've heard from her," she said quickly. Measuring her words more carefully, she looked him in the eye. "If it was my mom missing I'd want to know. I'd be pretty ticked if I found out she'd been missing for hours before I got a call."

"But what could they do? They'd just spend the night worrying."

"They could pray."

The lift of his brows told her that got to him.

"Okay. I'll call. But . . . You don't think they need to come home, do you?" Mitch was a leader, always in control. She'd never heard him sounding so unsure.

"No, not yet."

His shoulders visibly relaxed. She reached out to reassure him, the way she would have with Jill, but she pulled away before he noticed.

"While you call your kids, I'll start calling hospitals. And maybe check with the hotel again. Maybe someone will remember seeing her or . . . something."

"I already called there," he said, an edge to his voice. "They said they'd call if anyone remembered anything, but I guess it can't hurt to talk to them again."

She took her cell phone into the living room with the list of numbers Mitch had jotted down. In places, he'd pressed so hard with the pencil that it had sliced through to the next sheet of paper.

She heard him talking to Evan, then Katie. Mitch's voice changed as he tried to calm his daughter. "Katie, listen to me . . ." His tone was deliberately even—what Shelley thought of as his principal's voice. "It's going to be fine. I'm sure there's an explanation. I'll call you back as soon as we know anything, okay? Just say a prayer for Mom, okay, sweetie?"

Shelley understood Katie's fears. She had a bad feeling . . . a very bad feeling about tonight. That Jill had been in an accident—or worse. And yet—

Bits and pieces of a conversation she'd had with Jill a few weeks ago came back to her now— like darts. Not quite hitting a bull's eye, but close.

It had seemed innocuous enough—an old boyfriend had friended Jill on Facebook earlier this summer. She'd thought he was flirting with her just a little, and naturally, she'd been flattered.

Shelley hadn't thought much of it at the time, except it wasn't like Jill even to entertain such an overture.

Now, she had to wonder . . . Was there something else at play here?

3

Saturday, September 4

Shelley looked up from her phone, realizing Mitch had been silent in the kitchen for several minutes. She looked at the list of phone numbers. She'd only made one call. A lot of help she was.

She struggled to remember the last conversation she'd had with Jill. Jill had been crazy busy with the start of school and it had been several days—maybe a week—since they'd had a conversation that went beyond the everyday "Hey, can I borrow an egg?" But she and Jill went way back, and their friendship had survived the ebbs and flows of each of their lives. They shared secrets and trusted each other implicitly—and often vented to each other. Thinking out loud, they called it. How often had they laughingly said, "Who needs a shrink when I've got you?" after a particularly intense venting session?

But Jill had struggled recently—maybe more than Mitch knew—with how different her life would be after Katie left for college. And Shelley couldn't seem to help her through this rough patch like she always had before. It had shocked Shelley to see her confident, vibrant friend suddenly not seem to have a sense of herself. Questioning everything. Was she making a difference as a teacher? Had she been a good enough mother? Would she and Mitch still be happy together when it was just the two of them? And that thing with the old boyfriend was out of character for Jill. She'd never been a flirt.

Shelley had teased her about being in full-blown midlife crisis. But finally she'd steered her friend to a real shrink. Maybe she'd mistaken a serious emotional crisis or deep depression for something she never should have blown off so easily. She tried again to remember the last thing she and Jill had talked about.

Probably Katie going off to college. Or Evan. Jill constantly worried that she hadn't given her kids the life skills they needed to live on their own. It bothered Shelley that she had to think so hard to remember their last conversation.

But it had been a while since she and Jill had just done something fun together—gone shopping or to a movie or out to lunch. She should have made more of an effort. But it wasn't all her fault. Besides getting her classroom ready for a new school year, Jill had been helping Katie get ready for college. Jill was measuring out every moment with her daughter, and Shelley had made herself scarcer than usual, trying to give Jill her space. And Jill hadn't protested.

Shelley hated her own tendency to jealousy. Jill had ten times as many friends as she did—mostly fellow teachers. And she somehow managed to juggle them all and not make Shelley feel like she was anything less than her closest friend—most of the time anyway. Audrey and Katie had rolled their eyes and made gagging sounds the first time she and Jill had referred to each other as BFFs. But it was true. And in spite of Jill's wealth of friends, Shelley never doubted she and Jill would always be Best Friends Forever.

She had good intentions of doing things to broaden her own friendships—invitations for shopping trips and lunch-hour gatherings with her coworkers weren't rare. But she didn't need as many friends as Jill did. As long as she had Jill, she was content with the way things were.

Sighing, she went back to the kitchen where Mitch still sat at the table in the breakfast nook.

"So . . . the kids haven't heard from her?" She didn't need to ask. The answer was in his hunched shoulders and weary sigh.

"No." Mitch dragged his fingers through his hair. "Katie's pretty upset. I promised.I'd call her back in a couple of hours. Remind me, would you?"

"Sure." Knowing her tendency to forget,

Shelley set an alarm on her phone to remind them. "Hopefully by then we'll be calling with good news."

Mitch shook his head. "I don't see how it can be good . . . not at this point."

She had no words to refute him.

He motioned toward the list in her right hand. "Did you find anything?"

"No . . . I still have calls to make. I'll do that now. Do you want me to put on some coffee first?"

"That would be good." He took the list from her. "You make coffee. I'll make phone calls. Thanks."

She knew her way around Jill's kitchen as well as her own. Memories washed over her as she looked around the Brannons' beautiful home. She and Jill had spent many hours helping each other paint, hang wallpaper, or finish some home decorating project or another. Those hours had formed a bond between them that went far beyond mere next-door neighbors. She could hardly make it seem real that her friend was missing.

She opened the cupboard where the coffee was stored and her hand hovered over the small selection of containers. If she had any faith at all, she would choose decaf, trusting they'd all soon be sagging back to their beds in relief.

She pulled out a tin labeled ROBUST BLEND and measured it into the filter. Within a few minutes the soothing aroma wafted under her nose. She poured a cup for each of them and carried the coffee to the breakfast nook. She sat down across from Mitch. "It's going to be okay," she said, with more conviction than she felt. "Hey, would Jill have stopped somewhere for gas along the way?"

"She left with a full tank. I know that because I filled it up Tuesday night after she got home. But she might have stopped to fill up before she headed back." He brightened and held up a hand. "I know how we can find out. She's got our credit card account set up online. If I can remember the password I can check if she's used the credit card."

He went back to his office and returned with his laptop. Shelley sat across from him at the table while he checked the credit card statement.

"Here it is. There's a charge pending at a gas station in Kansas City, Kansas. Purchase made yesterday . . . But it doesn't say what time." He looked up at Shelley. "The hotel must have been on the Kansas side. I didn't realize that. That would mean she had a little farther to drive than she might have thought."

"Not seven hours farther." She immediately regretted her somber tone.

But Mitch agreed, frowning. "I can't imagine why she hasn't called. Why *someone* hasn't called. If she was in an accident, wouldn't they be trying to reach me? Even if she was unconscious, she'd have her ID on her. I just don't get it. She should have—"

The shrill ring of the landline phone made them both start.

Shelley almost cheered. "There she is!" A rush of relief went through her.

Mitch shoved back his chair and hurried to answer the phone. Shelley strained to hear his side of the conversation, but it was immediately apparent that it wasn't Jill. And whoever it was had upset Mitch.

"Did she *steal* it?" His forehead creased deeper.

Shelley leaned closer, and didn't even try to pretend she wasn't eavesdropping. This didn't sound good.

"I don't understand." Mitch scratched something on the notepad by the phone. "Why would she have done that . . . ? No. My wife is still not home. No one has seen her. She's missing, and I want to talk to that maid!"

Shelley got up and came over to stand on the other side of the bar counter.

"I don't care," Mitch shouted into the phone. "My wife was supposed to be home seven hours ago. You can't tell me there's not a connection here."

He made no effort to use his principal's voice now. What was going on?

He paced the length of the kitchen. "No. I want that woman held for questioning—" He

39

listened with clenched jaw. "Yes, and you can expect to hear from the police shortly, too. And my attorney."

After a few more heated words, Mitch turned to Shelley, his jaw slack. "This is Jill's hotel. A maid supposedly found some jewelry left in Jill's room."

"*Jewelry?* She doesn't even wear that much jewelry. Except for her wedding ring. Did they say what it was?"

"They're checking now."

"If she checked out at one o'clock, why would they just now be finding her stuff?"

"The guy said they found it when they cleaned the room—whenever that was. Apparently the night staff had made a note of my call earlier when I asked for Jill. They didn't realize the connection until they briefed the next shift and—" He held up a hand and pressed his phone closer to his ear.

Mitch slid a pen and pad toward Shelley, and she jotted down the descriptions as he relayed them. *A silver watch, a pair of silver earrings, and a diamond bracelet with a clasp.*

"Yes, but why?" he said into the phone. He glanced at Shelley and rolled his eyes, obviously impatient with the person he was talking to. "But why didn't someone call before to let us know the jewelry was left behind?"

Shelley stood by, listening, feeling a little like she was eavesdropping.

"No, don't mail anything," Mitch said, his brow furrowed. "If you could, please just hold the jewelry in the safe there until I contact you." He hung up and looked at Shelley, shaking his head. "To protect the privacy of their guests, they don't contact guests about lost items. Apparently they made an exception in this case since I'd already called looking for Jill."

"Why wouldn't they call? What if it was something important?"

"The guy said"—he glanced away, looking embarrassed—"some of their guests would prefer that their spouses not be informed that they had stayed at the hotel."

It took her a minute to get it. And she hated that when she did, it took her back to the conversation she'd had with Jill. But there was no way—

"Does anything there sound like Jill's jewelry?" Mitch slid the notepad closer.

His question surprised her. "You'd know better than I would, Mitch." She looked at the list again. "Jill so rarely wore jewelry, and this isn't much to go on. I remember her wearing a silver watch sometimes, but she never wears earrings. Does she? Did she even own a diamond bracelet?"

"Not that I know of. Not real diamonds for sure."

"But do you think she might have worn more jewelry than usual to a conference?"

He shrugged. "I don't know. She always says it

gets in the way at school. I guess she does sometimes wear a necklace or bracelet if she's dressing up . . . like for a wedding or something. The kids got her a bracelet for Christmas a couple years ago and she wears that sometimes. Mostly just when they're around though. For their sake."

"She did have pierced ears though. Remember? She sneaked out and had it done when she was in high school." She smiled, remembering Jill's hilarious account of the event.

Mitch chuckled. "Yes, and her mom found out and grounded her for the whole summer."

"But I can't remember her ever wearing earrings since I've known her."

His smile faded. "She doesn't. Hasn't for a long time."

"Maybe there was a dressy banquet at the conference?"

"No. I'm sure there wouldn't have been. Not at this conference. Why would she have taken that stuff with her?"

"And then left it there?" It didn't make sense. "Is it possible someone else left the jewelry behind? A previous hotel guest. Did they say where in the room they found it?"

"On the bathroom counter. If someone else left it, Jill would have seen it first thing when she checked in. And she would have reported it right away."

Shelley nodded. Jill would never have let

someone worry about a lost treasure. And the watch did sound like one she'd seen Jill wear.

Mitch put an ear to the phone again. "I'm calling the police. Something's fishy."

4

"Sir, you can meet us at the hotel if you like." The police officer's tone struck Mitch as condescending and he gripped the cell phone tighter. Then quickly reminded himself it was probably studied patience on the officer's part. Mitch glanced at Shelley, who stood across from him, listening to his end of the conversation. Hopefully she would keep him from saying something he'd regret.

"Just let us know what time you'll be arriving," the officer said.

"Like I told the guy at the hotel, I live five hours away, and I don't want to be away from home in case my wife shows up here. Or in case . . . some hospital calls looking for me. But once my wife is home, we will come up and pick up the jewelry." He still wasn't convinced the jewelry belonged to Jill in the first place.

"I understand, sir. And we'll keep her belongings safe. I assure you we're doing everything we can from our end. Right now we have no cause to believe this has any connection to your

43

wife's whereabouts. Our detectives questioned the employee and the hotel manager shortly after you reported the incident. It appears your wife's things were left behind. Whether accidentally or on purpose, we couldn't—"

"What do you mean on purpose?"

"As I started to say, sir, there's no way to determine whether the items were left behind accidentally or intentionally, but it does appear the hotel employee acted exactly according to the hotel's policy and turned in the abandoned property as soon as it was discovered."

"Abandoned? I'm sorry, but do you have *any* reason to think my wife left it there"—he groped for a word—". . . willfully?" His patience was thinning fast.

"Sir, that is always a possibility in situations like this. Not knowing anything about your situation, we have no way of determining that. But I can tell you that it *is* the case in most skips— disappearances, I mean."

"I'll tell you about my 'situation'—" His blood reached a slow boil. "My wife and I are very happily married, and I promise you she did not intentionally disappear. Anyone who knows us will vouch for that." He looked to Shelley for validation, calming a notch at her nod of agreement. "I'm telling you that something is very wrong and you need to take this seriously and find out what it is!"

Shelley cleared her throat softly, but pointedly. It had the effect he knew she intended. He lowered his voice, felt his blood pressure go back toward simmer. "I'm sorry," he told the officer. "I—I know you're doing everything you can. Thank you. How should I get in touch—"

Shelley tapped the notepad he was writing on. "The jewelry," she mouthed.

In his anger, he'd forgotten that Shelley had suggested they ask the police for a more detailed description of the jewelry since the hotel hadn't been very clear. "Sir," he said into the phone, "could you please describe the jewelry they found? The stuff my wife supposedly left in her hotel room?"

"Let me check the report. Just a moment."

He covered the phone. "Thank you," he told Shelley. "I'm not thinking straight. If it wasn't for you I'd—"

"Mr. Brannon?" The officer was back on the line. "What they sent over isn't a very clear image, but it looks like a silver bracelet-type watch, a pair of—"

"Wait. Let me write this down."

Shelley leaned in, reading over his shoulder.

"There's the watch, a bracelet—possibly diamond? —and a pair of silver and black tear-drop earrings and some sort of hair thing. The word they wrote looks like *scrunchy*"—he spelled it—"whatever that is?" The officer chuckled.

Mitch jotted the items on the notepad. He showed it to Shelley, who gave a nod, even though the shrug that accompanied it said she wasn't altogether certain.

"Yes," he said into the phone. "I think those are Jill's things—my wife's things." He wasn't at all sure, but he wasn't about to risk his chance to view the jewelry and be certain for himself. Hopefully Katie would recognize it. *Please, God, don't let this go that far.* It killed him even to imagine having to call the kids back and tell them Jill still wasn't home. That she was . . . *missing.* "May I call this number back to check on the investigation?"

"Let me give you another number to call first." The officer read off a toll-free number. Mitch dutifully jotted it down below the others on what was becoming an extensive list. He had the distinct impression he was being pawned off on some rookie, but he thanked the cop and hung up.

"They think she walked out on me," he said through gritted teeth.

"What? That's . . . crazy. They *said* that?"

"Not in so many words, but their questions made it obvious that's what they think."

"They—they're probably just trying to cover all the bases."

"It's ridiculous!" He made a fist and wished he could punch something. "They'll bend over backward to cover for some idiot who's slinking around in hotels having affairs, but they won't start searching for a woman whose family is worried sick about her until they're sure she *wants* to be found?"

Shelley gave him a sympathetic look but didn't respond to his comment. Instead, she picked up the notepad he'd been writing on. "Do you want me to call this number?"

"Not yet." He looked at the clock for the thousandth time. It was almost five a.m. Twelve hours now since Jill should have returned home. Nine at the very least, allowing for traffic and stops she might have made. "I think it's time to call the kids. And I suppose I need to call Jill's folks."

Shelley nodded.

He picked up the phone but immediately put it down again. "Maybe I'll wait at least until six. Let them get a little more sleep. It's still the middle of the night in their time zone." Jill's parents lived in a retirement community near Colorado Springs. Her father was in poor health, and at eighty-three increasingly confused.

She shrugged. "I guess there's nothing they could do right now anyway."

"Do you think I should have the kids come home?" Imaginary conversations played through his mind like a horror movie. "Should I have them come home?" He could tell by the look she gave him that it wasn't the first time he'd asked her that. "I'm sorry. I . . . I feel like I'm going crazy."

"Who wouldn't be, Mitch? This is unbelievable. I think the kids will want to come home. But hopefully by morning something will turn up . . . We'll have heard from Jill," she corrected, realizing how her "something will turn up" could be taken.

"I'm starting to think it's not going to be good news when we finally do hear. I want to protect the kids if that happens. But I have no clue how—"

"Shhh," she said. "We have to stay positive. I'm sure there's an explanation. You'll probably be laughing about this over lunch with Jill a few hours from now."

He appreciated her optimism, wished he could muster some of it himself. But he had a bad feeling about this. He couldn't let himself think what life without Jill would be like. Yet, even as he tried to push the thoughts away, a virtual movie played in his mind—he and the kids standing at a grave. Jill's grave.

He looked down at his hands and saw they were trembling.

"Are you okay?"

"You know . . . I've heard how your life supposedly passes in front of you in those brief moments before you die, but I never thought the life of the person you love most in the world would pass in front of you . . ." He let his words

48

trail off, afraid of what Shelley would think if she knew how he was thinking.

"But don't you remember, Mitch? We practically had the kids' funerals planned that night they were late getting home." She must have read his thoughts.

"I remember."

"I'm sure it's an even stronger reaction when it's your spouse. That whole two-shall-become-one thing . . ."

Her answer surprised him a little. She had been divorced since Audrey was a toddler, and from what Jill had told him, Shelley didn't have much respect for the institution of marriage. But he nodded and dared to give voice to his thoughts. "If I lose Jill I might as well die."

"Mitch . . ." She put a hand on his arm. "You're not going to lose Jill. You're *not*. We won't stop praying until we find her."

He'd been shooting up desperate prayers all night. He looked down at Shelley. "I think I need to call Evan again. And you need to go home and get some sleep."

"No. I'll leave if you want some privacy, but I won't be able to sleep until she gets home."

Her quiet confidence that Jill *would* come home bolstered him. "Thanks, Shelley. It . . . it's good to have somebody here."

"I'll put on another pot of coffee."

Hearing her behind him in the kitchen gave him

the courage to dial Evan's number. He took the phone to the table in the breakfast nook.

"Yeah? Dad? Is that you?"

When had their son's voice gotten so deep?

"Man, it's like five o'clock in the morning," Evan mumbled. "What's goin' on? Is everything okay?"

Mitch swallowed the boulder that suddenly lodged in his throat. "I'm sorry to wake you up, bud, but I need to talk to you. Are you awake?"

He heard rustling and then a door closing and water running. "Yeah. Yeah, I'm awake. Is Mom okay?"

Why hadn't he rehearsed how to say this? Evan was going to think there'd been an accident. "We're not sure what's going on, but . . . Mom's still not home . . . and she's not answering her phone."

"Whoa . . . Are you serious? What's the deal?"

"I don't know, buddy. We're doing everything we can to locate her, but I think . . . If she doesn't turn up in a couple of hours, maybe you and Katie should come home."

"Does Katie know?"

"I haven't talked to her since right after I talked to you late last night."

"What time was Mom supposed to be home?"

"I was expecting her around six last night. But I didn't really start worrying until eight or so when she still wasn't answering her phone."

"What? That's, like, ten hours. Or more. Man, that's crazy. But—Where could she be? Why wouldn't she be home yet?"

"I don't know, bud. But we need to pray. I'm starting to get pretty concerned."

"Did you call the highway patrol? Maybe she was in an accident."

"We've called them. No accidents reported. We've called everybody we can think of. And—"

"Who's 'we'?"

"What?"

"You said, 'We've called them.' "

"Oh. Shelley's here with me. Helping make calls. And we'll keep calling and looking until—"

"Oh, man . . . This is wild." Evan huffed into the phone. "Okay. I'll get Katie and we'll come home. It'll probably be . . . at least one or so before we can get there."

"Okay, but—" He didn't want the kids to drive six hours for nothing. He needed to think this through, but he couldn't seem to make his thoughts coherent. "Yeah, you go pick up Katie, but give me a call before you leave. Mom could walk through the door any minute, and I'd hate to have you get too far down the road for nothing." He didn't feel the conviction of his words. "And listen, give me fifteen minutes before you call your sister, will you? I want to talk to her first."

"Yeah, sure. I'll wait. But we're coming home as soon as we can. This is crazy."

Mitch didn't argue with him. "Drive careful, Evan. Don't speed. We don't need—" He bit back the rest of the lecture he wanted to give. "Please . . ." His voice broke. "Pray. Just . . . pray for Mom."

"I will, Dad. We will."

He hung up the phone and sighed.

"Did he take it okay?" Shelley asked.

"I think all I did was succeed in scaring the kid to death. I would give anything if Jill would walk through that door before I have to call Katie and tell her—"

The ring of his phone interrupted him, and Evan's number appeared on the screen. "Hey, bud."

"Dad, did you check the search app for Mom's phone?"

"What search app?"

"I helped her set it up last time I was home. She was excited about it—you know how she was always losing her phone."

Mitch felt like he'd been handed a lifeline. "But how do I do a search without her phone?"

"You need to get on Mom's laptop."

That took the wind out of him. "She has her laptop with her."

"Oh. Well . . . You should still be able to find it from your computer if you log in as Mom. Do you know her password?"

"Maybe. Hang on a sec." He went to his laptop at the kitchen counter. "Where do I go?"

He typed in the address Evan gave him.

"Do you know her password?"

"Not for sure," Mitch said, "but I know a couple I can try." He entered their e-mail password and got an error message. He tried the password he'd used to get into their credit card account. Same message. He bit back a curse.

"Dad, are you on your laptop?"

"Yes."

"Try going to the computer in the den. Maybe Mom has saved passwords on that one."

"Hang on . . . It'll take a while to boot up." It seemed like forever, but when he finally got online and went to the first address Evan had given him, it logged "Jill" in immediately. "Got it!"

Evan cheered into the phone. "Okay, now click on the phone icon . . ." a map popped up on the screen and a spinning arrow indicated the computer was searching for the phone. The map zoomed in and a green dot appeared beside a callout. "It says 'located one minute ago.' "

"Where, Dad? Where is it?"

He zoomed out and tried to figure out where that dot on the map was. Zooming one more level, he recognized the cross streets. "It's the hotel! It's showing the phone is at the hotel in Kansas City. Mom must still be there." *Then why wasn't she answering her phone?*

"Call them, Dad. You've gotta call the hotel!"

5

With trembling hands, Mitch dialed the hotel. Shelley stood beside him, bracing her forearms on the kitchen bar counter, her eyes wide with hope.

He asked for hotel security and was routed to the concierge. He explained how the app had indicated that Jill's cell phone was on the premises.

"I'm not familiar with that particular phone app, sir." The concierge sounded hesitant. "I *can* tell you that we would not reveal any information about one of our guests without their permission. I can connect you to the room of a guest if you'd like."

"No, you don't understand." He clenched his fists. "My wife checked out of your hotel sixteen hours ago. That's the last time anyone has heard from her. I already explained everything to your security people a few hours ago. Like I told them, the police are looking for my wife." Mitch wasn't positive whether that had actually happened yet, but anything that might grease the wheels . . .

"I'm not sure how I can help you. If her phone is here, perhaps your wife hasn't actually checked out? I could dial her room for you if you'll give me her name."

He bit back a growl of frustration. "Her name is Jill Brannon." He spelled the surname for the concierge. It was worth a try.

"One moment please." A brief pause. "I'm sorry, we don't have a guest by that name staying here. Is there anything else I can help you with?"

"May I speak to your supervisor, please?"

"Sir, I am the supervisor on duty at this time. Would you like me to contact hotel security and let you discuss this with them?"

If he didn't need the phone so badly, he would have put it through the window. "No, I'll just call the police at this point."

"Sir, I assure you—"

Mitch ended the call. "Where's that list of numbers?"

Shelley grabbed it off the end of the kitchen bar and handed it to him. He called the detective in Kansas City and explained what had happened.

Twenty minutes later, with the knot in his gut growing ever tighter, the phone rang.

It was the detective. "We've found your wife's phone. It was on the floor of the parking garage at the hotel."

"What happened?"

The silence on the detective's end sent Mitch's heart into his throat.

But when the man finally spoke, he seemed more stymied by Mitch's question than anything. "We don't know. We're looking at every possible angle. We can't rule out anything at this point. But there's no indication of foul play. No sign of forced entry into the hotel room she stayed in, no sign of a struggle in the parking garage. And the hotel says they find cell phones dropped or left behind almost every day."

"Yes, but that can't be a coincidence, finding her phone like that. Her car isn't still in the parking garage there, is it? It's a gray Camry, license num—"

"No, sir. That's the first place we looked. It's not here. Like I said, Mr. Brannon, we're not ruling anything out. I assure you we are taking this seriously and doing everything we possibly can with what we have to go on."

Shelley poured herself another coffee and filled a mug for Mitch. She was worried about him. He'd seemed strong after talking to the hotel earlier, but after he called Evan back, and then called Katie to tell her what was happening, he'd hung up and gone out onto the back deck without speaking.

Now, half an hour later he was still out there, his back to her, looking off across the lawn. She couldn't even imagine the thoughts that must be going through his head . . .

She carried the coffee out to the deck. A sliver of sun lined the ridge behind the tidy row of homes on Chanticleer Lane. Daylight meant that

Jill had now been missing overnight. Still, the sun was a welcome sight.

Balancing the mugs, she slid the door shut behind her with her foot and spoke Mitch's name softly. He turned to face her, his eyes red-rimmed, his hair spiked every which way, as if he'd tried to comb it with his fingers. Holding out a steaming mug, she longed to put an arm around him, offer him the support of a friend. But for a world of reasons, she didn't dare.

"Thanks." He took the cup from her and looked back across the yard.

It tore her apart to see him so broken up.

She'd called her daughter a few minutes ago and explained what was happening. She warned Audrey not to tell anyone about Jill yet—Mitch still hadn't contacted Jill's parents in Colorado—but to please pray. And pray hard.

She shivered. The morning air was cool, but that wasn't why she was trembling. Her best friend had seemingly vanished, and she didn't have a clue how to help.

Where *was* Jill right now? She couldn't let herself believe that Jill might truly be gone. But when she pondered the possibility that her friend might be lying in a ditch, injured and frightened somewhere—or even abducted by some psycho—and wondering why the people she loved weren't coming to save her . . . Shelley shuddered.

She hadn't felt this helpless since Audrey was

two and got a gash on her forehead after falling off a swing. Shelley winced, remembering. She'd had to hold her precious, screaming daughter down, a white cloth covering Audrey's sweet face, while Dr. Melson stitched for twenty minutes. Oh, that this could end as well as that had, with nothing but a thin scar to show for the trauma.

But the more minutes that ticked off the clock, the more she feared that wasn't going to happen. "Are Evan and Katie coming home?" she asked softly.

Mitch nodded. "It sounded like they would get on the road pretty quick. They'll probably be home right after lunch." He shook his head slowly, then without warning slapped a palm hard on the deck table.

The iron table rattled and shuddered. "There's got to be something else we can do!" Without explanation, he slid the door open and went inside.

Shelley followed, not sure if he wanted her company.

But he motioned her over to the kitchen bar counter and reached for his laptop. "The Sylvia police said Jill's info would be on the highway patrol website sometime today." He slid onto a high stool and opened Google.

As images loaded on the screen, Shelley leaned over his shoulder, squinting because she'd misplaced her reading glasses somewhere in the chaos of papers and maps and quickly jotted notes on the counter. Mitch scrolled through the information and they read the text together in silence.

She could almost feel Mitch's spirits flag.

"Can this be right?" For at least the tenth time since she'd arrived, he raked a hand through his hair. "Almost 700 unsolved missing persons cases in Missouri alone?" He clicked on another link.

The images that loaded nauseated Shelley. Photos of bodies—dead bodies posed for macabre ID photos. Deceased persons whose bodies had been found but never identified. "How can that be?" she whispered.

"I don't know." In the gray light the computer screen cast Mitch's face seemed bled of color. "How could a person go missing and not have someone care enough to come looking for them. Look at this . . ." He shook his head slowly.

"It makes me ill." She reached over his shoulder and closed the laptop. "Jill's not there. Maybe we should call the hospitals again. And the Highway Patrol. Maybe now that it's light someone will see her car if it went off the road."

He straightened a little and his face brightened, as though he hadn't thought of that yet.

But the images swirling in her mind weren't anything a hospital could fix.

She pulled herself back from the cusp of a cauldron of dark thoughts and forced herself to think of best-case scenarios. As she'd told Mitch after they listened to Jill's message on the answering machine once again, Jill *could* be a little ditzy, especially when she was distracted. It was totally conceivable that she'd been rushing around trying to check out of the hotel and that she'd put her cell phone on the roof of her car while she packed up the last of her things. Heaven knew Shelley had done that enough times herself. If Jill had called Mitch from the lobby, or even before she left her room, it was possible she'd driven for a couple of hours or more before she realized she didn't have her phone.

Shelley knew if it had been her, she wouldn't have gone back to get it. She would have kept driving, eager to get home, and would have just waited to call the hotel when she got home . . . asked them to mail the phone to her. And then she would have e-mailed Audrey and Jill—the two who called her phone most frequently—and explained why she wasn't answering her phone.

But none of that explained why Jill wasn't home yet and Shelley couldn't stretch her optimism any farther. Jill should have been home long ago. Something had gone terribly, terribly wrong.

Mitch briefly touched her arm. "Let's go make some more calls."

She followed, picked up her phone, and dialed the next number on the long list of hospitals in the towns along Interstate 55.

...

Mitch put down his phone and looked across the table at Shelley, who had just hung up her cell phone. "Anything?"

She shook her head. "Sorry. Nothing."

"Then that's it. It's like she disappeared into thin air."

It was seven a.m. Shelley had called the last hospital on their list. He'd called the police in Sylvia, the Clemons County sheriff's office, and the officer in Kansas City that he'd talked to last night. The Sylvia police had issued bulletins, and Highway Patrol throughout a tristate area had been given the make and model of Jill's vehicle and the circumstances of her disappearance.

Mitch had called a few close friends and colleagues and asked them to pray, and to let him know if they thought of any place Jill might be. And against his better judgment, he'd let Shelley call their pastor and ask him to put the news on the church's prayer chain. He didn't want this to go public yet. But in a town the size of Sylvia, and with Jill missing overnight now, it was probably too late for that.

He needed to call Jill's parents soon. It was still early in Colorado, but they would probably be waking up within the next hour. He blew out a breath. "I don't know what else I can do."

"You've got to get some sleep, Mitch. Before the kids get home." Evan and Katie had probably left by now, but it would be a good five or six hours before they got here.

"You've been awake as long as I have. Why don't you go home and try to rest a little. I think I'm going to head toward Kansas City. I'll take the route Jill would have taken. I want to be here when the kids get home so I won't make it all the way to the hotel, but I can't just sit here and do nothing."

"Mitch, you can't make a trip like that when you've been awake for over twenty-four hours. Get some sleep first. Please."

He knew she was right, but he wasn't sure he *could* sleep. He was afraid of the dreams that would manifest themselves in living color if he let down his guard. Already snippets of horrific images had nudged into his mind. Jill in trouble, screaming his name, and him, utterly helpless to get to her, because he didn't know where she was.

"Did you hear me?" Shelley was saying.

He shook off the terror, blinking eyelids that felt like sandpaper. "I'm sorry. What'd you say?"

"I'm going to go home and sleep for a couple hours. Please, Mitch, you do the same. A little shut-eye and a hot shower and then you'll be fit to drive. I'll come back over"—she looked at the clock—"say, eight thirty." We can drive Jill's route for a couple of hours before the kids are due in. Okay?"

She was right, and he agreed reluctantly. "I'll

62

have my cell phone in my hand. If you hear from her—"

"She's not going to call me first, Mitch."

"Yeah. Okay." They were both so weary they weren't even making sense.

"Don't worry. If I hear anything I'll wake you up." She gave him a nudge in the direction of the master bedroom. "Now get some sleep. I mean it. We are no good to Jill like this."

He walked her to the door. "Thanks for—being here. For helping me make all the calls. I think I might have gone mad if you hadn't—"

"Shhh." She held a finger to her lips. "Get some sleep."

He gave a halfhearted salute and watched her walk across the lawn to her own front door.

He went inside and turned out the kitchen lights, then thought better of it and flipped them back on. And the living room and dining room lights, too. If Jill came home he wanted her to be welcomed with every light blazing.

He trudged back to the bedroom. He sat on the edge of the overstuffed chair and took off his shoes. His side of the bed was unmade, just as he'd left it yesterday. Jill made the bed first thing every morning. The only time she ever left it unmade was when they had plans to crawl back in bed together on a Sunday afternoon. But she'd been at the conference for two days and his side had stayed rumpled.

Now, he went around to her side of the bed and tossed her fancy pillows onto the floor. He turned the covers down and, fully dressed, crawled beneath the down comforter. Maybe if he slept on her side the bed wouldn't feel so empty.

Would he ever share this bed with Jill again? This whole crazy thing seemed like a dream.

He sent up one last desperate prayer—*God, please bring her home*—before everything faded to black.

6

Shelley jolted at the blare of the alarm on her cell phone. Her heart raced, and her stomach felt like it housed a heavy stone. For a split second, she hoped maybe last night was all a dream, but the memories rushed back, all too vivid. *Jill was missing.*

She hurried to the window that looked out over the Brannons' driveway. Maybe by some miracle Jill had come home while she was sleeping. Her heart sank when she saw the empty driveway. But Jill wouldn't have parked on the drive. She would have parked in the garage like always. And maybe Mitch hadn't called, not wanting to wake her.

With fresh hope, she took a quick shower, threw on some clean clothes, put her hair in a ponytail, and started out the door. She stopped short on the front step. If Jill *had* come home she and Mitch were no doubt sleeping. She hated to call in case that was true, but she couldn't just not go over there either.

A mist floated over the still-green lawn like a wraith, and the air held the chill promise of autumn. Shelley fished her cell phone from her jeans pocket. Her finger was poised over Mitch's name when the phone rang. She jumped, then laughed at her own skittishness. "Hello?"

"Hey, I'm sorry to wake you, but—"

"No, it's okay. I was up. Any word yet?"

"No. And please go back to sleep. I just didn't want you to worry if you came over later and I was gone. I'm going to head toward Kansas City and get as far as I can before I need to turn around to beat the kids home. But there's no reason we both need to go. You get some sleep. I'll let you know the minute I hear anything."

"Did you get *any* sleep, Mitch?"

"A little."

She hoped her pause conveyed her skepticism.

"No, I slept," he said. "I really did. How about you?"

"Pretty good. For a couple of hours. Please let me come with you. I do not want to have to explain to your kids that you fell asleep at the wheel."

He frowned. "You're sure you don't mind?"

"Of course not." She hitched her purse up on

her shoulder, made sure her front door was locked, and started across the lawn. "You don't want to be alone now, Mitch—and neither do I."

"Okay. If you're sure. I wouldn't mind the company. I'll drive the car over if you're ready."

"I'm halfway to your front door now."

"Oh. Okay. Yes, I see you."

She looked up and saw him waving at the open door.

"I'll go get the car. Meet you there." He motioned in the direction of the garage. "We can drive through for coffee."

The garage door was already going up by the time she got there. She climbed in the passenger seat—Jill's seat—and Mitch backed out while she buckled herself in.

"So, no word at all?"

"Nothing. I talked to the kids just a few minutes ago."

"How are they holding up?"

"As well as can be expected. I told them to call my cell every hour or so." He rounded the curve of their cul-de-sac. "Maybe it was crazy for me to have them come home. I won't be able to live with myself if they have an accident, but I—"

"Mitch!" A patrol car was turning onto their street. "Maybe they've found her."

He made a swift U-turn and followed the officer back around. Sure enough, the vehicle turned into the Brannons' driveway. Mitch pulled in behind it, jumped out of the car and ran to meet the two officers who climbed from the patrol car.

Shelley got out, too, but stood beside the car, not wanting to intrude. The patrol car bore the insignia of the Missouri Highway Patrol. Her hands trembled. There must have been an accident.

Shelley could only hear snatches of the conversation, but Mitch's expression was grim as he spoke with the older Highway Patrol officer, the driver of the patrol car. She read disappointment in Mitch's slumped shoulders, but it didn't look like grief. She gathered the Highway Patrol didn't have *any* news about Jill. Apparently they were only here to question Mitch. At least maybe they would begin a serious search now.

The officers started toward the house, and Mitch motioned for Shelley to follow them. "Do you want me to go home until they're done talking to you?"

"No." A look of near panic crossed his face. "I'd really appreciate it if you'd come with me to talk to them. You know Jill almost as well as I do . . . You might remember something I've forgotten."

She felt strangely honored that he wanted her there. The officers gravitated toward the kitchen table and Mitch pulled a chair out for Shelley. "This is our next-door neighbor and Jill's best friend," he told the men.

The older man introduced himself as Detective Marcus Simonides. Shelley didn't like the way he looked at her. As if he was trying to figure out what her and Mitch's relationship was. And thinking the worst.

Mitch offered to make coffee.

The detective declined for both of them. "This will only take a few minutes. We just need to ask you some questions about your wife."

Mitch sat down beside Shelley, and for the next twenty minutes the detective bombarded him with questions, occasionally asking Shelley to answer the same question Mitch had just answered. Did Jill seem depressed or upset about anything recently? Was there anyone who had reason to be angry with her? A parent of one of her students, perhaps? Had she and Mitch argued before she left for the conference?

Detective Simonides scooted his chair back. "I'd like to take a look around the house if I may?"

"Yes, of course." Mitch seemed surprised. "But . . . Jill hasn't been here since Wednesday morning. She took a lot of her things with her. Clothing and her laptop and such."

After what seemed to Shelley like a rather perfunctory inspection of the house, Detective Simonides went through another battery of questions about Jill. Mitch answered calmly, but she didn't miss the quaver in his voice.

"Is there anywhere you can think of that Jill might have gone instead of coming home? Did she have family in the area, or friends . . . ?"

Mitch shook his head. "Our kids are in college at the University of Kansas, but I've already called them. They're on their way home now."

Shelley couldn't remember if Jill's old boy-friend lived near Kansas City, or was just going to be in town at the same time as Jill. But if Mitch didn't know about the guy, now was not the time to break the news to him.

Simonides scribbled in a small notebook. "Any other place you can think of she might have gone?"

"We have a cabin down on Lake Norfork, in the Ozarks . . . Arkansas. But she wouldn't go there. Not by herself."

"You're sure?"

"Positive," Mitch said. "We have some friends —the Marleys—who live down there year-round. I can ask them to go by the house and see if everything looks okay. But that'd be the last place I'd look."

Shelley knew that was true. Jill tolerated the lake for Mitch and the kids' sake. She complained —as much as Jill ever complained—about sand and sunburns and overpriced groceries and no air-conditioning in August.

The detective asked Mitch to play the message Jill had left on the answering machine. It was haunting to hear her voice again, and to wonder if these might be the last words her friend had ever spoken.

When Mitch took his seat after the recording ended, the questions turned more personal. It became apparent to Shelley that they were trying to determine if Mitch could somehow be responsible for Jill's disappearance.

Shelley understood the spouse was always the first suspect in cases like this, but anyone who knew Mitch and Jill would know this line of questioning was a waste of time. "Mitch . . ." She touched his wrist and immediately regretted it when she saw the detective take note of the contact. She decided it would be best to aim her question at Simonides. "Shouldn't he have an attorney present?"

"No." Mitch's tone was harsh, but she didn't think his words were aimed at her. "I have nothing to hide, and I don't want to hold up this search. I'll answer whatever you ask, but if you think I had anything to do with this, you're just wasting valuable time. You can ask anyone who knows Jill and me."

Simonides held up a hand, looking sympathetic. "You understand I have to ask these questions?"

"Yes, sir. I understand." Mitch waved his arm in a let's-get-on-with-it motion.

"Is there someone who can verify your where-abouts yesterday, Mr. Brannon?"

"Yes, sir. I was at work all day. Until about five-thirty."

Shelley was grateful that literally hundreds of students and teachers could confirm his alibi. And another cadre of teachers from all over the state could testify that Jill had been at the conference up until she checked out of the hotel in Kansas City, presumably around one fifteen p.m.

"What about after you got home? Can anyone confirm you were here?"

"Mitch called me around eight o'clock, asking if I'd heard from Jill."

"Do you know if that call came from a home phone or a cell phone?"

"A cell phone—" She remembered something. "But I went out on my back deck right after I talked to him. Mitch was standing right out there." She motioned toward the rear of the house. "I saw him. We can see each other from our decks . . . It's how Jill and I first met, in fact."

The detective jotted something on his notepad. "It was pretty dark by eight o'clock. You're positive it was Mr. Brannon you saw?"

"Yes. The lights were on. We've lived next door to each other for over fifteen years. I know it was him."

The detective didn't respond but turned back to Mitch. "So what about between five thirty and eight when you called Ms. Austin? Is there anyone who could say they saw you during that window of time?"

"Window of opportunity" is what he meant. Shelley shook her head. Did they seriously think Mitch had something to do with Jill's disappearance?

Mitch rubbed his temples. "I called Jill's phone. Ten or twelve times. And left probably half as many messages. I don't know if you can check her phone and tell where those calls came from or—"

"That phone was found at the hotel where your wife was staying."

"Yes, they told us." He explained about Evan helping him use the phone-finder app. "Can we get her phone back? Maybe there's something on there that would help."

"It's in evidence in Kansas City now. Everything will be gone over with a fine-tooth comb." He looked at Mitch with piercing eyes. "But you'll get her things back at some point."

A chill went through him. It was almost like Simonides was talking about "personal effects." He didn't like the sound of that. "Do you think someone . . . took her? Abducted her?"

The detective softened visibly. "We don't have any reason to believe that at this point. The phone case was scuffed, but the phone wasn't damaged. We were able to check her messages and track the phone's activity."

"Shouldn't that help you find her?"

"It would be better if she still had it with her."

"So . . . what do we do now?"

"We'll need to check your computers here at the house. We'll need copies of any credit cards Mrs. Brannon might have with her. We've got bulletins out on her and the vehicle. We're working with the local police . . . doing everything we can."

"How can I help?"

Simonides glanced at the other officer, then back at Mitch. "First thing you might want to do is think long and hard about whether you can prove where you were between the hours of five thirty and eight p.m. last night."

7

"I know the husband is always the first suspect, but . . ." Mitch gripped the steering wheel, trying to keep Shelley from seeing how badly his hands were shaking. "The guy made me feel almost guilty. Like maybe somehow it *is* my fault."

"That's ridiculous, Mitch. Of course it's not your fault. I am so sorry you had to go through that whole ugly interview."

Being questioned by the Highway Patrol's Missing Persons detective had shaken him more than he realized—and made it far too real that

Jill was missing. This likely wasn't going to end with a simple misunderstanding, or the discovery that Jill had car trouble or took a wrong turn and ended up in Illinois. He couldn't let himself think about the probable ways it *would* end.

The officers had taken information about Jill's car, and copied everything in the house that might contain what they called her "electronic signature"—his, too. Computer hard drives, his cell phone, even the answering machine.

For one awful moment, Mitch had been afraid they would erase Jill's voice from the machine. The last words she'd had for him. Words he'd listened to a dozen times, trying to decipher them beyond face value.

He'd been strangely embarrassed, too, by the intimacy of Jill's last message—her intimation that she was bringing him a "treat." Hearing it played in the presence of the officers—and Shelley—somehow cheapened the innocent, playful message from his wife.

After Simonides and the other patrolman left, he and Shelley had driven through Sylvia's small-town version of Starbucks before heading north on I-55. The mist had lifted a few minutes ago, and traffic was fairly light for a Saturday morning.

"Are you sure this is the route Jill took?" Shelley stared intently out the passenger side window. "Is there any other way she could have come?"

He gave a humorless chuckle. "This is Missouri after all. There are probably a dozen different ways she *could* have come, but I don't know why she would've gone any way but the Interstate. It's the only route we've ever taken to Kansas City. And she was in a hurry to get home . . ." He narrowed his eyes at her. "Why did you ask that?"

She shook her head. Rather emphatically, he thought.

"No reason. I'm just trying to think of every possible angle. She has to be *somewhere*."

Mitch nodded, staring out the windshield and to the left, past the ditches and into the woods beyond where the trees were still fully clothed in green leaves barely tipped in autumn's yellow and gold. Even on this gray Saturday, he could peer into caverns of winter darkness beneath the outspread branches. "Her car is the same color," he said, not realizing he'd spoken aloud until Shelley looked at him, her brow furrowed.

"Her Camry is that same gray color as the woods. It would be a miracle if we could see it in there."

"Then we'll pray for a miracle."

He'd been praying for just that, but if Jill was out there somewhere in the vast acreage flanking this ribbon of highway, how would they ever find her? *Jill, where are you? Please, God . . . Show us where to look.*

For almost an hour, they drove along in silence, he and Shelley each scanning their respective sides of the four-lane highway. He kept the speedometer below sixty and cars whizzed past them.

Today's weather was similar to yesterday's—overcast but not foggy—and the sun tried valiantly to shine through the veil of clouds. There'd been no precipitation, and the temperatures weren't cold enough for the roads to get icy. Still, if she'd been stranded somewhere overnight, it would have been freezing. He tried to imagine Jill making this drive yesterday. Tried to think the way she might have thought. That brought a smile.

"What?" Shelley tilted her head, eyeing him.

"I was just . . . thinking. Trying to think like Jill. You can imagine how that's working out."

Shelley's laughter was a welcome distraction. "Jill always said you two had personalities like oil and water, never mind the whole 'men are from Mars' thing. But . . . I'm sure you're right that she took the Interstate. I'm not sure I would have, but she—"

"Why not?" He tapped the Cruise button again. "You think she might have come another way?"

"I just know that sometimes, especially in the spring or fall, I like to take the back roads. See something new, just get lost in thought or sing at the top of my lungs and not worry about causing other drivers to crash laughing."

He grinned at the image.

But Shelley winced. "I'm sorry. I wasn't thinking."

"What?"

She frowned. "Making jokes about accidents."

"Oh. I didn't even give that a thought. Frankly, I could use a few jokes about now," he said wryly. But despite his words, he sobered. He couldn't even let himself think about what the future might hold. What his kids might have to face before this day was over.

He looked at the clock on the dash. "We'd probably better head back. I want to be there when the kids get home. I don't know what else to do. I feel . . . torn."

"Mitch, if we could see where Jill went off the road—if that's what happened—so can the police. They'll find her. Right now, your kids need you."

"I know." At the next exit he slowed and eased off the Interstate. Weekend traffic was picking up, and he started to turn off onto the exit ramp.

But Shelley pointed to a highway billboard. "Hey, slow down." There was excitement in her voice. "I've been there before . . . with Jill."

He pulled the Saturn over to the side of the road and followed Shelley's line of vision to a sign advertising a colony of antique shops.

"The antique shops?"

"Yes. Jill talked me into stopping there when we were coming back from that bed-and-breakfast weekend a few years ago. She loved the place. In fact, that's where she bought the green dresser that's in your dining room. That was when I was driving the Escape, and we just barely managed to get that dresser in the back."

"Oh, sure. I remember. You helped her refinish it, didn't you?"

She nodded, looking as nostalgic as he felt.

"I kind of remember her telling me about the place. We were always going to go back and explor—" He clipped off the word. Would they ever get a chance to do all the things they'd meant to do together?

The look Shelley gave him said she was having similar thoughts.

"I gave her such a hard time about buying all that junk," he said. "Most of it any normal person would have tossed in the trash. But she so seldom spends money on herself . . . And she always managed to turn trash into treasure."

He turned the car around again and headed in the direction the sign pointed. "Do you think she might have come this way?"

Shelley craned her neck to look up at the billboard through the windshield. "Maybe. We took county roads all the way back to Sylvia that day. It was fall. A little later in the year than this,

I think. I remember the leaves were turning . . . really pretty. Jill loved it."

"It's a long shot, but . . . Maybe she decided to come this way again. Check out the stores again . . ."

Shelley frowned. "If she left Kansas City after one, I don't know if the shops would have still been open by the time she got here . . ."

"No," he agreed. "Probably not on a Friday afternoon before a holiday."

"She might not have thought of that though. Do you think she would have taken the same back roads home?"

"I don't know." He'd always felt like he knew Jill almost as well as he knew himself. Now, he wasn't sure about anything.

They wound through gravel roads deeper into the woods. They were on the fringes of a conservation area and houses were few and far between.

Shelley looked up at the canopy of trees overhead. "It's a lot denser and more overgrown than I remember. It would be easy to get lost out here. And without her cell phone . . ."

Mitch heard hope in her voice. And even as he wondered how far these acres of trees stretched, he dared to entertain hope himself. These roads were washboard-rough and only wide enough for one car in places. She could have gotten the car stuck or even gone off the road. It was a long shot.

But at least it was a shot.

8

"She doesn't look familiar." The proprietor of the antique mall slipped off cat-eye glasses and handed the photo of Jill back to Mitch. "But we get a lot of people through here on a weekend, especially with the holiday. Doesn't mean she wasn't here. You said it was last night?" The woman looked from him to Shelley and back again. "May I ask what this is about?"

"Yes. This is . . . my wife. She was driving home from a conference in Kansas City last night and she . . . didn't arrive home when we expected her." Mitch hadn't considered that showing Jill's photo around would mean he'd need to explain why he was asking questions. Neither had he considered that having Shelley with him would feel a little awkward.

Strangely, a forgotten memory surfaced. When the kids were in high school, Jill had offered Shelley a ride home from an out-of-town basketball game. But at the last minute, Jill hadn't been able to attend—he couldn't even remember why now. But he did remember how awkward it felt walking out of the high school to the parking lot beside Shelley, and realizing that they were getting looks from other Sylvia fans, who must have wondered why he and Shelley were getting in a car together—alone—to make the hour-long ride home.

He and Jill had always been careful about appearances. Knowing the damage small-town gossip could do, and given their positions in the school system, they'd chosen not to travel—or even have lunch—alone with a member of the opposite sex if they could help it. But until the inquisitive looks he'd received that night, he'd never felt uncomfortable with Shelley. His interactions with her had always involved Jill, and the close friendship the two women shared made Shelley seem more like a sister to him.

He didn't owe this stranger any explanations, but he sensed her curiosity, and in light of the suspicious attitude that the detective had shown toward Shelley, he wondered if it had been unwise to bring her along. He didn't need witnesses who could testify they'd seen him and Shelley alone together an hour from home. But after all, they *were* searching for Jill.

"Have you called the police?" the woman asked, sounding a little incredulous.

"Yes. The authorities are looking for her." He thanked the proprietor for her time and started to leave, but turned back. "Are any of your employees here today that were working yesterday? Would you mind if I spoke with them?"

"I'm sorry, but my weekend staff is all that's here today."

Mitch wondered if she was telling the truth, but he certainly couldn't fault her for being cautious. "I understand," he said. "Thank you very much for your time."

Her demeanor softened at that. "I could keep the photo if you like"—she reached for it—"and ask when they come in Monday if anyone remembers her."

He clutched Jill's photo to his chest. Why hadn't he thought to bring copies? "I'm sorry, this is the only one I have with me. And I'm sure she'll be back by Monday."

"Of course. I certainly hope so. I could make a photocopy if you like."

"Yes. Please," Shelley said. "That would be great."

"Yes, thank you." He reluctantly turned the photo over to the woman, and the two of them waited by the cash register while she went into a back room.

She came out a few minutes later with a stack of color copies of Jill's photo. "Thought maybe you'd be talking to others who'd need a copy to keep."

"Thanks so much." He took the copies from her. "Oh, I'm sorry. Can I pay you for the copies? I . . . I'm not thinking straight."

"Well, of course you're not. And you don't need to pay me. It's the least I can do. I'll say a prayer you find her quickly."

He held the door for Shelley and they got back in the car, immersed in their separate thoughts.

He drove slowly, winding along the rough back roads. His neck ached from craning to peer into the dense forest on either side of them.

Shelley was quiet beside him, rubbing her own neck. He could almost see the hope seeping out of her with every mile that drew them closer to home. He felt the same.

He called Evan's cell phone around noon and drove a little faster when he realized the kids were in danger of beating them home. He didn't want them to come home to an empty house.

The thought brought him up short. No matter how many people crossed the threshold, their house would feel empty until Jill was found.

His cell phone rang and he whipped it out of his pocket. "Yes?"

"Mitchell? What is going on?" Jill's mother.

"Miriam. Hello. What do you mean?" Surely she couldn't know.

"I couldn't sleep so I took my coffee in to the computer. I was on Facebook, and Katie had written something about her mother being missing? I don't always get the things these young people write about, but Katie sounded serious. I called the house and no one answered. Jill's not answering her cell phone. Please tell me this is some sort of joke."

Mitch sighed into the phone. What had Katie

been thinking to post on Facebook? "I wish it was a joke, Miriam. I was going to call you, but I didn't want to wake you before we had any real news." He broke the news to her as gently as possible. After Miriam settled down, they agreed there was no reason for her and Bert to make the trip to Missouri yet.

"I think I won't say anything to Bert until I really have to," Jill's mother said. "He hasn't been well at all." It sounded like there was more to that than Miriam was willing to reveal just then.

"Well, don't let him watch TV then," Mitch said.

"Mitch? Is this that serious? Why do you think it would make the national news? Is there something you're not telling me?"

"No, Miriam. We're praying Jill shows up before the story makes the news at all, but if it should, I wouldn't want to risk it for Bert's sake. He doesn't get on Facebook, does he?"

"Oh, heavens, no. He doesn't even know how to turn the computer on. And he can't hear the TV, but I'll monitor him."

Mitch tried to encourage Jill's mother before he hung up, but his words rang false even in his own ears. Beside him, Shelley looked stricken, as if hearing him tell Jill's mother had made what was happening all too real.

When they pulled into the driveway a few minutes later, Evan and Katie were in the driveway waiting. Seeing them, he felt at once

84

comforted and bereft. Having the kids home made it all too real that Jill was not.

TP yipped his pleasure, jumping up on Evan and Katie in turn, whining, and licking Katie's face. Watching them made Shelley miss Audrey desperately. She wished she'd called her daughter home, too. At the same time, she prayed it never became so serious that she'd have to call Audrey home. But she'd lost a lot of the hope she'd been hanging on to back on those forested roads she and Mitch had just driven.

Katie laughed and let TP wash her face with his pink-black tongue, but when Mitch nudged the dog out of the way and took his kids into his arms, Katie burst into tears and clung to her dad. Shelley could see that it was everything Mitch could do to hold it together himself.

"Dad?" Evan's voice cracked. "They still haven't found her?"

Evan had stayed in Lawrence over the summer and Shelley hadn't seen him since last Christmas. His voice was lower than she remembered, and he'd filled out, no longer the lanky athlete.

"No, bud. Nothing yet." Mitch reached up and ruffled Evan's hair as if he were still a little boy.

"I don't get it. How could she just disappear? What do they think happened?"

"I wish we knew. We literally don't have a *clue*."

She caught Mitch's eye. "I'll leave you guys alone," she said quietly. "I'll be at home if you need—"

"No. It's okay. Please stay. Unless you need to get some sleep."

"No. I—I'd prefer to stay. Thanks." She was glad. It would have killed her to go home and sit alone, wondering what was going on.

Mitch ushered them all into the family room and plopped onto the sofa with a kid on either side of him.

While he filled them in on the search and everything leading up to now, Shelley put water on to boil for tea and hot cocoa. She could still hear their conversation, but being apart from them in the kitchen made her feel less like an intruder on this intimate family gathering.

She stirred a cup of hot chocolate and added it to the tray she was preparing. When the drinks were finished, she carried the tray over and set it on the coffee table.

"Thanks, Shelley," Mitch and Katie said in unison.

"Do you guys want something to eat? I'd be glad to make some sandwiches."

They all declined.

"I'm not hungry," Katie said, putting a hand to her stomach. "How's Audrey liking school this year?"

"It's going real well. Thanks for asking, Katie."

It touched her that Jill's daughter would think to ask about Audrey at a time like this. And perhaps she was imagining it, but Evan seemed very interested in her reply. She had dared to entertain hopes that Audrey and Evan might get back together one day. After they both finished school. Now, something about Evan's interest made Shelley wonder if he and Audrey had been talking.

No doubt news about Evan and Katie's mom was all over cyberspace. There was no keeping anything secret in this age of social media.

Secrets. Her mind swam with conversations she'd had with Jill. Recent conversations. There was no reason to share them. Least of all with Mitch. And she'd promised Jill she wouldn't. That whole thing with her ex had no bearing on this.

But what if it did? The things they'd shared in confidence had seemed petty at the time. Even frivolous. For fifteen years, she and Jill had shared everything—like two teenagers whispering and giggling together. They'd often compared their friendship to that of sisters.

It had been no different the night Jill shared that her old boyfriend had contacted her. Shelley could tell Jill was flattered by his attention, but she'd never entertained any serious intentions of accepting the guy's invitation.

She knew the decision Jill had made, but what if something had changed her mind? What if she'd gotten to Kansas City and decided—

No. Not Jill. Jill would never have done anything to put her marriage in jeopardy. Shelley bit her lower lip. If she was wrong about this, she would never forgive herself. But if she breached Jill's trust and said something to Mitch, *Jill* might never forgive her.

Maybe she could tell the authorities. Ask them to keep her confidence and not say anything to Mitch. But there was no guarantee they would do that. And telling the police might even put the news on the front page and embarrass Jill to death. Embarrass the whole family.

Besides, the last thing Shelley wanted to do was talk to that detective from the Highway Patrol. He intimidated her. And she didn't appreciate the way he looked at her—as if she knew things she wasn't telling.

She curbed a sigh. She'd always loved having a friend with whom she could share her deepest hopes and fears, but right now, she hated being the keeper of Jill Brannon's secrets.

9

Monday, September 6

"It shouldn't even *be* a case," Evan Brannon lurched off the sofa and shouted at the TV. A local news anchor had just referred to "the case of a forty-four-year-old Sylvia woman who went missing Friday" on the noon newscast.

Mitch knew exactly what his son meant. That the news media labeled Jill's disappearance a "case" made it sound like they didn't expect her to be found. Or to come home.

He ran a hand over two and a half days' worth of stubble on his jaw. He'd never felt so helpless in his life. He felt torn in a thousand directions, needing to be there for Evan and Katie, who were devastated and in shock—like he was. But he also felt a need to ride herd on the authorities, who, in his opinion, had done far too much speculating and far too little actual *searching* for Jill. But his hands were tied. Marcus Simonides had warned him about "going vigilante" on him. Until the detective gave him the go-ahead, he wasn't to take any action without talking to Missing Persons first. "I've had too many families organizing their own search parties and trampling evidence in the process," the detective had told him. "If people want to help, they need to clear it with law enforcement first. This is what we do every day, Mr. Brannon, so I'm asking you to trust us and let us handle it."

He stared at a stack of cards and notes on the coffee table—cards people had brought by along with a generous offering of casseroles and cakes. There was no mail delivery today because of the Labor Day holiday, but if this stack of cards was any indication, he expected a flood of envelopes in their mailbox tomorrow. He'd appreciated people's thoughtfulness—until he opened the first envelope that contained a *sympathy* card! *Thinking of you on the loss of your loved one.* He'd immediately stuffed the card in the bottom of the garbage can in the garage before the kids could discover it. But that wasn't the only one. At least half a dozen people had chosen cards obviously meant for the family of someone who'd *died*. Did people actually think Hallmark had made a card just for such an occasion when they saw one that read "the loss of your loved one"?

The thought made him feel petty and ungrateful. It *was* comforting to know that in the days since Jill had gone missing, so many people were praying for them. And for Jill.

He should probably turn off the TV for his kids' sake. But he couldn't. Instead, he leaned forward, praying for any morsel of hope the anchor could toss him. Sadly, he'd learned more from TV reporters than he had from the authorities who were supposedly looking for his wife.

"A spokesperson for the Missouri Highway Patrol says there is virtually no trail to follow in the disappearance of Jill Brannon," the weekend news anchor said, wearing something a little too close to a smile for Mitch's taste. "The third-grade teacher from Sylvia was last seen Friday at a Kansas City, Kansas, hotel where she had attended a conference. Authorities say Jill Brannon's cell phone was used shortly after one p.m. Friday when she left a message for her husband. The phone was later discovered in the hotel's parking garage, and according to information from the Missouri State Highway Patrol's Missing Persons Unit, the trail goes cold from there."

The scene on the television screen changed to a reporter with her back to the camera, holding a microphone up to a patrolman behind a messy desk. "Ordinarily in a case like this," he said, "we'd have search parties out scouring the countryside, search-and-rescue dogs combing the scene. But after searching the hotel where the missing woman's cell phone was discovered, we have virtually no idea of where to go from there. We're essentially flying blind. There's no lead on the vehicle, no cell phone GPS to track, none of the usual evidence. I can tell you, it's a frustrating situation . . ."

The audio clipped off the patrolman's words and cut back to the studio. The photo of Jill that Mitch had given local police—last year's school photo—flashed on the screen to the anchor's voiceover. "Authorities are asking anyone with information about Jill Brannon to contact the number that appears at the bottom of your screen."

The anchor pivoted her chair to face another camera, smiled, and switched to a less somber tone for a story about a homeless woman caught camping out in empty lakeside homes and the angry Osage Beach homeowners who wanted to have her prosecuted. Mitch had trouble feeling much empathy. People needed to count their blessings. There were far worse things that could happen.

He put an arm around Evan, but he was all out of comforting words. Maybe it was his imagination, but every authority he'd spoken to over the past two days since Jill had vanished left him feeling that they suspected Jill had *chosen* to disappear. It helped somewhat that every person who actually *knew* Jill—knew their marriage, knew her love for her children, knew her passion for her career and her love for her third-graders— didn't believe for a minute that Jill had walked out on him.

The weekend had passed in a blur of police interviews, and subsequent news reports. Mitch still had trouble believing they were real. They were about him. About *them*.

He stole a worried glance at Katie, curled in the corner of the overstuffed chair that was Jill's favorite. TP curled at her feet on the ottoman, a place he would have been banished from if Jill were here. But Mitch wasn't about to enforce that rule. Not now. Seeing his daughter's beautiful face swollen and smudged with tears, he wondered when he'd ever again see the little-girl dimples that hid until she smiled.

Tuesday, September 7

On Tuesday morning, when a television reporter mentioned that Mitch had been questioned, Katie's eyes grew wide. "Did they seriously think you had something to do with this, Dad?"

He should have been relieved that the authorities apparently had decided he couldn't have been involved in Jill's disappearance. But he was too stunned over the fact that there had been no leads in Jill's case whatsoever. She'd seemingly disappeared without a trace . . . into thin air . . . off the face of the earth. Listening to the news reports was like a storm of clichés.

He grabbed the remote and turned off the TV. Evan and Katie didn't protest. "We need to decide what . . . to do." He swallowed hard. "I don't want you guys to miss any more school."

They stared at him as if he'd lost his mind. "We're *not* going back, Dad." Katie rose to her knees in the oversized chair. Beside her, TP's ears pricked. "There's no way I could go back! Not until we find Mom."

"Then let's find her." He rose from the sofa and went for his car keys. He might be crazy, but he couldn't sit around doing nothing.

"Where are we going?" Evan croaked, following him into the kitchen.

"I don't know, but if I stay in this house for another second I'll go stark raving mad. Shelley and I drove halfway to Kansas City . . . took the route we think Mom would have taken. But we didn't go all the way there. Maybe we need to do that."

Evan shrugged. "Beats sitting here. Let's go."

Katie appeared in the doorway. "Maybe I should stay here. In case Mom comes home . . . While we're gone."

"I don't think—" He'd started to tell her that wasn't going to happen, and hated the realization that he was beginning to believe that possibility more than he believed they would ever find Jill. But he couldn't take away Katie's hope. That wasn't fair. "Maybe we could call Shelley," he said. "We can leave a note, and let Mom know Shelley is home. But remember, Mom has our cell phone numbers. She's going to call us if she can."

"No, Dad," Evan said. "She might not have the numbers. Not if she doesn't have her phone. Everything's in memory. Do you know *my* number without looking?"

He'd thought of that. And no, he couldn't have called either of the kids without using his phone's memory. It was a sobering thought.

But Jill knew their home phone number—unless she had a head injury, or some other trauma, and couldn't even remember her own name. It was the stuff movies were made of. But when he started entertaining a host of even stranger scenarios, few of which had happy endings, he had to force the thoughts away.

After the barrage of calls from reporters and well-meaning friends when the news of Jill's disappearance went public, he'd been tempted to unplug their home phone. But he didn't. Already, only four days later, the calls had dwindled to a trickle. Now he worried Jill's story would be forgotten.

But Jill would have called home if she could. His kids knew that.

TP trotted into the kitchen and Katie knelt to hug his thick neck. Her eyes held a haunted look. "Call Shelley. I can't stay here."

Mitch fished his cell phone from his pocket and punched Shelley's name—and realized he couldn't even have called next door without that memory feature on his phone. Waiting for Shelley to answer, he tore off a sheet of paper from the magnetic notepad stuck to the fridge and slid it across the counter to Evan. "Write your phone numbers down for me . . . yours and Katie's."

Shelley answered on the second ring. Mitch could tell by the way her voice lilted when she said "Hello" that she was hoping for good news. Oh, how he wished he could give her that gift.

"Hey, the kids and I are going to drive to Kansas City. See if we can spot anything. Are you going to be home for a few hours?"

"Of course. Do you want me to come over . . . in case she comes back while you're gone?"

"No. Thanks, but you don't need to do that. We'll leave a note for her, and tell her to go over there if she comes home before we get back." Shelley was still holding out hope, and that thought buoyed him. But he didn't know how much longer he could go on acting as if he expected Jill to show up any minute. *If that was going to happen, it would have happened by now.* He tried to shut out the hopeless voice.

"Sure. I'll be here. As long as you need me."

"Thanks, Shelley."

"Mitch—"

"Yes?" There was something in her voice that he couldn't pin down. Something ominous.

"I think . . . Maybe we need to talk before you go. Just for a minute. There are some things I think . . . you need to know."

He glanced at Evan and Katie, very aware of their eyes on him. "Can it wait?"

He heard her intake of breath, and the quick sigh that followed. "It might be nothing," she said. "But . . . if you're going to Kansas City, I think maybe I need to talk to you first."

"Okay . . ." He turned away from his kids. "Can I come over now?"

"I'll meet you at the back door."

What was this about? He couldn't imagine. He made excuses to the kids and went through the back door and across the yard, where Jill and Shelley had practically worn a path over the years.

Shelley was waiting on the back deck when Mitch arrived. She invited him in.

"Hey . . . What's going on?"

"Mitch . . ." She looked at the floor, then pulled out a tall stool at the kitchen bar and sat down.

Her voice wavered, and that fact made Mitch steel himself. "What's wrong, Shelley?"

"This is probably nothing. And Jill will never forgive me, but . . . I would feel awful if it did turn out to be significant."

He waited, unable even to imagine what she might have been keeping from him all these hours.

Shelley seemed to be waiting for him to sit down too, so he pulled out a stool and perched beside her at the counter.

"A few weeks ago—maybe early July—Jill got a friend invite on Facebook from an old boyfriend. Greg somebody . . . ? She said he was the first boyfriend she'd ever had . . ."

"Greg Hamaker."

"I don't know if she ever told me his last name, but . . . well, she friended him. On Facebook." She held up her hands, palms out. "There was *nothing* between them, Mitch. I'm *sure* of that. But she had a few conversations with him—only through Facebook. Just friendly chitchat."

Mitch pulled out a bar stool and straddled it, trying not to look as stunned as he felt. Jill hadn't said a word. She had dated Greg off and on through most of high school. Mitch had never met the guy, but he knew about him. Greg lived in Kansas now, was on his second marriage, and was "a total jerk" according to Jill. Though Mitch suspected she played up the jerk aspect for his sake. Jill wouldn't have dated a *total* jerk for three years. Still, he and Jill never kept old relationships secret from each other. Never kept any secrets. At least that's what he'd always thought.

Greg was only a high school fling. Maybe they'd seen each other once or twice her first semester of college, but never after he and Jill started dating. Still . . . Three years. That wasn't something a woman took lightly.

In fact, Jill admitted once that she'd thought

she would end up marrying Greg. "Until I met you," she was always quick to add when the subject came up.

Shelley closed her eyes and pressed her lips together. It was obvious she had more to tell.

After a long minute of silence, he prodded her. "So what are you saying? What does this have to do with us going to Kansas City?"

"Apparently Greg was going to be in Kansas City this weekend. Had meetings near her hotel. When he found out Jill would be in town, he invited her to have lunch with him."

That knocked the wind out of him. "Did—she go?"

Shelley shook her head. "No. At least I don't think so. She said she wasn't going to. . . ."

"But you think she could have?" That didn't even sound like his wife. "She considered it?"

"For a little bit. But . . . when she realized she wouldn't have told you about it, she decided it wouldn't be wise to go."

"What do you mean she wouldn't have told me about it?" He braced the ball of his foot hard on the lowest rung of the bar stool. It was an effort to keep his tone steady. He hated this feeling of Shelley holding these things over him.

"I just mean . . . She knew you wouldn't want her to go, so she said she'd either have to tell you, or just not go. I'm almost positive she'd decided not to go." She looked him in the eye as if willing him to believe her. "That's why I didn't say anything in the beginning."

"So why are you telling me now? You must think there's at least the possibility that she went."

"I truly don't think she would have met him without telling you, Mitch. But—well, what if I'm wrong? Maybe I should have said something before, but I just kept thinking she would show up any minute. I feel like a jerk betraying her confidence . . . But now . . . What if there is something to this?"

She found no sympathy in his eyes.

"Did she say where Greg lives now? He doesn't live in Kansas City?"

"A suburb, I think. I'm not sure. It sounded like he was coming into town on business. From where, I don't know. I found him on Facebook, but he has most of his info hidden. Do you know Jill's Facebook password? You could see more information if you could log in to her account."

"I don't know anything about Facebook. Jill only got on there when the kids did. I don't think she ever got on there unless she was seeing what the kids were up to."

Shelley bit her lip and looked away.

"What the—" He shook his head. "Am I wrong? She *did* spend time on Facebook? What else don't I know about my own wife?"

"No . . . It's not like that, Mitch. But Jill did have quite a few friends on Facebook. I mean,

100

she wasn't just on there to creep on the kids. Do you think Katie might know her password?"

His mind was reeling. "I doubt it. But maybe we can figure it out." He huffed in frustration. "This is the stuff we warn our teachers and students about. What was Jill thinking?"

"It's just a tool, Mitch. Facebook is perfectly safe if you're cautious."

He inhaled and blew out a slow breath. "Do you think Jill and Greg were—" He scrubbed his face with his palms, unable to finish the sentence.

"No. Of course not. They were just friends. You know that. And old friends. I honestly don't think she'd talked to him in years. At least she was surprised to hear from him—on Facebook, I mean. But surely you know women well enough to know that a first boyfriend—especially for as long as Jill dated Greg—always holds a special place in a woman's heart. But," she added quickly, "Jill was—*is*—head over heels in love with you, Mitch. I have absolutely *no* doubt of that."

He hadn't missed Shelley speaking of Jill in past tense. He'd caught himself doing the same. It disturbed him deeply. And made him question his faith that God would take care of Jill. Now he questioned everything he'd thought about his marriage to Jill.

"Mitch . . ." Shelley put a hand on his arm as if she knew his thoughts. "Jill would never do anything to put your marriage in jeopardy. I *know* that. And I think Greg's invitation was just . . . friendly. I don't think he was coming on to her or anything."

"But she was flattered." It wasn't a question.

"Of course she was. Any woman would be."

"But why didn't she tell me?"

"Because she knew it would make you question her love. Like you are right now. And if she wasn't going to see him there was no reason to tell you and get you all stirred up."

"She told you that?"

"Not in so many words. But I know Jill well enough to know that's true. And for what it's worth, when she was deciding if she should meet him"—she cringed as if she wished she hadn't mentioned that again—"I reminded her of my story." She looked at him like he should know what she was talking about.

"Which story is that?"

"Oh . . . Maybe you don't know. Tom left me after connecting with an old girlfriend at a reunion."

"Ohhh. No, I guess I didn't know that."

"It's okay. I shouldn't have expected you to. Anyway, Jill knew it wasn't something to take lightly. That's why I would almost swear that she didn't meet him. But if there's any chance . . . I thought I should mention it."

"Yes. I'm glad you did." He ran a hand over his face, looking distraught.

"Just so you know, Mitch, Jill didn't keep secrets from you. In fact, the first time I ever confided in her, she wouldn't let me continue until I understood that you and she were 'one' and that she wasn't comfortable keeping anything from you."

He pondered her words, mildly consoled. "So what am I supposed to tell my kids?"

"Why do you need to tell them anything? I just thought you might want to talk to Greg. If there's any chance at all that Jill did decide to see him in Kansas City, maybe it would be"—she shrugged—"a lead. Or at least a place to start."

"I guess it's better than what we have now. Which is pretty much nothing."

"If Katie doesn't know Jill's password I wonder if the police can somehow get into her Facebook account."

"They made copies of our hard drive at home. And I signed something for them to get into her computer at school. You'd think they would have checked it out already." He had talked to Carol once, but hadn't thought to ask Jill's principal if the police had actually confiscated her work computer or copied the hard drive like they'd done with their home computer.

A chilling thought came to him, and he dared to voice it. "Do you think the police could track if there's been any activity on Jill's laptop?"

"I don't know. They've surely checked the

obvious things already. Her credit cards, phone records." Shelley tilted her head. "You don't really think she just—disappeared . . . of her own free will, I mean?"

"Do you? It seems like you knew her better than I ever did."

"Stop it, Mitch. That's not true. Wives share things with girlfriends sometimes that husbands don't necessarily need to know."

"You don't think husbands need to know when their wives are seeing old boyfriends?" He didn't even attempt to keep the bitter incredulity from his voice.

"That's not fair, Mitch. Jill was not seeing him. He contacted *her*. She didn't start it. It was one lunch invitation—between friends. And I would almost swear that she declined. So please don't jump to conclusions." She put her head in her hands with a sigh. "I never should have said anything."

He forced himself to calm down. "No. I'm sorry. I didn't mean to take it out on you. I'm just exhausted. And worried sick. I'm glad you told me. I need to know everything I possibly can if I'm going to find her. I'm sorry I got so upset. Please don't hold anything back."

She sighed again and Mitch steeled himself.

"Okay," she said. "Then maybe there are a couple of other things I should tell you."

10

"Mitch, Jill loves you to pieces. You've got to believe that." Shelley's forehead furrowed and she didn't seem able to meet his gaze.

Mitch rubbed circles on the speckled countertop, trying to brace himself for what she might reveal next.

"I think she held a lot back from you because she wasn't sure how you would react. Or maybe she was still trying to wrap her mind around everything with Katie going to college—"

"But she talked to me about that. We talked. I know she was—" He grasped for a word, anger roiling inside him. How dare Shelley Austin insinuate that there were things Jill would confide in a friend and hide from *him*. He measured his next words. "I know Jill was almost in mourning over Katie leaving. Believe me, she talked about that plenty."

"Did she mention that she was afraid you two would grow apart now that the kids are gone? That she was afraid you wouldn't find her interesting anymore?"

"What?" Where was this coming from? "That's ridiculous! She's the most interesting woman I know."

Shelley held up a hand. "I know. That's what I

told her. But she was struggling. Kind of a midlife crisis, I think. Enough that she saw a counselor. But maybe she told you that. . . ."

His heart sank. And he could see in Shelley's eyes that she knew Jill *hadn't* told him. Was she just patronizing him now? It didn't matter. What mattered was that his wife had been seeing a counselor and he'd been completely unaware. Had she missed school for those appointments? How could he have been so blind? What kind of fool was he that he'd thought everything was fine between them? "I didn't know. I guess I'm utterly clueless," he finally said.

"No. Jill wanted it that way."

He looked at her askance. "She wanted me utterly clueless?"

Shelley gave a little laugh, and strangely, it offered him a tiny spark of hope.

"No," she said. "She didn't want you to know about the counselor. She knew it would only worry you. Make you think something was wrong between the two of you."

"But obviously there *was* something wrong!"

"No. It wasn't like that. She went because of her fears for the future. She felt like they were out of proportion to reality. It really didn't have anything to do with you. That's why she didn't tell you."

"It had everything to do with me! How could it not, if she was worried I wouldn't find her attractive, that I—" He couldn't even bring himself to voice Jill's fears. Was it any wonder she'd had to see a counselor? Was he that uncaring that she hadn't felt she could talk to him about these fears?

"Mitch, she just wanted some help getting through a rough patch. She knew how crazy things were with you at work, and she didn't want to bother you with something she felt she should be able to get over by herself."

"And of course, when an old boyfriend called, she was flattered." He closed his eyes.

"I'm sure she was, but that's not the point. Not at all. Jill just didn't want to bother you with what she felt were her own issues. She knew if she told you, you'd take the blame—which you're only proving by your reaction right now." She gave a telling smile at that, but just as quickly, turned serious again. "And it *wasn't* your fault."

He wished he could believe her. But this wasn't the time for self-flagellation. "The kids are waiting. And they've got to be wondering what this"—he motioned between them—"is all about. I need to get back."

"Of course."

He slid off the kitchen stool and started for the back door. "I think I need to talk to Greg Hamaker—just for my own peace of mind."

She nodded and followed him to the door. "Yes, I think you should."

107

What on earth would he tell Evan and Katie? He didn't want to plant even a hint of doubt in their minds about their mother. Even if those doubts had already crept into his own.

"I'm sorry, Mitch. I—should have said something earlier."

"Yes. You should have."

With one hand gripping the cold doorknob of her back door, Shelley stared at Mitch. His words—*Yes, you should have*—hit her squarely in the chest. Was he right? She'd thought she was helping Jill by keeping the confidence. Now she wasn't so sure.

"I'm truly sorry, Mitch. I feel like a traitor to Jill, and—*worse* to you. Maybe I shouldn't have said anything, but—"

"I've got to let Simonides know about Greg Hamaker. And I hope to heaven they don't call off the search when they find out."

"What are you talking about?"

"Don't you see? This makes it look like something was wrong in Paradise—like Jill might have had a reason to leave." He fished his phone out of his pocket and turned away, dismissing her. But while he waited for the call to go through, he turned back. "Would you mind telling the kids I'm on my way? I'd like to get on the road right away."

"Mitch, please believe me when I tell you that

Jill loves you more than anything in this world," she said again, pleading, feeling responsible for the deep V that now seemed a permanent fixture between Mitch's eyebrows. "There's no way there was anything going on between her and Greg."

Ignoring her, he turned away again and spoke into the phone.

Stinging from his tacit rebuke, she started across the narrow alleyway connecting their backyards. He'd made it clear that he was finished hearing anything she had to say.

She'd felt like a traitor—and an instrument of torture besides—sharing the things Jill had confided in her. But she would have felt worse keeping quiet when Jill's secrets might hold a clue to where she was now. Still, she believed what she'd told him. Jill would never have betrayed him.

She quickened her steps. Mitch's kids were waiting. When she reached the Brannons' back door, she turned to see Mitch still talking on the phone.

When he came in through the back door a few minutes later, she could almost see him put on a new demeanor the way he might pull on an itchy sweater. Mitch grabbed his jacket off the back of a kitchen chair. "Are you guys ready to go?"

In answer they moved toward the back door, eyeing Shelley as if wondering whether she was going with them. Or maybe wondering what she and Mitch had been talking about. But they said nothing, and she didn't try to explain.

She slipped her hoodie off and hung it on the chair where Mitch's jacket had been. Giving Katie a quick hug, she tried to make her voice matter-of-fact. "I'm going to stay here at the house in case your mom comes home or tries to call."

She thought Katie looked relieved and wondered if it was because she wasn't coming with them, or because someone would be at home for Jill.

They gathered jackets from the mudroom closet and water bottles from the fridge and filed out the door.

She stood in the door between the garage and the kitchen and waved, whispering a prayer to send them off. "Give them a miracle, God. Please let them find her."

The garage door closed behind them, and Shelley retreated back into the kitchen. The house was bathed in silence. She realized that, except for stepping into the garage to feed TP when they were on vacation, she'd never been alone in Mitch and Jill's house. It felt . . . odd. As if she were trespassing. She walked through the rooms, almost feeling Jill's spirit in the very walls of the house. Her touch was everywhere. Along with visible reminders of the friendship she and Jill had shared all these years.

She walked down the hallway past Mitch's study, to the bedrooms, peeking into each room, not even sure what she was looking for. Jill had made a halfhearted attempt to turn Evan's room into an office for herself, but the floral overstuffed chair and the plastic basketball hoop hanging over the door made an eclectic potpourri of elementary school teacher and teenage boy.

Back in the dining room Shelley ran a hand across the antique sideboard she and Jill had refinished together back when crackle paint was all the rage. It looked outdated and too countrified for Shelley's taste now, but when she'd said as much recently and suggested repainting the piece, Jill had feigned a gasp. "You had better not go all modern on me, Shelley Austin."

She smiled at the memory and brushed a microscopic crumb off the sideboard. This was the "dresser" she and Jill had bought and wrestled into her old Escape at the antique shop they'd driven past on the way back from Kansas City. The day after Jill disappeared.

Was that only four days ago? Her throat clogged with tears. What would she do if her friend didn't come back? She couldn't imagine life without Jill next door. She lost her breath at the next thought that came.

If Jill was gone, would Mitch stay here, or would he move away?

Her sigh echoed through the empty rooms, but it failed to answer her question.

11

"I win!" Shelley's cheer rang false, yet Mitch silently thanked God that she was here with them, keeping Evan and Katie busy playing some card game. He sat in his easy chair, pretending to read the newspaper, but keeping a watchful eye on his kids, dreading what they might have to go through in the next hours and days.

He'd sometimes felt annoyed with Shelley Austin when she took Jill's time or energy away from him. It was pure selfishness. Shelley was a great friend to Jill. The kind who always had Jill's best interests at heart, and would have done anything for her. He made a mental note to be more appreciative of their friendship when this was all over.

The four of them had been huddled in the family room around the large flat-screen TV ever since he and the kids returned from a fruitless drive to Kansas City and back. While they were gone Shelley had baked—in their kitchen—making chocolate chip cookies from Jill's recipe for Evan and Katie. The sweet smell wafted through the house—just the right touch, and true comfort food for his kids. And even though he had no appetite, he ate one of her cookies just to show his appreciation for her thoughtfulness.

Shelley's news about Jill and Greg Hamaker was eating him alive. He'd relayed the disturbing information to Detective Simonides, along with the news that Jill had been seeing a counselor. He'd even driven by Hamaker's office, a brokerage firm in Kansas City. But of course, it was closed for the Labor Day holiday. Even if it had been open, Mitch wouldn't have confronted Hamaker while Evan and Katie were with him. He hoped his kids would never have to hear the man's name.

He grabbed the remote and punched the volume down, leaving it just loud enough so they could hear if anything came over the news.

News had traveled quickly through town, and even before he and the kids returned, Shelley had fielded concerned neighbors and friends bearing casseroles. Now, the doorbell rang yet again, and without Mitch asking her to, Shelley jumped up to answer it.

He heard her making gracious excuses for him and the kids, and thank someone for an offering of food—no doubt another lasagna, or a chicken and rice casserole to add to the collection. He checked the cynical, ungrateful thought. It meant the world to him that so many had remembered them with food and phone calls and prayers. But it all had a much too funereal feel to it. And he was not ready to go there.

The front door closed, and he heard Shelley

in the kitchen, opening the refrigerator and rearranging its contents to make room. If he closed his eyes, he could almost imagine it was an ordinary day and it was Jill in the kitchen, puttering and creating the homey sounds he'd too often taken for granted until now.

A minute later, when Shelley plopped down cross-legged on the floor in front of the coffee table, he waited to catch her eye. "I'm going to go in the den and make some phone calls," he said softly. "Do you mind getting the door if anyone else comes?"

"Of course. Go on. I've got it."

"Thanks." He started down the hallway, dreading the task he'd put off until the kids were occupied. TP gave a little whine and lumbered off the sofa, following after him. "No, boy. You stay."

Shelley called the dog, and TP looked up at Mitch as if asking permission. "It's okay, fella. Stay. Stay with Shelley."

He mouthed his thanks to her and went down the hall to the den, closing the door behind him. He settled in his chair, grabbed a pencil from the Cardinals mug by the telephone, and punched in the number Detective Simonides had given him.

After being put on hold twice, he was finally connected to the detective.

He dispensed with niceties. "This is Mitch Brannon. Do you have any news for us?"

"I'm sorry. Nothing. I've gotta tell you, I've never had a case with so few clues."

"Will they get some search dogs looking, or is that something I'd have to arrange privately?"

"We had a K-9 dog at the hotel the day her phone was found and turned up nothing. If we had something—*anything* to go on, we'd put together a K-9 team, but we have to have some kind of lead. We can't just start from zero."

"Can't you just have them follow the routes she might have taken?" He knew he sounded as desperate as he felt.

"Mr. Brannon, the area between the hotel and your house covers hundreds of miles of Interstate and highways. Thousands if you consider all the city streets and back roads she could have taken, assuming she even headed that direction . . ." The detective's voice trailed off, and Mitch could tell his patience was thinning.

"What about the counselor my wife was seeing? Were you able to talk to him?"

"Yes. We've spoken with him." Simonides hesitated. "You realize there are confidentiality laws that preclude—"

"Yes, but surely they have to make an exception for something like this. If someone is in danger . . ."

"It's been more than six weeks since the counselor last saw your wife, but he did not believe there was anything about her emotional

115

state that would have led her to do anything . . . rash. He felt she was mentally stable. That's all I can say."

Mitch's mind reeled. He did triage on the barrage of questions from his mental list and asked the one that rose to the top. "Did you talk to Greg Hamaker?"

"Yes. But he didn't have any new information. There's nothing there."

"Did he know Jill was missing?"

"Not until we told him."

"Either that or he's a good liar."

Simonides cleared his throat. "Mr. Hamaker didn't deny that he'd invited your wife to get together over coffee while she was in Kansas City for the conference. He said she first agreed to meet, but then she called him from the hotel and canceled. I think he's on the up-and-up. We can see the call to him in her phone's history. Around noon, just like he said. He's been cooperative— agreed to share the brief communication he had with her on Facebook, and there's nothing there to indicate anything more than he told us. And his alibi checks out. He was in meetings in Kansas City shortly after he talked to Jill. But don't worry, we're keeping an eye on him."

A rush of relief was quickly replaced by chagrin. Jill had canceled, yes, but she'd first agreed to meet with Greg. Why? Had she been looking to renew that friendship? That *romance?*

Had he been so blind that he couldn't see she was unhappy in their marriage?

No. He gripped the pencil so hard his knuckles went white. No, he had too many memories—recent memories—that supported his belief. They had a good marriage. No one could convince him otherwise. But it hurt that Jill had considered meeting Greg at all without telling him. He and Jill had some hard things to talk about when they found her.

He was almost afraid to ask his next question. "Does this change—the search. You're not going to quit searching, are you . . . because of this?"

"No, sir. As long as we have reason to believe your wife did not leave of her own volition, we will search for her."

He hung up, knowing he should have told Simonides his plans—asked permission even—but he didn't want to risk that the detective would try to dissuade him. He had to talk to Greg Hamaker himself. Hear for himself what the man had to say.

It hadn't taken him three minutes on Google to find Hamaker's business address and a phone number. A home phone, he was pretty sure, since it came via a local area-wide phone directory.

"Hello?" The feminine voice sounded wary.

He hesitated. He hadn't thought of Hamaker's wife. He wondered if she knew about Greg's invitation to Jill. The answer to that question would tell him a lot about the guy's intentions, but he would give Hamaker a chance first. "May I speak to Greg, please?"

"May I tell him who's calling?"

"This is Mitchell Brannon."

"You're . . . Jill's husband." It wasn't a question.

"Yes. Is Greg there?"

"The police have already talked to him. I . . . I don't know what else you want from him."

"Mrs. Hamak—I'm sorry . . . Is this Greg's wife?"

A long pause. "Yes."

"I'm just trying to get any information I possibly can about my wife. You probably know that Greg and Jill were high school . . . friends. I know they'd been in con—" He clipped off the word. He didn't want to hurt an innocent woman, but if Hamaker had any information about Jill, he didn't have a choice. He tried to make his tone caring. "I know they'd been in contact in the weeks before Jill disappeared. On Facebook. I'm hoping your husband might be able to shed some light on what happened. We have nothing else to go on. I'm just—I'm desperate for anything at all that might give us a clue to where my wife is."

She sighed. "Just a moment. I'll get Greg."

He heard their murmured conversation in the background, then a terse reply. "This is Greg."

"Greg, this is Mitch Brannon—Jill's husband. I take it you've heard that she's missing."

"Yes, I—I'm sorry. I truly am, but I don't appreciate you calling my wife and disrupting my family. And I don't appreciate the police breathing down my neck. You wouldn't know anything about that, would you?"

Mitch clenched his fist tighter around the pencil. "You are one of the last people Jill talked to. And the police are asking about it because she didn't tell anyone that you two were meeting in Kansas City."

"Like I told the detective, Jill declined my invitation."

"But she first accepted?"

"Just a moment."

Mitch couldn't hear all of the muffled conversation, but he got the impression that Hamaker had asked his wife to leave the room.

"Listen, Brannon. Your wife and I are old friends. I hadn't talked to Jill since college. We connected on Facebook, I found out she was going to be in town, and I suggested we get together for coffee. She called and canceled. End of story."

"No, it's not the end of the story, because my wife never came home. And if you know something you're not tell—"

"Listen, Brannon, I am sincerely sorry about Jill. I was shocked to hear about it. But like I said, I've told the police everything I know. There's nothing more to say, and I don't wish to be involved further. If you have anything else to say, please talk to that detective. I have nothing more to offer."

The phone went dead. The guy had hung up on him. Didn't that indicate some level of guilt?

But what if he was telling the truth? Mitch tried to put himself in Hamaker's place. Not that he would ever try to connect with one of his old girlfriends without Jill being there, or at least knowing about it. But if he had been the last one to see a friend alive, how awful—how mortified—he would feel to be a suspect. He would worry about his reputation with the school district and the community. If Hamaker was innocent as he claimed, he and his family must be worried that this would affect their livelihood.

And yes, it had probably caused some strife between the guy and his wife. It wasn't fair to ruin another man's life just because he was suffering. He needed to let it go.

But he couldn't. Something about Hamaker's attitude wouldn't let him dismiss it so easily. He needed to look the man in the eye. Only then could he be sure he was telling the truth.

12

Wednesday, September 8

"I'm sorry, Mr. Hamaker is out of the office. Did you have an appointment?" The well-dressed woman behind the desk of Hamaker & Associates was friendly enough, but Mitch thought she looked rather cautious. He wondered if the police had confronted Greg here in his office.

"I don't have an appointment, but I need to speak with Mr. Hamaker. With Greg."

"May I ask what this is concerning?"

"It's a personal matter. I'd rather not say."

"I can give you his number." The receptionist slid a business card from a brass display on the shiny desktop and handed it to him. "You may leave a voice message and have him return your call when he's available."

"Thank you, but it really is urgent that I speak with him in person. When do you expect him back?"

"Probably around two o'clock, but he has appointments all afternoon. Would you like to set up an appointment for later this week?"

"No. I'm here from out of town. I drove quite a distance to speak with him. May I ask where he is right now? Maybe I can catch him at lunch or—"

"I'm sorry, I'm not free to give out that information."

Mitch looked at his watch. An hour and a half before Hamaker was due back. "Could I wait for him in his office?"

"You're welcome to wait here in reception." The woman was definitely getting suspicious. "I would recommend leaving a voice mail message for him though. I could call for you, if you like. But he'll need to know what this is concerning."

"Yes. I guess . . . that would be good."

"Your name?"

"Mitchell . . . Mr. Mitchell." It wasn't exactly a lie. "He'll know what it's about."

Hamaker probably wouldn't make the connection, but Mitch was banking on curiosity getting the better of him. Mitch started to take a seat in a plush leather chair at one end of the reception room, but an idea came and he changed his mind.

He thanked the receptionist and reached for the door. "I'll be back in about an hour."

He went out to the parking lot and drove around behind the building. Just as he suspected, there was a reserved space for G. Hamaker. Mitch pulled his car into a space beneath a tree across from the executive parking. His chances of getting to talk to Hamaker were far greater if he caught him before he went inside the building.

He pulled out his cell phone and checked his messages and then his e-mails. More condolences and a text from Shelley letting him know the kids were doing fine. *I'm winning at gin.*

He smiled, grateful again that Shelley had been willing to come over and keep the kids company—and cover for him, since he hadn't told Evan and Katie where he was going.

The purr of a car's motor and a flash of silver made him look up. A late-model Lexus slid into G. Hamaker's parking lot. Mitch wiped sweaty palms on his thighs and got out of the car.

He took a deep breath. *Here goes.* "Mr. Hamaker?"

The man who turned to face him was nothing like Mitch remembered from Jill's high school photos—or from the images on Hamaker & Associates' website, for that matter. His graying blond hair was clipped short and he wore wire-rimmed glasses. He was taller than Mitch expected and looked like he spent his lunch hours at the gym. "Yes?"

Mitch strode toward him, arm outstretched in a manner friendlier—and far braver—than he felt. "I'm Mitchell Brannon. Jill's husband."

Greg Hamaker shook his hand, though he seemed reluctant. "How can I help you?"

"We spoke on the phone last night . . . I just have a few more questions. I thought it might be better if we talked in person."

"I told you everything I know."

"Please. Could I take just a moment of your

time? I'll keep it short, I promise. I know you're busy." It took every ounce of self-restraint he had to maintain the polite, diplomatic demeanor. "I wonder if Jill said anything—either when she accepted your invitation or when she called to cancel it—that might tell you what her state of mind was."

"She seemed to be . . . herself. What I remember of her. It had been a long time since we'd talked."

"But she did accept your invitation initially? To get together?"

"Listen, Brannon, I've told the police everything I know. That's who you should be talking to. You had no right to call my house and you have no right to come to my place of business and—"

"And you had no right to invite my wife on a date!" He was losing it and he knew it, but he couldn't seem to stop the accusation from leaving his lips.

"I meant nothing at all by the invitation. It was a simple lunch between friends. If Jill implied otherwise, she was mistaken. The only thing—"

"She didn't *imply* anything because she didn't tell me about it. Period."

"I don't know why that makes *me* a suspect. I did nothing wrong. Jill called me the day we were supposed to have lunch and said it wasn't going to work out. She didn't give me a reason and I didn't press her. End of story. Now I wish you'd lay off and leave me alone." He started for the back door to the building, fists clenching at his side, but before he entered, he turned on Mitch. "You've turned this into a federal case and it's threatening my marriage. If you try to contact me again, if you set foot on my property again, I will call the police and have you escorted off."

Was he serious? "Well, excuse me if I have inconvenienced you in any way." He immediately regretted his sarcasm and worked to control the rage roiling inside him. "Listen . . . I'm trying to find my wife who has apparently vanished into thin air. Surely you can put yourself in my shoes and see that you'd want to talk to me if I was the last one who'd been in contact with your wife before she went missing."

"I have cooperated with the authorities in every way. I've told everything I know. You're harassing me for information I don't have. I'm finished." With that, he grabbed the fancy door handle and disappeared into the building.

Deflated and trembling, Mitch crossed the parking lot and got into his car. Something about Greg Hamaker's story didn't ring true. Mitch didn't trust the man any farther than he could throw him, but they couldn't get a conviction on a hunch.

What now? He put the key in the ignition, but he was too upset to drive. He gripped the steering wheel and closed his eyes.

He had no inkling of where to turn next. Every avenue had been exhausted. Even the police and the missing persons agencies were at a loss. He only had one recourse, and though he knew it was the most powerful thing at his disposal, right now it felt futile. But he had nothing else. Nothing.

If he'd been anywhere but his car, he would have slid to his knees. Instead, he bowed over the steering wheel and rested his forehead on his hands. "God please . . . Help me. Help Jill. Help *us* . . ."

He hadn't shed a tear since this whole nightmare had begun, but he wept now. Wept bitterly—and prayed for all he was worth.

Thursday, September 9

Mitch grabbed the remote and turned the TV up a notch, wishing Evan and Katie didn't have to hear it, but not willing to miss what the reporter would say. The TV had been on day and night for five days now.

Jill had now been missing for almost one hundred forty hours, and it seemed with every hour that passed, the authorities scaled back their efforts. It didn't help that everything had been closed for the holiday weekend and now they were playing catch-up at every level.

Simonides had chewed Mitch out for

confronting Greg Hamaker. "You need to let us handle this investigation. If you have any information, if you think of anything else, you let us know and we'll handle it. But you can't go hunting down people who've already been cleared. We will keep you apprised of what's going on, but the last thing we need is vigilantes taking things into their own hands."

Mitch apologized, knowing he deserved the reprimand. The detective softened a little, and assured Mitch they were doing everything possible, and that Jill would remain on the active missing persons databases as long as there was no proof she hadn't disappeared voluntarily. But Mitch sensed that Simonides was beginning to believe—or maybe had always believed—that Jill didn't wish to be found.

They would never convince him of that. Never.

Over the last four days, besides interviewing as many of the teachers in attendance at Jill's conference as they could track down, the authorities had talked to friends and family. Those same friends and family had formed unofficial search parties, combing the countryside between Kansas City and Sylvia for any clue that might lead to Jill's whereabouts.

Complete strangers from as far away as St. Louis, Cape Girardeau, and even Springfield had joined the search, but when Mitch looked at a map and saw the intricate web of intersecting county roads and back roads—all the possible routes Jill could have taken if she veered from the Interstate and main highways, his optimism flagged. The area was so wide with virtually *nothing* to go on, that it felt like the proverbial hunt for a needle in a haystack. There was a bit of comfort in knowing they all—authorities and civilians alike—were doing everything they possibly could to locate Jill. Still, none of it mattered if it didn't bring her home.

Shelley's presence in their home had cheered the kids up a little. And him. Mitch wasn't sure how they would have managed without her. As word spread through their little town of Sylvia and beyond, the doorbell rang again and again with neighbors, church friends, and coworkers from his school and Jill's, offering their condolences and prayers.

Shelley had come over each morning as soon as she saw lights on in their windows, and she stayed each evening until Mitch insisted she go home. In between, she kept up with the kids' laundry and answered the door—thanking friends and fiercely turning away the reporters that hounded them.

Tonight, as had become their habit, the four of them ate supper in front of the TV, a Mexican dish someone from church had brought by and Shelley had warmed up.

"I've got next week off from work," she said, trying, he knew, to sound casual.

"The whole week?"

"Yes, so whatever you need me to do, I'll be available."

He knew Shelley well enough not to argue, and he silently blessed Jill's friend for everything she'd offered them at a time like this.

"Evan, I think you and Katie ought to find out about getting your class assignments sent home. I don't want you guys to be too far behind when you get back to school, and it'll help the time go faster while we wait."

Katie glared at him. "Dad, how can we even think about school right now?"

Evan shook his head in agreement. "There's no way I could concentrate on anything else. And besides, I wouldn't know who to call to get our stuff."

"A few more days won't matter, will it?" Shelley said softly. "Maybe I can help you guys check with the school tomorrow . . ." She looked between Evan and Katie. "We could at least get some online reading assignments so you guys aren't swamped when you get back."

He appreciated her diplomacy. As much as he wanted Evan and Katie here, with every hour that went by with no word on Jill, he feared what his precious kids might have to experience when news finally came. As much as their presence comforted him, it was tempting to just send them back to school. It about killed him to imagine having to see their anguish if bad news came to the house about Jill, and he—

He couldn't finish the thought. Not even in his mind.

"I know how you feel, guys. I don't think I'd be worth anything at work either."

"You don't have to work tomorrow, do you?" Shelley looked appalled.

"No . . . My superintendent insisted I take the rest of the week off." Mitch knew he wasn't in any shape to go back to work yet, but the thought of sitting around watching television, waiting for some morsel of information, was something he couldn't let himself think about.

They all turned at the sound of scratching on the patio doors. TP sat on the other side, looking in the French doors. Mitch went to let him in. If the look in TP's eyes was any indication, the dog was in mourning along with the rest of them. And yet, TP had quit looking for Jill after that first night. Mitch took TP's head in his hands and caressed it, even as he turned away from the doggie breath that wafted up to him. "Come on, boy. Come inside. You could use a Milk-Bone." He grabbed a treat from the laundry room and followed the dog back to the family room.

Shelley reached out to stroke TP's neck as he brushed by on his way to Katie's chair. The dog plopped down beside Katie, who seemed to have taken Jill's place in his affections.

"Hey! Turn up the TV!" Evan set down his plate and grabbed the remote. "It's about Mom."

"Still no sign of the Sylvia teacher missing since Friday. Brannon failed to return to her home in this small south-central Missouri town after attending an educator's conference in Kansas City, Kansas."

They sat like statues, listening as the anchor-woman gave a dispassionate—and disheartening—report.

"That's right here! In Sylvia." Katie pointed to the images on the screen. "That's our house!" She had her laptop open on her lap and immediately started typing furiously—no doubt keeping her classmates who were away at colleges across the country up to date on everything that was happening.

"Katie? You're being careful about what you post, I hope? I'd hate for—"

"Dad, I don't need a lecture. I'm being careful."

He let it go, but after the brouhaha with Miriam finding out about Jill on Facebook, he'd warned both the kids about being careful what personal information they put out there.

The news camera pulled back and panned their neighborhood. The television footage zoomed in on their front door, then briefly showed Shelley's house, and the Claremonts' to the north.

Mitch hated that his situation had brought the media down on their little town. Still, he was grateful they'd been able to keep the press mostly at bay until now. At least they hadn't invaded his back yard or accosted them leaving the driveway like he'd seen with other media circuses. And if the publicity helped them find Jill he would let them sit at his dinner table. . .

"According to statistics from the Missing Persons Unit of the Missouri State Highway Patrol, Brannon's is one of more than one thousand active missing persons reports in the state.

"The third-grade teacher was last seen by a fellow teacher in the lobby of the Royale Suites hotel in Kansas City. Her vehicle, a gray 2007 Toyota Camry, has never been located, and a message she left her husband on the couple's home answering machine gave no indication that Brannon was in danger or under duress.

"A spokesperson for the Missouri State Highway Patrol said when a person is declared missing by a state law enforcement agency, that person's name is added to a database. The agency serves as a liaison between the public and the law enforcement agency."

The story cut to an interview with a stony-faced Highway Patrol spokesperson at his desk. He spoke without emotion, as if he were speaking of a nameless, faceless person. Not Jill.

"It is feasible that some persons who remain in the database are not in fact in harm's way. Sometimes, for any number of reasons, an adult or juvenile may decide to 'disappear.' Unless he's wanted by law enforcement agencies for a crime, if an adult doesn't want to be found, that's their prerogative."

The anchor gave a pithy recap and the screen flashed to a different story.

The four of them sat around the TV, dazed.

"A thousand people?" Katie's voice held a hush that could have been awe.

"What is wrong with them?" Evan sneered. "How could there be a thousand people missing in one state?"

If Mitch hadn't been sure before, he was convinced now. And convicted. If Jill was going to be found, he would have to find her himself.

"Dad! Look at this!" Katie crawled off the sofa and brought her open laptop over to him, turning the screen so he could see.

He craned his neck to cut the glare. "What am I looking at?"

"I don't know." She looked like she'd seen a ghost. "Mom just tweeted 'Happy birthday' to me!"

"What?" His pulse raced. "What are you talking about?"

"She just posted a tweet for my birthday—on Twitter!"

"Just now, you mean? You heard from Mom just now?" He could scarcely breathe.

"Yes!" She peered at the computer. "The time stamp says it was just two minutes ago!"

"Are you sure? You're sure it's her? On Twitter?" Mitch bent to look over her shoulder at the laptop screen, not daring to hope.

Evan slid off the couch and scooted over to where he sat. "No," he said, sounding deflated. "I know what it is."

His demeanor punctured hopes Mitch hadn't quite realized he'd entertained. "What's the deal? It's not Mom?"

"No. It's her," Evan said. "Sort of. It's a tweet she scheduled . . . that day I helped her download all those apps and stuff. Last summer . . . Remember? I showed her how to schedule tweets ahead of time, and she tested it out on our birthdays."

He turned to Shelley. "You'll get one, too, Shelley. On your birthday." He turned to Mitch. "You would've too, Dad . . . if you were on Twitter."

"You're positive Mom couldn't have tweeted it just now?" He held his breath, hoping against hope.

Evan looked almost disgusted with him. "Dad, do you really think she's going to disappear, and

134

then her first communication with us is wishing Katie happy birthday—online—like nothing was wrong?" He did a double take at his sister. "Hey, wait. It's your birthday? *Today?*"

"Oh!" A little gasp escaped Shelley's lips.

Katie looked sheepish, and Mitch's breath caught, for a different reason this time.

September 9. How could he have forgotten his daughter's birthday?

"Oh, sweetie . . ." He pulled her into the crook of his arm. "I am so sorry, honey!" Of all the years to forget . . . He wanted to crawl in a hole.

Katie shrugged. "It's okay, Dad. It's not important."

"Of course it's important. *You* are important. Forgive me, honey. With everything that's been going on—I'm so sorry, kiddo. It won't happen again."

She sniffled and melted into him, her shoulders shaking. He felt sick to his stomach, but he sensed easy forgiveness in her demeanor, too. He stroked her hair and held her until she shrugged out of his embrace. "At least Mom—remembered. Even if it wasn't on the day."

"Of course she remembered."

And he hadn't. Jill had always been the one to handle dates and celebrations and remembering the things that were really important.

Oh, Jill . . . Honey, where are you? I need you.

● ● ●

That night, while Shelley helped him empty the dishwasher, he sought assurance that Katie could forgive him. "I feel like such a heel. There's just been so much going on and—It just . . . never once crossed my mind."

"Katie knows that, Mitch. She's a sweet girl. She's not going to hold this against you."

"I know, but—Of all the times to pull a boneheaded stunt like that." He shook his head.

She set down the stack of dishes she'd carried over to the cupboard. "You know, in a way, it's kind of neat that Jill did that. She had no way of knowing how much that tweet would mean. But for Katie to know Jill was thinking of this birthday, even months before the date came, is pretty special."

"Yeah. Thank goodness *somebody* remembered."

"I should have remembered, too," Shelley said. "But nobody is thinking straight. Katie knows that," she said again.

A hopeful fantasy played in his mind—him getting to tell Jill all about how much that birthday wish had meant. Oh, please God. *Let this be more than wishful thinking.*

Was Jill somewhere right now thinking about Katie, and wishing she could be home for her birthday? But where? How could that be? More and more, thinking about what it meant if Jill was still alive was harder than thinking . . . the worst.

He was losing hope.

Even so, forgetting Katie's birthday was a wake-up call for him. He might have to face losing Jill. But no matter what happened, he had to be there for his kids.

Still, he felt torn in a thousand directions. Yes, Evan and Katie were devastated and in shock like he was. If they faced the worst, his kids would need him desperately. But he also needed to ride herd on the authorities who, in his opinion, had done far too much speculating and far too little actual *searching* for Jill.

He felt the stone in his belly grow heavier by the second.

For Jill's sake, he had to find a way to help his kids go on with their lives. Even if it meant doing that without her.

Which he prayed to God it didn't.

NOVEMBER

13

Monday, November 1

Mitch had just walked in the back door from work when the front doorbell rang. He hadn't seen a car behind him on the street. It was probably Shelley. It was odd she was using the front door though.

Through the living room windows he viewed the tracery of branches of the massive elms that grew in the front yard. Most years, by this first day of November, those trees wore white streamers of toilet paper, courtesy of overgrown trick-or-treaters who couldn't resist the target of their principal's home. But last night, Halloween had passed without incident. The pranksters had passed him by, no doubt out of respect for what had happened. He couldn't find it in him to be grateful.

He reached for the door and opened it, anticipating that smile of Shelley's that always lifted his spirits.

Marcus Simonides stood there, in uniform, with a package in his hands—one of those padded manila envelopes—and a somber look on his face. Mitch's gut twisted. "What is it? Has some-thing happen—"

141

"May I come in?"

Wordlessly, his heart racing, Mitch led the detective through the house to the kitchen table where they'd talked that first day Jill went missing. Hard to believe he'd spent most of two months without Jill now. And yet, in other ways, it seemed like a lifetime.

"You've found something?"

"No. No, I'm sorry. But I wanted to return your wife's things—her phone, and the jewelry that was found in the hotel. There's really no reason for it to be held in evidence any longer." He held out the envelope. "We weren't able to pull any prints off anything other than partial prints from the maid who found the jewelry—and Jill's, of course. We have photographs and recordings on file if we should need them at a later date."

Mitch took the envelope and undid the clasp —one of those old-fashioned string and loop fasteners. "Does this mean—that you're giving up? Closing the case?"

Simonides held up a hand and shook his head emphatically. "No. Absolutely not. The case stays open until we find her." He looked briefly at his lap and Mitch knew exactly what he was thinking: *dead or alive.*

Mitch shrugged out of his jacket and offered to take the detective's overcoat.

Simonides waved him off and pushed back his chair. "I just thought you might like to have these things. Or your daughter might. The jewelry, I mean."

Mitch couldn't imagine Katie wanting these pieces that would only be a reminder of that awful day. He doubted whether he would even mention that the jewelry had been returned. But he opened the envelope and peered inside, wondering again why Jill would have left her watch and the other jewelry behind in a hotel room she'd already checked out of. Why she would have taken any jewelry with her in the first place, when she so rarely wore it. So many unanswered questions.

The detective rose and offered his hand. "We'll keep you posted if we have any new leads. You have the numbers to call if you think of anything else, or if Jill should contact you."

Mitch nodded, feeling this was a dismissal, in spite of Simonides's reassurance to the contrary. He walked with the detective to the door and stood on the porch, watching the patrol car drive away.

He looked across the lawn at this neighborhood that Jill had loved so much. Almost overnight the trees had donned costumes of russet and purple and gold, and the sun cast dappled shadows on the still-green lawn. Fall had always been Jill's favorite time of year and the beauty all around him now, the very air, made him ache for her.

Feeling a weight in his chest, he went back inside and slumped on the sofa, resting his forearms on his thighs, head in his hands. "God, where is she? Please, Lord . . . Even if she's— *dead* . . . I need to know where she is. Please, God. I'm begging you. . . ."

He'd pled with God before, and far more passionately. With far more hope. It scared him to realize that he'd become almost . . . resigned.

A soft knock on the front door brought his head up.

"Mitch?"

Shelley. He rose, smoothing a palm over his hair, and went to open the door again.

Her worried eyes met his. "Is everything okay? I saw the patrol car here and—"

"Everything's fine. They were just returning Jill's things—her phone and the jewelry she left at the hotel."

"Why? Don't they need it? For evidence or . . . something?"

"Simonides said they took pictures, recordings. He thought Katie might want to have the jewelry. For sentimental reasons."

"Oh . . ." Shelley frowned and shook her head. "I could be wrong, but I don't think that's a good idea. At least not now."

"That's what I thought. It would just be a bad reminder."

"I agree. So, it is Jill's jewelry? I mean, you recognize everything?"

"It's her watch. I'm pretty sure. The other stuff

144

I honestly couldn't say. Do you think you'd know if you saw it?"

"Maybe. I can take a look."

"Come on back to the kitchen." He led the way, and after slipping the phone out first, he spilled the rest of the contents of the envelope onto the table.

"Yes, that's her watch." Shelley picked up the bracelet, holding it gingerly, as if she was afraid of contaminating evidence. "I'm not sure about the bracelet—or these earrings. She hardly ever wore jewelry . . ." She dangled one of the earrings between her fingers, holding it up to the light. "Didn't that guy say something about a hair scrunchy, too? Was that in there?" She motioned toward the envelope.

Mitch opened the padded envelope wide and tapped the open end on the table. "There's nothing else in here. But yes, I do remember them saying there was some hair thing they found with the jewelry."

"Yes. I wonder why they wouldn't have returned that, too?"

He shrugged. "Maybe since it didn't have sentimental value like the jewelry? I don't know."

"You don't think they kept it for . . . DNA, do you?" She winced. "Sorry. Too many episodes of *CSI*."

He shook his head. "I can't watch that stuff anymore."

"No. Believe me, you shouldn't."

"That first day they went through the house, they had trouble finding anything to take for DNA testing. Because she had all her stuff at the conference with her. They ended up taking this travel toothbrush that I'm not sure she'd used more than once—and an old hairbrush she rarely used. But it had a strand of her hair still in it." The thought of that single strand of hair brought a lump to his throat.

"Looks like they didn't return those things either." Shelley looked pointedly at the empty envelope.

He hadn't thought of that. And he didn't want to think about why they'd probably kept them.

"Is that Jill's phone?"

He nodded. "Simonides said they made recordings of everything." He picked up the phone and slid open the keyboard. "I'll need to find a charger for it."

"Can I see?" Shelley reached for the phone and inspected it. "I might have one of those universal connectors. If Audrey didn't take it to school with her."

"Hey, I think we've got one around here somewhere." He went back to the den and found what he was looking for.

He plugged in the phone, waited for it to power up, then pressed some buttons, searching for voice mail. "I never did like her phone."

"It's almost like mine," Shelley said. "May I?"

He handed her the phone, and she clicked through several screens, expertly pressing keys.

Mitch started as his own voice filled the room. *Where are you? I'm going to fire up the grill. Let me know when I should put the steaks on . . .*

The room tilted and he gripped the edge of the table. The events of that September day came back to him like it was yesterday, except now he saw so vividly how everything had changed in the space of a phone call. And here they were, two months later, and Jill never had come home.

Shelley must have read his thoughts. She snapped the phone shut, silencing the recording. "I'm sorry," she whispered.

He shook his head. It wasn't her fault. Yet he couldn't seem to find his voice to tell her so. From somewhere outside the sound of a car revving its engine penetrated the walls of the house.

"It still doesn't seem real, does it," she said softly.

"No . . . It doesn't."

His cell phone burred from his belt, making them both jump. He slipped out his phone and checked the caller ID. "It's Jill's mom. I'd better take this." He nodded toward Jill's phone. "Would you mind scrolling through her messages and see if there's anything there the police might have missed? There's no way they could pick up on what's behind some of the text messages and even voice mail. I'll listen too, but some of it, you'd get better than I would."

"Sure." Once more, she slid the keyboard out and bent her head over Jill's phone.

Mitch's phone rang again and he clicked to answer. "Hello, Miriam."

"Hello, Mitchell. Is there any news?"

"I'm sorry, no." Miriam had called him every other day since the kids had gone back to school. He didn't begrudge her the calls, but he felt guilty every time he had to tell her that there was nothing new. "You know I'll call you the minute we hear anything, Miriam."

"Why haven't they found her yet? This is ridiculous. You'd think with all the satellites and TV cameras at every stoplight and that Goggle thing on the Internet, they could surely find her."

In spite of everything they'd both been through these past weeks, he curbed a smile at his mother-in-law's gaffe. "I know. It does seem like they should have news for us by now. But I talked to the detective again just tonight, and he assured me they're doing everything possible to locate her. Shelley's here right now going through Jill's mes—" He stopped.

He'd been going to tell her about Jill's phone being returned, but thought better of it. He'd given Bert and Miriam only the bare details, not wanting to worry them needlessly, and right now he couldn't remember if he'd ever told them about Jill's phone showing up at the hotel.

"Oh? Shelley's there?" Miriam seemed not to notice his abrupt U-turn. "Tell her hello."

"I'll tell her." He winked at Shelley, knowing Miriam always spoke at high enough decibels that Shelley was probably hearing every word.

"She's such a good friend to Jill. Always has been."

"Awww," Shelley mouthed, placing a hand over her heart. "Tell her and Bert hello from Audrey and me."

Mitch relayed the greeting.

"You and the kids are coming for Thanksgiving, of course," Miriam said. It was not a question.

"Oh—" Mitch was caught off guard. He and Jill and the kids had spent every Thanksgiving since their marriage in Colorado with Jill's parents. Last year they'd picked up Evan at college on their drive through. But on the way home, after dropping Evan off, and with Katie asleep in the backseat, Jill had wept over the decline they'd seen in her father. "I have a feeling this may have been our last Thanksgiving together."

The memory jolted Mitch. Had her words been prophetic?

"Why would God take Dad away when we're losing Katie next year, too," Jill had asked him.

And instead of comforting her, he'd repri-manded her for being such a pessimist. "You don't know that you won't have your dad next year, Jill." That only made her cry harder. Oh, what he wouldn't give for a do-over on that conversation.

Now, under the circumstances, he couldn't bring himself to tell Miriam they wouldn't be there for Thanksgiving. He'd been needing to go see Jill's parents anyway. The holidays made a good excuse. "We'll be there, don't you worry. I'll give you a call sometime next week and let you know when to expect us."

"Well, I want you to know I am setting six places at the table. I fully expect Jill to be with you by then."

"I'm praying the same thing, Mom." He rarely called Miriam "Mom," but it seemed right just now, though the curious look Shelley gave him made him feel awkward. He turned away and spoke into the phone. "Give Bert our love. We'll see you in a few weeks."

He hung up and turned back to Shelley, surprised to see her eyes brimming with tears. "What's wrong?"

She handed the phone back to him, dabbing at the corner of her eye with her pinkie finger.

"Did you find something?"

She shook her head, swallowing hard. "Just a lot of messages back and forth between us. Jill and me. You and Jill. It's . . . sweet. She was—*is* always so sweet." Her voice broke. "I miss her."

"Yeah, me too."

He took a step toward her and reached to give her a hug. She reciprocated, putting her arms around him. He almost flinched. It had been so long—so very long—since he'd had the arms of someone made of warm flesh and blood around him. *Oh, God, I miss her so much.*

"Let me know if I can do anything, Mitch," she said, pulling away, patting his back like she might've with one of the kids.

He looked at the floor, feeling a little uncomfortable.

But Shelley seemed not to notice. "Let me know if I can do anything. You know where I live."

He smiled at her little joke. "I will. Thanks, Shelley."

She hooked a thumb behind her. "I'll let myself out the back if that's okay."

"Sure." He waved, then turned back to pick up Jill's phone. It took him a few seconds to figure the thing out, but when he found her voice mail function, he scrolled through the names, willing there to be a clue they'd somehow missed.

The majority of the calls and messages were between Jill and him, Shelley, the kids, and a couple of teachers in her school. He listened to a few of the voice mails, choking up to hear Evan and Katie's playful messages to their mom. This little device held a microcosm of their lives— the life of the family he'd too often taken for granted. He played half a dozen more messages.

When he came to the last voice mail from Katie, he couldn't hold back the tears any longer.

He closed his eyes and pressed the phone against his cheek. Katie's sweet, little-girl voice floated up to him.

Hey, Mommy! I miss you. Thanks for the M&Ms you hid in my luggage. That was a nice surprise. Well . . . just wanted to say thanks. Tell Daddy hi.

None of them could have known then that they were talking to Jill for the last time.

The thought hung in the air like an omen, and his breath caught. He snapped the phone shut. And for the first time since this all started, he could not muster an atom of hope that he would ever see Jill again.

14

Thursday, November 25

"Evan, please pass the mashed potatoes around again." Miriam lifted a bowl of her famous creamed corn and started it around the festively decorated dining room table. The traditional honeycomb paper turkey sat on the buffet, and the Christmas tree was already up in the living room of the town house Jill's parents had retired to three years ago.

"And for heaven's sake," Miriam said, "put

some of those spuds on your plate. Look at all this food. You're all eating like a bunch of birds."

"No, thanks, Grandma. I'm stuffed." Evan puffed out his belly and patted it. "But everything tastes great. Maybe leftovers later, okay?"

Miriam made a *tsk tsk* sound with her tongue and put another spoonful of cranberry salad on Bert's plate.

Mitch took the bowl of corn from her and put a small scoop on his own plate. He nudged Katie under the table, encouraging her to do the same. Either he didn't communicate very well or Katie purposely ignored him.

Miriam's idle chatter was getting on his nerves, and yet he understood why she felt compelled to hover over them all, talking nonstop in a falsely cheery falsetto. Her prayers to have Jill home by Thanksgiving had not been answered. Jill's absence was palpable, and even Bert—who hadn't said a dozen words since they'd arrived in Colorado Springs last night—seemed to be aware that this was not the typical happy family Thanksgiving they were accustomed to.

Mitch thought Bert had declined further, and wondered if Jill's father was even aware of what had happened with his daughter. Like always, Bert was affectionate with Evan and Katie and seemed to know they were family, but Mitch noticed he hadn't addressed either of his grand-children by name, and he didn't ply them with questions about college or tease them about the latest boyfriend or girlfriend as he'd always done.

Miriam seemed to be trying to make up for Bert's lethargy and prattled on about this and that. When dinner was over Mitch helped Miriam and Katie carry dirty dishes into the kitchen.

As he scraped plates into the garbage disposal and rinsed silverware for the dishwasher, he felt Katie's attention on him. He turned to see her watching him with eyes wide and jaw dramatically agape.

"What?"

Katie gave an exaggerated blink. "I think I'm in shock."

Miriam snickered, obviously in cahoots with her granddaughter.

"What?" he said again. "You've never seen a man do dishes?"

"Not on Thanksgiving Day, we haven't," said Miriam. "At least not in this house. Or yours either." She poked a finger at his chest.

Katie shook her head. "Wow, Dad, if Mom could see you now . . ."

"Listen, baby girl, I'll have you know I've reformed since you left for college. I not only do dishes, I've even been known to run the vacuum a time or two."

Miriam and Katie gasped in unison, then dissolved into giggles.

It felt good to laugh—and to talk about Jill in a

conversation that didn't revolve around her disappearance.

Miriam playfully swatted at him with a dish towel. "Get out of here! This kitchen isn't big enough for a man. Go watch your football game."

"Okay, okay . . . Just let me rinse these dishes first."

Miriam gave him a pointed look. "Now, how are Katie and I supposed to talk girl talk with you hanging around? I need to hear the scoop on this new boyfriend."

"*Is* there a new boyfriend?" Mitch looked from Katie to Miriam and back again. "I didn't even know there was an old one."

Katie's cheeks flushed a becoming shade of pink. "I was going to tell you, but I didn't want stupid Evan to give me a hard time."

"So there *is* a boyfriend. Wow. How have you managed to keep this a secret from your brother, living on the same campus and all?"

She gave an enigmatic smile. "We have our methods."

Miriam giggled like a teenager. "Well, do tell. Come on! Out with it!"

Katie glanced past Mitch toward the living room. The TV droned football. Seeming satisfied that her brother was otherwise occupied, she spoke in a hushed tone. "Well, his name is Brandon. He's from Lawrence—so he lives at home—and he's a biology major. He's super

155

sweet and his family is awesome. He has two little sisters. They're only in middle school, but they're, like, the sisters I never had."

This sounded serious. Why hadn't Katie mentioned this boy before? He tried to keep his voice casual. "So, how did you meet him?"

"He's in my psychology class. He's a sophomore, but—"

"Oooh, an older man?" Miriam wiggled penciled eyebrows.

Katie giggled. "Yes, but since I took Psych 1 through the community college, we're in the same class."

"What does he look like? A hunk, I'm sure. Or a fox? Or . . . what is it you kids say now . . . ?" Miriam's eyebrows went up. "Is he *hot?*"

Katie cracked up at that, but she huddled in close to her grandmother. "He is *smokin'* hot. You should see him, Grandma. He's got these baby blue eyes that just—" She looked up and cut her eyes at Mitch.

"Hey, don't mind me," he teased. "You two talk all you want. I'm just the kitchen help." He grabbed the dishrag and started swabbing an already spotless section of the countertop.

Katie groaned and turned back to her grandmother, describing this KU boy in glowing —and too graphic for his taste—terms. Did he really need to know that his daughter was taken with a guy who was "ripped"? It bothered him that in all the phone conversations they'd had in the last three months, Katie had never mentioned she was dating someone. Still, it warmed his heart to see Miriam playing Jill's role—and Katie eating it up.

"Oh, and look, Grandma—you, too, Dad"—she pulled a necklace from beneath her collar—"he gave me this. Said it was a Thanksgiving present. Isn't that *soooo* sweet?"

Miriam admired the necklace and patted Katie's cheek, but Mitch sensed a sudden dip in Miriam's enthusiasm. Maybe she was just remembering similar conversations with Jill. Physically, Katie looked more like the Brannon side of the family, but she had Jill's mannerisms, and Miriam couldn't help but notice. And remember.

"It's real pretty, honey," he offered.

Miriam gave a little frown. "I hope it wasn't too expensive."

Mitch had thought the same thing.

"Your mother had a boyfriend who used to give her little trinkets like that—before she met your sweet dad, of course." Miriam gave Mitch's cheek a patronizing pat before turning back to Katie. "Jill—your mom—thought it was nice, too, until the guy started using those gifts to manipulate her."

It had to be Greg Hamaker Miriam was referring to. He was pretty much the only guy Jill had dated in high school.

"Oh, Brandon isn't like that." Katie shook her head and turned to Mitch. "Hey, Dad, you know what we thought of the other night, me and Brandon? If men took their wives' names when they got married, Brandon would be Brandon Brannon. Isn't that a hoot?"

He stared at her. "You're not getting married, are you?"

"No! Give me a break, Dad. I'm only a freshman." She rolled her eyes. "We were just talking. Don't freak out."

He shrugged. Still, how could that Brandon Brannon tidbit have even come up if she hadn't been discussing the subject of marriage with this guy? Suddenly Mitch was not a fan of Brandon whatever-his-real-last-name-was.

A faraway look came to Miriam's eyes. "I'll never forget when your mom told me Mitchell Brannon had asked her to marry him."

Mitch's heart lurched at the memories that washed over him. He struggled not to let his emotions show.

It helped when Katie gave him a playful look and hopped up on the kitchen counter, settling in for Miriam's story.

Mitch took his time finishing the dishes, enjoying seeing this side of his daughter. And basking in the memories of his and Jill's courtship.

Later, when Katie had fallen asleep on the sofa,

Mitch sought out Miriam at the dining room table, where she was putting away the good silver.

"You mentioned the boyfriend who manipulated Jill with gifts . . ."

She looked up, curiosity in her gaze. "Greg Hamaker. You knew him, didn't you?"

He shook his head. "I knew about him." There was no reason for Miriam to know about his confrontation with Hamaker. Or his suspicions. "You said he gave Jill trinkets. Like what?"

"Oh, goodness, I don't remember. Jewelry mostly. A necklace or bracelet . . . any little gift he could give to bribe her into getting back together after one of their breakups. They had a pretty rocky time of it."

"Yeah, Jill talked about that."

Miriam shook her head. "It didn't take much to make him mad, and every time he'd have one of his blowups, I'd be sure that would be the last straw and she would finally break up with him for good. But then he'd come crawling back with some trinket." She shook her head. "Peace offerings, Jill called them. But they were bribes, pure and simple. I don't think he ever gave her anything of value—it was just costume jewelry and baubles. And flowers. Lots of flowers. Bert and I tried to get her to give it all back to him when they finally did break up, just so he couldn't hold anything over her head. But I don't know if she ever did. I guess there are a lot of things we may never know now." That faraway look came back to her eyes. "If we . . . don't find Jill, please promise me you and the kids will stay in touch."

"Oh, Miriam. Of course we would."

"Colorado's a long way away. And the kids will both have their own lives, their own families. I know that, but—"

"Hey . . ." He put an arm around her shoulders, surprised at how thin she'd gotten. "Let's don't give up hope, okay?"

"Oh, I haven't given up hope, Mitchell. But when you're eighty, the hope you're banking on isn't necessarily for this side of Heaven."

She looked up at him, and the sadness in her eyes tore him apart. Because he knew it wasn't as much for herself as it was for him.

Sunday, November 28

"Mom! Why didn't you call me?" Audrey's words came out on a sob, and Shelley tried not to let her own alarm color her tone.

"Audrey . . . Honey, I'm sorry." There was something going on that her daughter wasn't saying. Shelley had just gotten back to Sylvia after driving down to see Audrey over Thanksgiving. "Remember, I stopped in Poplar Bluff to have lunch with Aunt Mona, and well . . . then I discovered this little antique shop downtown. I

160

guess I stayed longer than I thought. But I should have called you anyway. I'm sorry."

"I thought something happened to you. Why didn't you answer my texts?"

"Honey, I told you . . . You know how phone service is between there and Cape. Past Cape Girardeau, I didn't have more than two bars until I was almost back to Sylvia, and by then I figured you'd already be in bed. I knew you had early classes tomorrow and I didn't want to wake you."

"Okay," Audrey sniffed. "I'm sorry I got so upset."

"Is everything okay? Is there something you're not telling me?" They'd had such a good time together in Springfield, and Shelley hadn't sensed anything amiss.

"Nothing's wrong. It's just . . . after what happened to Evan's mom . . . I worry about you." Her voice rose on another sob.

"Oh, Audrey, I'm sorry. But think about it, honey. The chances of that happening to two best friends is practically nil." She didn't tell Audrey that on more than a few nights, she, too, had awakened in a cold sweat from a terrifying dream. Rarely could she remember what the dream was about, but she always woke with Jill on her mind and couldn't deny the source of those dreams. It still didn't seem real that her friend was gone. And that they had no idea what had happened to her.

"I know that's probably true, Mom, but . . . I've always thought our little town and our house was safe, and look what happened. It just scared me. That's all."

"But honey, it didn't happen in Sylvia. Whatever happened . . . to Jill . . . most likely happened before she ever left Kansas City." She tried not to think how similar Springfield was to Kansas City when it came to crime rates and danger. "I do understand why you were worried though. It's been unsettling for all of us. I can't even imagine what Evan and Katie must be going through."

"Well, actually, Mom, I can. That's why I was so upset when you didn't call."

"I'm sorry, honey. I promise it won't happen—"

"Mom, if I ever lost you"—Audrey's voice cracked—"I'd be completely alone. At least Evan and Katie still have their dad."

Shelley had thought it was a good sign that she and Audrey hadn't talked much at all about Jill while she'd been in Springfield. Now she realized they'd both probably held back from mentioning Jill Brannon for fear of upsetting the other.

She talked to Audrey for another twenty minutes, carrying her phone through the house while she unpacked her suitcase and got ready for bed.

"Honey, I could talk all night," she said when she could tell Audrey had calmed down. "But you have class and I have to work tomorrow so I'm going to say good night."

"Okay. I love you, Mom."

"Love you, too, honey. Sweet dreams."

"I'd settle for no dreams."

"Yeah, me too. I'll pray for that." She hung up, overwhelmed with love for her daughter, and missing her as if she hadn't seen her for months.

It was times like this that she missed Jill the most. When she longed desperately for the friend she'd always run to for assurance. Her eyes fell on a ceramic shaving mug that sat on her dresser. The mug was filled with a "bouquet" of antique magnifying glasses—one of those accidental collections she'd accumulated after Jill saw her admire a jade-handled magnifier in a shop once.

"You need that," Jill had said. When Shelley left it behind—not wanting to tell her friend that it was simply not in her budget—Jill went back and bought it and presented it to her for her birthday several weeks later. Since then, whenever she and Jill scoured the flea markets and antique malls, old magnifying glasses were on her list of things to search out. Between Jill's gifts and her own finds, she'd collected almost a dozen of the ornate little pieces. She reached for the jade-handled one and dusted off the round glass, then held it over the palm of her hand, studying the intricate creases that crisscrossed each other. "Oh, Jill," she whispered. "Where are you? I miss you."

She'd tried to ignore the realization that Jill was the only real friend she'd had. Sure, she and Audrey had a warm mother–daughter friendship, and there were people she considered friends at work and at church, but no one she'd share her deepest desires and longings with. No one she would have confessed her sins to. Not like with Jill.

She walked through the house and checked the locks one more time. At the front door, she remembered that she hadn't checked the porch for deliveries since arriving home. She was expecting a package—a birthday gift for Jill that had been on back order so long she'd forgotten about it. Ironically, the day before Thanksgiving she'd gotten notification it had finally shipped.

Jill. Would she ever get to see her friend's face when she opened the gift? Shelley usually purchased her gifts at cost through Serendipity, but flipping through a specialty catalog last month, she'd found some little long-handled baskets for making s'mores over an open fire and thought they'd be perfect for the Brannons' lake house. It had always been fun choosing gifts for Jill, because no matter what Shelley picked out, Jill was thrilled. Mitch gave his wife a hard time about being too "easily entertained." Maybe so, but it was one of the qualities that had drawn Shelley to Jill—that quality of taking extraordinary delight in everyday things.

She stepped out on the front porch. Sure enough, her package was leaning against the sidelight. Had probably been there since Friday. She took comfort in the fact that the little town of Sylvia was apparently deemed safe enough that UPS or FedEx would still leave a package on the porch.

She picked it up and reached for the door. Instinctively, she looked up the street before going inside. Everything was dark at the Brannons'. The streetlight at the edge of her property caused the giant oak in the front yard next door to cast long shadows across the cul de sac. She'd always felt safer having the Brannons —having Mitch—next door. But tonight the darkness between them made her shiver.

15

Monday, November 29

The phone rang at eight p.m. and Mitch went to answer it, his mind still trying to track the evening news he was watching. He quickly refocused when he saw the Caller ID. The number was Marcus Simonides's. The detective had been faithful about calling Mitch weekly to update him on Jill's case, but he'd always called during work hours.

He picked up, his pulse racing. "Yes?"

"Mitch? Simonides here. I don't have anything new on Jill—didn't want to alarm you," he said quickly.

Mitch waited for the "however" he heard in the detective's tone.

"I did want to let you know that there will be a new detective assigned to your case from this point on. His name is Cody Fredriks, and he'll be calling you in the next few days to introduce himself."

"You mean . . . you're off the case?"

"I'll still be touching base, working with Officer Fredriks any time there's new evidence or a break in the case. But Fredriks will be your main contact with Missing Persons now. He's been briefed and he's up to speed on Jill's case, so you can—"

"Why the change?"

"Just routine shifts of duty." Something in his voice said he was hedging.

Mitch didn't like the sound of it. Judging by what Simonides said—and the new officer's given name—the guy was barely shaving yet. He knew what it meant and why Simonides was hedging: they were passing Jill's case off to a rookie. It was hard not to think that meant something. *They don't expect to solve this case.*

After giving him the new extension to reach Fredriks, Simonides made excuses and ended the call.

Feeling deflated, Mitch let TP out one last time

and stood in the dark on the front porch waiting, contemplating what the phone call meant.

The Lab barked twice and took off toward Shelley's house next door. "TP! Get back over here!"

The stupid dog had never obeyed him like it did Jill. Especially after a few days at the kennel. Mitch reached inside and flipped on the porch light, then trotted barefoot onto the lawn calling for TP. Despite the fact that Christmas was only three weeks away, the day had been warm—in the midsixties. But now the grass was damp and icy cold. He was a tenderfoot anyway, and considered running back in for his shoes, but he'd be chasing TP four blocks if he gave the mutt a head start.

He tiptoed cautiously through the mulch in a flower bed at the edge of their property. "TP!" he hissed, not wishing to wake the whole neighborhood and certainly not wishing to wake up one neighbor in particular. "Get over here right now!"

Silhouetted under the streetlight in front of Shelley's house, TP's ears pricked, but the dog made no acknowledgment that he'd heard his master's order.

Mitch picked his way across the wet grass, muttering to himself.

Musical laughter floated across to him on the night air, and he looked up to see Shelley standing on her porch wearing a fleece hoodie. She was obviously enjoying his antics.

He gave a self-conscious laugh. "If I didn't know better, I'd think you called my dog just to put me through my paces."

"Me? I was merely picking up a package from the front porch when this rabid dog came charging onto my property." TP pranced around Shelley's ankles and she knelt on the porch steps and gave the Lab a good scratching behind his ears.

"Come on, now . . . Don't reward his bad behavior."

"Sorry." She smiled up at him, gave TP one last pat and nudged him in Mitch's direction. "How are you doing?" Her tone held much more than the rhetorical greeting.

He hesitated. "Doing okay." They hadn't talked about Jill since that day Simonides had delivered Jill's phone and the jewelry. He'd purposely avoided it. Avoided *her*. What else was there to say? He quickly changed the subject. "You were in Springfield for Thanksgiving, right? How's Audrey?"

"She's doing great. We had a good time. And I stopped by to see my aunt Mona on the way home, too."

"That's nice."

"And you guys went to Jill's folks?"

"We did. It was . . . hard. Her dad has really gone downhill since last time we saw him. I'm not sure he's even aware of—everything that's

168

happened with Jill. And the first day we were there, Miriam burst into tears every time Jill's name was mentioned. But she and Katie had some good time together."

"Oh, that's nice. I've always loved Jill's mom."

"Yeah . . . I thought it would be good for the kids to go out there, but . . . I'm not so sure it was good for me. It was hard to drop them off in Lawrence and drive back here without them."

"Oh, Mitch. I'm so sorry. I can't even imagine . . ." Shelley straightened and wrapped the pink hoodie tighter around her. She wore gray fleece pajama pants and she was barefoot. In the dim glow from the porch light she looked so vulnerable and . . . feminine.

He looked away, missing Jill so desperately the ache was physical. Missing the kids. Missing everything about the life he'd had just three short months ago.

As if she'd heard his thoughts, Shelley whispered, "I miss her."

"Yeah. Me too."

"I found this little antique shop in Poplar Bluff on the way home from Springfield, and it was just the kind of place Jill loved. I kept seeing things I wanted to show her. Things I knew she would snap up the minute she saw them. It seemed like she should be just one aisle over, calling *me* over to see something she'd found that she knew I would love." Her voice broke. "I left without buying anything. It was just too hard."

He looked pointedly at her bare feet. "You'd better get inside. It's freezing out here. Come on, TP. Do your business and let this lady be."

"I'm fine. I needed some fresh air. Is . . . is there anything new . . . at all?" She didn't have to spell out what she meant.

"No. Nothing." He climbed the three steps to the porch so Shelley could stay under the overhang out of the wind.

She wrapped her arms around her body and leaned her back against the door. "I haven't heard anything for a couple of weeks now. It . . . it seems like the local news has completely quit covering it. I hope that doesn't mean they've . . ." She fumbled for a word, trying, he knew, to avoid suggesting they'd given up.

"No. I . . . just talked to Simonides tonight . . . He assured me the case is still open. There's just nothing to go on." He didn't trust his voice to tell her about the case being relegated to a new officer—and about what he suspected that meant.

"How are you doing, Mitch? How are you *really* doing?" Her eyes sought his, and she tucked a loose strand of hair behind her ear.

The simple action touched him in a way he didn't want to acknowledge. "I'm okay. As long as I keep busy it's not too bad." That was a lie, but he didn't dare tell her the truth—

"Mitch, nobody *expects* you to be back to normal yet. You know that, don't you?"

He stared at her. "What brought that on?"

"I see you. I know you, Mitch . . . Maybe better than you think."

He suddenly felt naked. He'd shared thoughts far too personal while they'd driven the roads between Kansas City and Sylvia. And from the things Shelley confided that she and Jill had talked about, Shelley probably knew even more about him than he knew about her. Things he'd just as soon have her not know. It was disconcerting to have her look at him and read his thoughts.

The truth was, for weeks now, he'd been walking around like an automaton. Barely eating, staying up too late watching TV and combing the Internet for any piece of news that might hold a clue to where Jill was. And when he did sleep, it was fitful and dream-laced. He attempted a grin. "So you don't think I'm back to normal?"

"No. I don't." Her expression remained serious. "And I'd think something was wrong with you if you were."

"What am I supposed to do?" The infernal lump that had taken up permanent residence in his throat threatened to strangle him, and it was all he could do not to turn tail and run back home.

Shelley tilted her head. "What do you mean?"

He felt a dam opening inside him, felt all the pent-up emotions of past weeks rushing to his

171

throat. He hadn't been able to weep in those early weeks when it had first happened. But he'd made up for lost time these past few weeks, weeping sometimes till his throat was raw and he finally fell asleep. Worse, his emotions betrayed him at the least provocation. He'd choked up at a staff meeting last week when someone casually mentioned that the third-grade teacher's position had been filled at the elementary school—Jill's position. He didn't think anyone noticed—or would have cared if they did—but he cared.

"How am I supposed to go on like nothing's happened, Shelley? How? My work is suffering, my faith is suffering. I feel like . . . like I'm on the verge of crashing and burning all the time. If I just knew. I think I could deal with—just about anything if I just knew what happened to her. It is killing me not to know. To think she might be out there somewhere . . ." He felt powerless to stop the flow of words, despite the fact that something told him Shelley was *not* the one to confide in.

But it was too late.

She reached out and put a hand on his shoulder. "Oh, Mitch . . . I'm so sorry you're having to go through this. I'll never understand why God let this happen. And . . . please forgive me. Those were thoughtless words. I didn't think before I—"

"No. It's okay." Even in the darkness he could see the pain in her expression. He felt like a heel.

"I didn't mean to unload like that." He shook his head and took half a step back.

He slid from beneath her touch and bent to pick up a tattered geranium leaf that lay beside a large flowerpot at the bottom of the porch steps. He mashed the leaf between his fingers. Its pungent citrus scent brought him to his senses, as if it were smelling salts. "I'd better get back." He turned to scan the yard, whistling softly for TP.

The dog trotted up, sniffing at Shelley's bare toes. She gave him a perfunctory pat on the head.

"Come on, boy. Let's go."

"Mitch, wait . . ."

He turned back, waiting.

"It's been almost three months. Do you really think she's coming back? Do you have any reason to hope for that?"

Her words stunned him. He felt the muscles in his neck tense. "Why would you say that? You *don't* think she's coming back?" He studied her, wondering. "Is there something you're not telling me? Something else I don't know?"

"No, Mitch. No. It's not that. It's just, if she was . . . *alive* . . . they would have found her by now. You say it's making you crazy thinking that she might be out there. But . . . how could she be. After this long? Not in these cold nights. I want to believe, but . . . I'm sorry. I just can't anymore. At some point, don't you have to just accept . . . that she's probably not coming back?"

He shook his head slowly, not believing what he was hearing. Her, of all people. "I can't listen to this." He grabbed TP by the collar and half dragged him across the lawn.

Behind him, Shelley called his name. He walked faster, ignored her. He couldn't listen to her. She was a traitor. He was hanging on by a slender thread of hope as it was.

If he listened to her, he would have nothing left at all.

JANUARY

16

Saturday, January 1

Mitch woke to the smell of bacon and pancakes. He rolled over in bed and looked at the clock. *Nine a.m.?* That couldn't be right. He'd waited up until after one a.m. for Katie to come home from a New Year's Eve party, but he hadn't expected to sleep half the morning away.

He crawled out of bed, threw on yesterday's jeans and flannel shirt, and padded barefoot out to the kitchen.

"Morning, lazy bones." Katie flipped a pancake before stirring the pan of scrambled eggs on the stove.

"What are you doing up so early?"

"Hey, some of us have work to do."

"Yeah, right. Says the girl without a job."

"I've gotta start packing."

"Packing? I thought you weren't going back until Friday."

"I'm not, but I've got a lot of stuff to pack."

He pulled a plate down from the cupboard and held it out to her. "Hit me."

She laughed. "Don't try to be hip, Papa. It's not a good look on you." She flipped a pancake onto his plate and dished half the eggs beside it.

"Why are you in such a chipper mood this morning? And where's your brother?" He hadn't heard Evan come in last night.

"He's still sleeping. I'm guessing he might be up around . . . oh, three or four at the earliest." She tilted her head and studied Mitch. "And how come you waited up for me and not for him?"

"He's older."

"Not that much older."

"He's a boy."

"So?"

"So, I don't worry as much about him as I do you."

"That's really not fair at all, you know. And sexist. You need to take sensitivity training."

He rolled his eyes at her. "I won't wait up for you next New Year's Eve. How's that."

"Promise?"

"No, I do not promise."

"That's because you know you won't stick to it."

"How about we'll talk about it this time next year?" He popped a bite of eggs in his mouth to keep from laughing.

She narrowed her eyes and gave a little growl, but she was smiling.

While they shared the morning paper in companionable silence, she kept him supplied with pancakes until he thought he might pop. He tried not to think about how quiet this house would be again after the kids went back to school.

Katie seemed to sense his melancholy and heaved a sigh too immense for his little girl.

He looked up from the sports page. "You okay?"

"Are you going to be okay? After we leave?"

He was immediately sorry for spoiling her good mood. She'd handled the holidays with such courage, making Christmas Day special by insisting on cooking a big dinner. And bossing him and Evan around. It had ended up being a surprisingly happy day, though they'd shed plenty of tears for Jill.

The three of them had gone to Colorado the day after Christmas, and seeing Bert's continued decline, they'd ended up staying almost a week, helping Miriam with the house and some business matters.

He thought Evan and Katie had actually been relieved to stay in Colorado. And he understood why. Being at home, especially during the holidays, was too much of a reminder that Jill wasn't there.

He'd been relieved to stay away, too. For the same reasons. And for different ones.

He forced a smile and patted her hand. "Don't you worry about me, little girl. You just go back and enjoy college. And keep your grades up, of course. Don't forget why you're there." He winked, hoping he'd staved off a black cloud.

But she sighed again. "Dad? Could I . . . have something of Mom's to take back to school with me? I mean . . . I have stuff you guys got me for my birthday and everything, but is there something that actually belonged to Mom that I could have? Just . . . to remember her by." She swallowed hard, her voice wavering.

He reached across the table and covered her hand with his. "Oh, honey—"

"And pictures. I've been looking through the picture albums we have, and there are hardly any pictures of Mom. She's always the one *taking* the pictures." She started to cry. "Why didn't any of us ever take any pictures of *her?*"

Mitch wanted to weep with her. He rose and pulled her into a hug. "I'll find some of Mom's things for you, sweetie. I know she'd love that you asked, that you wanted them. And I'm sure we have some pictures—*somewhere*. I bet there are some at Mom's school, too. I'll talk to Carol."

"And what about Grandma? She has tons of pictures."

"You're right. You know, I wouldn't mind seeing some of those myself. I'll give her a call."

He'd mostly avoided looking at photos of Jill —although the one that had circulated in the media after she first went missing was emblazoned on his brain. But he thought he could handle it now.

And maybe it would do him some good.

Thursday, January 6

A box was waiting on the front porch when Mitch got home from work on Wednesday. Jill's mother had sent it second-day air via UPS. He brought the package in and put it on the dining room table. He dreaded opening that box almost as much as he dreaded going into the empty house. The kids were out with their friends one last night before heading back to school tomorrow morning, and he knew the house was going to feel like a mausoleum.

He let TP out and changed clothes. The box taunted him as he walked through the kitchen to find something for supper. Maybe he wouldn't open it. He didn't know if he was up for the task, up for the onslaught of memories the pictures were sure to bring. Maybe he'd just let Katie take it back with her.

But he wasn't sure what all Miriam might have sent, and he wanted to find out exactly what was in the package before he let Katie look through it. And besides, he'd promised her.

He went for the scissors and cut through the layers of brown paper and tape Miriam had swaddled it in. He removed the lid, summoning the courage to take this unwanted walk down memory lane.

The first packet of photos opened the floodgates. Their wedding photos—Jill, so young and beautiful, looking up at him with a radiant smile. He turned the small stack of photos over on his desk. This was too hard.

The next rubber-banded stack contained snapshots of Jill in the hospital with a wailing baby Evan. And then, just fourteen months later, precious Katie, looking as serene and unflappable in her infancy as Evan was wild. It was a miracle they'd had a second baby after all those colicky nights with Evan. Mitch shook his head, thinking how true to their earliest personality traits their son and daughter had remained.

He picked up another photo, disturbed that no matter how he tried, even as he grieved Jill, he couldn't seem to get Shelley out of his mind. He'd started to allow himself to consider what he would do if they'd still had no news about Jill a year from now. Or two years from now. Or three. If no clues turned up, if they never found anything, how long would it be before they could say definitively that Jill wasn't coming back?

And if by some miracle, they did find her, could the two of them find their way with each other again after everything that had happened in her absence? He closed his eyes. He'd already begun to forget what she looked like first thing in the morning. What it felt like to hold her in his arms. To kiss her.

And thoughts like that only made him think more of Shelley. Because he *could* imagine what it would feel like to kiss her. The thought startled him. He hadn't dared to admit, even to himself, the attraction he'd begun to feel for Shelley Austin. He scrubbed his face with his palms as if he could wash away the faithless thoughts.

He put the baby pictures back in the box and picked up the next batch of photos. Jill's senior class pictures, and high school events. Before he'd met her. He turned the stack upside down after looking at just a few. But something niggled at the back of his mind.

He went back to the last photo and looked at it again. It was a close-up of Jill dressed in an evening gown—probably prom night. Her hair was pinned up in big curls on her head—a little like she'd worn it for their wedding.

He held the photo at arm's length and studied it. He'd seen another picture of her in the same pose. He rummaged through the stack and found what he was looking for. Jill and Greg Hamaker stand-ing in front of a crepe paper arch. Another prom night, or some school dance. He looked at the close-up again. Jill looked so young. That sparkle in her eyes—those mesmerizing blue eyes of hers . . . But there was something else.

He looked again. *The earrings.* He knew hope was a great deceiver. He'd imagined clues before that never materialized. But of this, he was almost certain.

He scrambled off the couch and hurried into

the den. The manila envelope Simonides had returned to him was where he'd left it in the bottom drawer of his desk. Heart pounding, he spilled the contents onto the desktop.

He picked up one of the dangly silver and black earrings. There was no doubt—it was an exact match. Why would Jill have left *those* earrings at the hotel? Had they been some sort of . . . *message* for Greg Hamaker? Did she hope he would see the earrings she'd worn that night and remember a romantic prom date they'd shared?

No. That idea was almost laughable. If being married to Mitchell Brannon had taught Jill anything, it was that men rarely noticed things like earrings or hairstyles or shoes.

Still, this wasn't a coincidence. He didn't know how he knew, but he was certain of it.

Your mother had a boyfriend who used to give her little trinkets . . .

The conversation Miriam and Katie had at Thanksgiving played in his mind as if it had been recorded in stereo. Katie had chattered about her new boyfriend and Miriam had been all grandmotherly excitement. But she'd turned cool when Katie showed her the necklace that boy— Brandon —had given her. Miriam had said that Greg was always giving Jill "costume jewelry and baubles . . ."

Had the earrings in the photo been a gift from Greg? The same ones she'd left at the hotel more than twenty years later? Mitch looked at the other jewelry Simonides had returned. Was there a connection? He began to rifle through the photos, inspecting the jewelry Jill wore in each picture.

Ten minutes later, he found another possible match. A photo with Jill pinning a boutonniere on the lapel of Greg Hamaker's tux, showed her wearing a sparkly bracelet. He couldn't be sure it was the same bracelet she'd left at the hotel, but it was close enough to make him suspect.

He placed the two photos of Jill wearing the jewelry into the manila envelope with the jewelry and went back to the kitchen where he'd left his cell phone. He dialed Miriam in Colorado. Remaining as casual as he could, he explained to Miriam about seeing the photo of the jewelry that matched what Jill had left behind. "Do you remember if Greg Hamaker gave those pieces to Jill?" He described the jewelry briefly.

"The police asked us about those back in the beginning, when she first went missing. I couldn't remember any specific pieces he gave her. It was never anything of value. Mostly dime-store costume jewelry. If it'd been expensive we would have made her give it back when they broke up. But the boy was too cheap to give her anything really nice."

"Do you remember a pair of silver and black earrings she wore to her prom with a bright pink gown? The earrings are sort of a teardrop shape —the dangly kind."

"I can't say that I remember those. I wish I could, Mitchell. But it wouldn't surprise me if they were from Greg. You know Jill. She rarely spent money on herself. If she had any jewelry back then, it probably came from him. What . . . what do you think this means? Did that boy have something to do with Jill's disappearance?"

He hesitated. He didn't want to worry Jill's mother—or worse, get her hopes up. "I don't think so. He has a solid alibi. He may be a jerk, but I honestly don't think he would do anything sinister." He'd believed that after his first confrontation with Greg Hamaker, but now he couldn't say it with the same conviction.

"No," Miriam agreed. "But I'm glad she didn't marry him, Mitchell. I'm glad she waited for you."

He had to swallow a huge lump in his throat before he could reply. "I'm glad, too, Miriam."

17

Friday, January 7

Mitch parked in front of the office on a Kansas City street and tried to wrap his mind around the fact that, after all these months of nothing, suddenly there seemed to be a break, the first real glimmer of a clue.

"Lord," he whispered, "don't let me do anything foolish today." Maybe it was too late for that. He'd dressed for work this morning, pretending it was any normal day, and helped Evan and Katie pack up the car and head off to Lawrence. But once the kids were safely on the road, he'd called in to work and arranged to take yet another personal day. The district had been very lenient with him, allowing him extra days they probably couldn't afford for him to take off at this point in the school year. Still, this was too important.

Simonides had seemed dubious when Mitch called him last night and told him about finding the photo with the earrings and bracelet. The detective reminded Mitch that Greg Hamaker had witnesses on record who could testify he'd been in meetings at a hotel three blocks from Jill's hotel from the time she'd left her message on the answering machine at home, until late into the evening the day she disappeared.

But Simonides agreed to send Cody Fredriks to take a look at the photos. And probably not until Monday. The fact that Simonides was sending Fredriks instead of going himself told Mitch just how skeptical the detective was.

Well, he wasn't going to wait on them anymore. This was something he could do on his own. And no one had a bigger stake in the outcome than he did.

Mitch had taken a risk calling Hamaker for an

appointment—and to be honest, he wouldn't be totally shocked if the guy had ducked out by the time he got there. But he would take his chances. He had to find out if Greg Hamaker was hiding something.

Mitch lifted the ziplock bag that held the jewelry Jill had left behind in the hotel. "Do you recognize this? Is this jewelry you gave my wife?"

"What are you talking about?" Greg Hamaker's voice was steady, but his stance bordered on combative—feet planted on the carpet in front of his massive mahogany desk, his torso pitched forward as if he'd like to take a swing at Mitch. "I haven't given your wife anything."

"I'm talking about when you were in high school."

"You think I'm going to remember what I gave some girl in high school?" But Hamaker took the bag from him, turned it over, inspecting, then handed it back. "I don't recognize any of this. That doesn't mean I didn't give it to her, but do you remember what you gave your girlfriends twenty years ago?"

He had a point.

"Listen, man. I swear to you I don't know anything about Jill. I'm sorry I ever invited her. It was just supposed to be lunch with an old friend. She turned it into a federal offense and it's gone downhill from there."

"What do you mean she turned it into a federal offense?"

"Just what I've been saying. She called it off. Acted like I had ulterior motives."

"No. No one is accusing you of anything. I just need to know if you remember anything—*anything* at all—that might help us figure out what happened. Where she went after she left the hotel. We need as much information as possible."

"How many times do I have to tell you I've already told the authorities everything I know. I'm done with this." Hamaker turned and went back behind his desk, bracing his knuckles against the shiny surface.

"You only talked to her once, right? When she called to say she couldn't do lunch? Did she say why she was canceling?"

Hamaker puffed out his cheeks and scuffed the toe of a polished shoe on the carpet. "What do you want from me?"

Mitch sensed Hamaker softening, and he didn't want to blow it. "Please, Greg." He forced his voice down a few decibels. "Is there anything else you can think of? Anything at all—even if it seems insignificant . . ."

Hamaker blew out the breath he'd been holding. "Okay, listen . . . I'm going to tell you—and I'll probably regret it—I saw Jill at the hotel."

"Your hotel?" He didn't dare breathe.

"No. Her hotel. For about five minutes. Literally."

"Where at the hotel?"

"In the lobby. I was in meetings not three blocks from the Royale Suites, so I went there, just to say hello."

Mitch tensed. "So . . . you *talked* to her?"

"I tried. She wasn't very happy about me showing up."

"You told the police that?"

"I happened to be walking by the hotel on a break and thought it was ridiculous to be that close and not get a chance to just say hello . . . for old times' sake. She told me she backed out on lunch because she didn't think *you'd* be very happy about it. And yeah, I—gave her a hard time about it. Asked her if she was a kept woman. I was just joking, but that hacked her off. She launched into a lecture about what it took to have a happy marriage—whatever that has to do with anything."

Mitch could almost imagine that conversation. A band of long-held tension loosened inside him. Still, the man had lied to him. Lied to the police, apparently. He *had* seen Jill.

Mitch forced a calmness he didn't feel into his voice. "Do you remember what time it was when you saw her?"

"I don't know. I . . . had the concierge call her room, and she came down to the lobby. She had her luggage with her. Said she was just checking out."

"What time was that? Approximately. This could be important."

"I don't know. I didn't know at the time that I was going to have to account for every second of that day." He shrugged, sarcasm thick in his voice. "It must have been around one thirty, one forty-five." He thought for a minute. "Yeah, that's probably about right because I went and grabbed something to eat at my hotel after she called to cancel on me. It was after lunch when the concierge called, and I went to see her right after that. Like I said, I was there—in the lobby—five minutes tops. And I went directly back to my meetings from there. My alibi checks out. You can ask the—"

"But why didn't you tell the police all of this in the beginning? You held back evidence!" He clenched his fists at his sides, itching to strangle the man. "We needed everything we could get to—"

"Would *you* have told them?" Hamaker hissed. "If you were the last person to see someone alive? Listen, I did nothing wrong. I have enough problems with my wife as it is. The last thing I needed was being put under a microscope." He swore and then strode from behind his desk toward the door. "I don't owe you or the police or anybody else anything! I did *nothing* wrong.

And this conversation is over." He jerked open the door to the reception area and held it.

Mitch walked through the door, but turned before closing it behind him. "We'll see about that."

His disgust for the man swelled. How Jill could have dated someone like him for as long as she did? Maybe a younger Greg Hamaker had been a better man. But what made a man so centered on himself, so completely unmindful of another man's—another *family's*—suffering that he would withhold simple information that might have helped them before the trail went cold?

Mitch walked to his car, his breath forming wisps of steam in the frigid January air. He sat behind the wheel, shivering—as much from nerves as from the cold—too shook up to drive.

If Hamaker was remembering accurately, if he was telling the truth this time, Jill had encountered him in the lobby shortly after she'd left the message for Mitch at home. Did that explain why Jill sounded so happy, so . . . *herself* on the phone? Because she'd decided not to meet with Greg Hamaker? Because she'd told him off?

Maybe it even explained why she'd dropped her cell phone in the parking garage . . . He could picture it—Jill hurrying to her car, juggling her luggage, upset after encountering Greg. Flustered and in a hurry to get out of there, not realizing until she was well on the road that she'd dropped her phone.

Maybe Hamaker had even followed Jill to her car, harassing her. He'd lied before—or at least withheld part of the truth. Why should Mitch believe him now?

But if witnesses swore he'd been back in his meetings shortly after encountering Jill, how could he have done her harm without someone seeing something? Hearing her screams? Or . . . discovering her body?

He couldn't linger too long on that image. And he didn't want to believe that Greg Hamaker was capable of murder. Still, something didn't seem right.

Mitch put the key in the ignition and turned it. Four long months and finally he had a sliver of information. One new piece to a puzzle that was barely a frame. But was it possible that after all this time he might have found the piece that could finally lead him to Jill?

18

Saturday, January 8

According to the Missouri State Highway Patrol, Jill Brannon was listed as missing in the small south-central Missouri town of Sylvia after she failed to return from a conference in Kansas City, Kansas four months ago. The popular third grade teacher was last seen by fellow teachers in the lobby of a Kansas City, Kansas, hotel last September, and a message she left for her husband on their home answering machine gave no indication that Brannon was in danger or under duress.

Last September. He put down the newspaper and rubbed the bridge of his nose. The phrase made it seem a lifetime ago. The calendar said a brand-new year was under way, but Mitch still felt like he was living in the fog of last year's events. He didn't want to start a new year. Not without Jill.

He should have grown immune to these mentions of Jill in the news by now. But this one came after the detectives—both Fredriks and Simonides—had summarily dismissed Mitch's new suspicion about Greg Hamaker. Fredriks had—reluctantly, Mitch thought—contacted Hamaker again, but insisted there was nothing new worth pursuing, and asserted that Hamaker's alibi remained airtight.

And Simonides had reamed Mitch out for talking to Hamaker without their clearance. He felt like he'd been punched in the gut.

He smoothed a crease in the newspaper and forced himself to finish the article.

A spokesperson for the Missouri State Highway Patrol said that although less than two hundred of nearly one thousand persons reported missing in the state this year are still listed as "whereabouts unknown," many cases still in the database are no longer being actively investigated since some are more than fifty years old. But the spokesperson said law enforcement agencies are always looking for tips that could lead to solving a cold case.

Was this it? Was this what Jill's "obituary" looked like? A generic article in a newspaper— one most people would skim over in their rush to read the latest celebrity gossip or stock market news?

He wouldn't have it.

"If you're still speaking to me, could I ask a big favor?" Mitch had caught Shelley over the backyard fence, hoping to keep their conversation short and sweet.

"Why wouldn't I be speaking to you?" She rested her forearms on the chest-high gate that separated their backyards, and her narrowed eyes gave him the distinct impression that she knew exactly why he wouldn't be speaking to her.

Since that night when she'd revealed her doubts that Jill was even alive, he'd managed to mostly avoid Shelley. It hadn't been as hard as he'd thought to ensure that when their paths crossed, it didn't require more than a wave across the driveway. He and the kids had been gone over most of the Christmas holiday, and wintery weather had kept the entire city indoors for the past couple of weeks.

He'd made a halfhearted attempt to smooth things over with her—waving at her across their driveways, tossing her paper onto the porch on Sunday mornings, and clearing her front walk when it snowed. All things he'd done for his neighbor—Jill's friend—before he lost Jill.

But through the ordeal with Jill, Shelley had become a friend—not just Jill's friend, but his. And things had gotten . . . complicated. And now, somehow, they'd turned into strangers.

It still made him angry that Shelley had lost hope, but he'd overreacted and spoken too harshly to her that night. And he hated the rift between them. The truth was, he missed Shelley Austin. She was a tie to Jill, someone who knew *who* he was grieving. Someone who would let him talk on and on about Jill. Who even shared some of the same memories of her.

Looking at Shelley now, he saw the same sadness in her eyes that he saw when he looked in the mirror. And he felt a prompting to make things right between them. "Shelley—I owe you an apology. I shouldn't have spoken so harshly . . . that night. I know you were only being honest." And she was grieving, too. He sometimes forgot that.

Jill had been her best friend—really, Shelley's only close friend. Mitch could imagine how devastated Jill would have been if something had happened to Shelley. He'd never looked at it that way until this moment, and it broke his heart. And helped him understand her better. "I know you were just trying to process everything that happened. Same as I was. That wasn't fair of me and—"

"No, Mitch. Please. I'm the one who should be apologizing. I—" Tears welled in her eyes and she swallowed hard. "I was wrong to say the things I did. Please forgive me for being so negative. I didn't mean to . . . take away your hope. That truly wasn't my intent."

"Well, maybe you were right. Because . . . here we are all these weeks later and we still don't know any more than we did that night."

"So there hasn't been any news at all?"

"Fredriks—the guy who replaced Simonides—keeps assuring me her case is still open. But I don't know what they can be doing on it when they don't have any new leads. And then I give them something and they brush it off."

She frowned. "I don't understand. Has something . . . ? Do you have new information?"

He shook his head, and yanked off a withered strand of the honeysuckle vine that Jill had planted on their side of the fence. "Nothing new from the police. But"—he debated whether to tell her, but decided to go for it—"I had an interesting conversation with Greg Hamaker on Friday."

Her eyebrows rose, and he told her briefly about the encounter with Hamaker in Kansas City. "I still don't understand why she would have taken that jewelry," he said. "He says he doesn't remember, but I'm pretty sure it's stuff he gave her."

"Maybe she meant to give it back to him."

"Do you think he *asked* for it back?"

"I don't know why he would. It didn't have any value."

"But why else would she have taken it there? And left it in the hotel? After all this time . . . that doesn't make sense."

But Shelley shook her head. "I think it might make sense. If it were me, I would have given it back. I wouldn't want the guy to have one thing he could hold over me."

Mitch thought for a minute, trying to connect the dots and not liking where they were leading. "But then . . . when she left here, she must have thought she was going to see him. If she had the jewelry with her."

"But maybe this explains why she left the jewelry at the hotel, Mitch. Maybe she changed her mind about seeing Greg, but she didn't want to bring the jewelry home with her. I could see Jill doing that. It's what I would've done." The lilt in her tone told Mitch she felt certain that was what had happened.

"Unfortunately, I don't think Simonides thinks this has any bearing on Jill. Or maybe—" He hung his head. "Maybe he just thinks this gives credence to the scenario where Jill left of her own accord."

"No. We know that's not true!"

Mitch loved her adamance. "Either way, Shelley, I can't just sit around and do nothing. I've got to have some answers."

"I'm so sorry, Mitch. About . . . everything." She fixed her gaze on a spot beyond him, a faraway look in her eyes. He knew that look, knew she was remembering some little thing about Jill. But when their eyes met again, she brightened a little. "You said you wanted to ask a favor?"

"Yes. Would you mind too much taking care of TP for a few days?"

"Sure, I'd be glad to." There was curiosity in her smile, but it felt like an olive branch.

One he should have extended first. Weeks ago.

"So," she said, "are you going up to see your kids this weekend?"

"Actually, I was asking for Wednesday—of this week. I took a few days off from work. I'm going to search for Jill again."

"But . . . where would you search?" She looked at him like maybe she thought he'd finally gone over the edge.

"I'm not sure. I have a meeting at school Tuesday that I can't miss, but I'd like to leave early Wednesday morning. I'll feed TP before I leave, but would you mind letting him out when you come home for lunch, and again after work? It'll be the same the rest of the week. I'll be home after dark every night so I'll take care of him in the mornings."

He pretended not to see the skeptical look she shot him.

"Mitch, where can you look that hasn't already been searched?"

"I plan to drive the routes she could have taken from Kansas City. Even the back roads and out-of-the-way detours. I've mapped out some new—"

"Haven't they done that already? Along with half the city of Sylvia? We don't even know for sure that she ever left Kansas City, Mitch."

He shook his head. "I have to think she did. You heard the message she left. She'd left the hotel for sure. Filled up with gas, according to that credit card bill. It sounded like she was on her way home."

"It did, but . . ." She bit the corner of her bottom lip.

"There are still side roads she could have taken. Roads we haven't checked as closely. Side roads she could have made a wrong turn onto. Some of those roads aren't even on the map. And with the trees bare of leaves now, maybe I'll spot some-thing we missed before. It's a long

200

shot, I know. But . . . it's possible." He scuffed the ground with the toe of his sneaker. "I know you think I'm foolish, but I can't live in this limbo another day. I can't—"

"I don't think you're foolish." She sighed, looking near tears again. "I understand why you want to do that. Need to. But . . . Why do you think you'll find anything different than the police and Missing Persons, and all the others who've searched? So . . . you took time off from work?"

He nodded. "Believe me, they won't miss me. I've been worthless at work anyway. There has to be something they've missed. There *has* to. I have to find out what happened."

He looked down at the withered vines wrapped around his palm. "Even if I find out she's *dead*—" He sucked in a breath, shocked that he'd said it aloud. But he'd begun to think it more and more. *Dead.* After all these months, any other scenario was too agonizing to ponder.

"Do you think she might be, Mitch? Dead?" Her voice was a whisper, but at least she was brave enough to look him in the eye when she said it. And she didn't say *I told you so.*

"I don't know. I don't know what to think anymore. I just know I can't keep on like this. I can't . . . do nothing. I have to do something."

"Let me go with you. We can bring TP along. He might even be able to . . . I don't know . . . sniff out where Jill's been?"

He shook his head. "I doubt it. Not after all this time." He remembered something. "You know, TP was always antsy anytime Jill was gone. He was always her dog at heart. From the very beginning. The day she left for that conference he did his usual whining and sniffing at the garage door. But . . ." He studied Shelley, debating whether to share more, but he thought she would understand. "After that first night when Jill didn't come home, TP just . . . quit looking for her."

"Really?"

He nodded. It had seemed a small thing, but it disturbed him deeply. "They say animals have a sixth sense about these things."

"The kids came home that first night though. Maybe that was enough to satisfy him."

He shrugged. "I don't know."

"Are you saying . . . TP somehow knew Jill wasn't coming back?"

"No. I'm saying maybe he knows she *is* coming back. And he's just . . . I don't know"—he shrugged —"exercising canine patience or something."

She didn't respond, and he read skepticism—or worse—in her silence.

He knew it sounded a little crazy, but he'd reached a point where he was willing to risk seeming a little crazy. Because if he didn't do something, he would be certifiable. Time to change the subject. And make a confession. "I'm not just going to drive the roads."

"What do you mean?"

Should he tell her? Shelley was trustworthy, despite how worried he could tell she was about him. "There are people I need to talk to along the way. People who might have talked to Jill the day she disappeared. Maybe someone had a conversation with her, or overheard something that will give us a clue."

"You mean the people who were at the conference?"

"Yes. And the people at that gas station. And the hotel. Somebody had to have seen something. There has to be some kind of clue in all this. There just has to be."

"But didn't the police talk to those people already? And even if you could find them, would they remember anything they haven't already reported? How could you possibly track them all down after all this time?"

"I have a list."

"How?"

He shook his head. "I think it would be best if I didn't say." The former high school principal, whose place he'd filled, had mentioned that he knew the director of the professional development conference Jill had attended. One thing led to another, and when Mitch got back from Jill's folks' after Christmas, Jerry Boston had delivered a list of names to him—all the teachers who'd been on the conference roster, and the schools where they worked. But Shelley didn't need to know the details.

The skeptical expression on her face was clear.

Truth was, Mitch didn't know exactly how it had all come about. He hadn't asked Jerry how he got the list. Or about the legality of him using it. Teachers placed a high value on confidentiality—understandably—and it wasn't difficult to justify having the list in his possession. He didn't intend anyone harm. It wasn't like he had their home addresses and was harassing them in their living rooms. But he would do whatever it took to find Jill. There were almost a hundred names on the list, in thirty-eight school districts.

"Somebody has to remember something," he said. "Surely someone at the conference talked to Jill. Even if they didn't think their conversation was significant, there might be something that would hold a clue. And I want to talk to people—while they still might remember."

Shelley nodded, the crease in her brow remaining. But she surprised him with her next words. "Let me go with you. I might pick up on some clues you wouldn't."

He hated the truth of that. But she was right. Not only because his wife had confided secrets to Shelley that Jill had kept from him, but because Shelley was more sensitive and intuitive than he was. He had to admit that she would be a valuable asset in what he hoped to accomplish.

"I plan on coming back home each evening by a different route. It will mean long days. But I want to accomplish as much as possible with the few days I have. I was hoping to leave at sunrise every morning. And keep looking till after dark."

"That's okay with me."

He studied her for a long moment. "How are you going to get off work, Shelley? Haven't you used up all your vacation time already?"

"Don't worry about that. Can I come or not?"

He wanted to say yes. She *would* be an asset. And she was right—they could take TP with them.

Something told him to say no, but before he could examine why, he nodded. "Yes. If you're sure you can get off work. I've already made phone calls to some of the teachers on the list. I think we can talk to the rest in four days—and cover at least some of the roads I mapped out in the process. But I need to go during the week— when school is in session. You'd miss at least three days of work, unless you were supposed to work Saturday. Then you'd miss four. I thought I could talk to people Wednesday through Friday. Take a different route each day. Then Saturday, if you come with me, we'll see where we are."

She waved away his question. "I can get off."

"You're sure?" He sighed. "I'd really appreciate having you along. We can cover more territory if there are two of us to talk to people."

"I'm glad there's something I can do to help."

"Okay then . . . Let's do it."

That earned him a smile.

"I'd like to leave as soon as it's light Wednesday morning. Around seven or so? We probably won't be able to get hold of anyone at the schools until around nine, but we can drive to the farthest point on our route and then choose our routes back each night—starting with the ones she was mostly likely to have taken."

"Sounds good . . . I'll be ready."

Something about her demeanor restored a hope he hadn't felt in a very long time.

19

Tuesday, January 11

Shelley worked until eight Tuesday night, and it was well after dark when she got home. She quickly went through the house, turning on lamps. She hated how early the sun went down now that winter was here. She'd always hated the darkness, but it seemed to have taken on a more sinister quality since Jill had gone missing.

It startled her to realize how much time had passed since that awful day. She'd arranged to take the rest of the week off from work, even though her boss was not very happy about the idea. In a show of good faith, she'd stayed after closing tonight, and promised Jaclyn she would work after hours next week taking down the New Year's displays and putting out the rest of the Valentine's merchandise.

She pushed away the thoughts of work and let a twinge of excitement rise as she thought about a road trip with Mitch tomorrow. But she quickly checked her thoughts.

She changed clothes and went back to the kitchen and pulled the recipe box from a top cupboard. She'd been planning to make cookies to take to work. Valentine's cookies, since they were gearing up for the February holidays at the store. She could make the cookies and pack a lunch to take on the road with Mitch tomorrow instead.

But one look at the pink-iced heart-shaped cookies pictured in the recipe book, and she realized how awkward that would be, given the nature of the holiday—let alone given the nature of her feelings for Mitch.

"Okay, oatmeal it is," she said. Her voice echoed in the empty kitchen.

She had to keep reminding herself that no matter how solemn the purpose for their trip, she couldn't deny that she was eager to spend time with Mitch. Alone with him.

She felt like a traitor even thinking such thoughts. And even worse, the truth was she had very little hope that Jill was alive after all this time. She had nightmares imagining what might have happened to her friend, and as much as she wished she could muster the kind of hope Mitch had, something—something that seemed beyond simple intuition—seemed to tell her that Jill was gone.

But whether Mitch truly still had hope or simply needed closure, she was glad he'd agreed to let her come along. If she were to play armchair psychologist, she'd say that Mitch had worked through his initial anger and fear, and now the emotions he wrestled with were bewilderment and confusion. No one—least of all her—could, or should, rush him through the grief process before he was ready. And the strange circumstances of Jill's situation probably complicated the grieving process. He needed to get through this in his own time.

She turned on the oven, then measured sugar and sifted flour, remembering how much she'd enjoyed baking when Audrey had been home to enjoy the fruits of her efforts. As she put the first batch of cookies in the oven, a deep longing for the warm friendship she'd shared with Jill rose inside her. In a way, she thought it was God's gift to her—a dim shadow of the longing Mitch must be feeling for Jill. She needed that reminder.

Maybe she'd grieved too soon. Maybe it was wrong to give up hope. If Mitch caught even a hint that she felt their search was in vain, he would not want her with him on these trips to

Kansas City and back. And understandably so.

But maybe he doesn't really expect to find Jill alive. The thought took her breath away. She turned the mixer off and stared at the creamy batter in the mixing bowl that had been her grandmother's. "Oh, dear Lord," she whispered. "Please let us find Jill. And if that's not possible, let us find . . . *something.* Something that will let Mitch go on with his life. Something that will let us both go on."

Her hand trembled on the mixer. She understood that God knew her every thought, but it was still hard to admit to Him how much she struggled with her feelings toward Mitch. How deeply her romantic interest in her friend's husband had been rekindled throughout these months they'd remembered—and mourned—Jill together, comforting and consoling each other. Grief had a tendency to produce intimacy, but she'd allowed that closeness to taint what had begun as innocent affection and concern.

Ever so briefly, she toyed with the idea of backing out of the trip. But she'd already promised Mitch she'd go with him, and she could tell he was eager to have an extra set of eyes— and her insight regarding Jill. Besides, she'd already taken the time off from work. It was too late to back out now.

Don't make excuses, Austin. Just be honest. You want *to go with him.*

"Make my attitudes right, God. Please." By the time the sweet aroma of the first batch of cookies filled the house, she'd worked things out in her mind. She could manage this. Surely for a few days, she could set aside the longings of her heart and just be there for a friend in need.

Wednesday, January 12

A band of orange sunlight rimmed the eastern horizon as they headed north. Rounding a curve in the highway a few miles outside of Sylvia, Mitch flipped down the sun visor and looked over to the passenger seat, where Shelley sipped a cup of coffee. She'd brought a thermos full of the stuff and he was tempted to have her pour him a refill, but he'd wait until she was finished with hers.

He'd intended to pay for her meals, but without talking to him about it, she'd packed a cooler that would have fed half of Clemons County. Not for the first time, a twinge of guilt bit at him. He should have discouraged her more strongly from taking time off work to help him. He knew from comments Jill had made over the years that Shelley was barely scraping by. He doubted she was salaried at the gift shop downtown, yet she was sacrificing three—maybe four—days' pay to come with him. And now she was providing the food, too.

"Tomorrow I'll take care of lunch, but in the meantime . . ." He reached into the bag on the console between them and extracted another oatmeal cookie. He winked at Shelley. "You didn't want any of these, did you?"

She laughed. "It would be nice if you saved me one for lunch. The rest are all yours. Unless you want to share one with poor TP."

He glanced over the back of the seat where the dog was sacked out. "No, I'd hate to wake him up."

She rolled her eyes. "My, aren't you the thoughtful one?"

He acknowledged her sarcasm with a grin before stuffing the remainder of the cookie in his mouth. "Man, I haven't had a homemade cookie in a while. These are great."

He'd meant it as a compliment, not to garner pity, but Shelley gave him a smile full of regret.

He decided to tackle the subject head-on. Get it out of the way. "I got a little spoiled with our church bringing food those first few weeks, and all the goodies you made us. But I guess I'm going to need to learn how to cook for myself."

"You don't cook? I mean . . . you haven't cooked all this time?"

"Not much. I know how to make popcorn."

"Microwave popcorn?"

He nodded and managed to look sheepish.

"That's not cooking."

"Hey, I know my way to McDonald's." When the church's onslaught of casseroles stopped, he'd begun hitting the drive-through after work, and grabbing something at the convenience store for breakfast on the way to school. The scales were beginning to groan in protest. Not to mention his bank account. "But don't worry," he told her. "I caught this cooking show the other night on cable. It doesn't look too tough."

"What were they making?" She sounded skeptical.

"Beef Wellington."

She seemed to think that was hysterically funny.

"What?"

"That's like . . . the most challenging dish you could ever make."

"Um . . . I guess I didn't watch the whole show."

More laughter. "You might want to start with scrambled eggs or PB and J or something a little more intermediate. But you cook on the grill, right?"

"I haven't for a while. But I will once the weather gets nice again. But somehow a steak or burger doesn't quite cut it without all the trimmings." He sobered. "I didn't appreciate Jill's cooking like I should have. Especially when she'd come home from a full day of teaching to make me a full meal deal."

"She knew you appreciated her."

He shook his head. It ate at him that they'd

begun to speak of Jill in the past tense. "I'm not sure she did know. But if I ever get the chance, I'll never take her for granted again."

"She knew, Mitch. You don't need to beat yourself up about that."

He hoped she was right. And he meant what he'd said. If God gave him another chance, he would never fail to appreciate that everything good about him was because of the woman who'd completed him.

He loved Jill. He truly did. So why did it feel like he was trying to convince himself? Why had it become so difficult recently to think about what it would be like if Jill really did come home?

20

Thursday, January 13

Shelley looked up from the bench in the corridor of the tidy suburban elementary school in Lee's Summit, Missouri, a few miles outside of Kansas City. Mitch came down the hallway, and the hunch of his shoulders told her he hadn't been any more successful here than at the other schools they'd visited this morning. Yesterday had been a total bust, too.

"Any luck?" he asked. They'd split up at this school since there were two teachers here who'd been at Jill's conference. Shelley had finished early and waited in the hall for him. Hoping to cover more ground, Mitch had put schools with more than one teacher attending the conference at the top of the list. But it was a short list. By Friday they'd be talking to one teacher at a time, hoping beyond hope that the person had struck up a conversation with Jill at the conference, remembered their conversation after more than five months, and that the substance of their talk would yield some sort of clue.

Shelley wouldn't voice her thoughts, but it seemed like an exercise in futility if ever there was one.

She rose to meet him. "Sorry. Nothing. You?"

He shook his head, but didn't expound.

"Let's go find a place to eat our picnic. Take a little break."

"No." He motioned toward the front door. "We need to keep moving. We can eat in the car."

She managed a smile. "All right."

He grimaced and dipped his head. "I'm sorry. I didn't mean to be so short."

"No apology necessary. I know it wasn't aimed at me." Still, it stung. And maybe it was aimed at her.

But he put a hand to the small of her back as they went out through the front doors and his tone softened. "Do you mind too much if we eat on the road? I'll do the driving."

"No. I understand. I just thought you could use a break."

"I've only got a few days to do this, Shelley." He seemed to be weighing his words carefully. "I'd rather keep pushing and accomplish as much as possible while we've both got the time off."

"Mitch—" She bit her lower lip, struggling with how much to say.

Turning away and striding ahead of her across the parking lot, he aimed his keys at his Saturn and the lights flashed. When they reached the car, he opened the door, but didn't get in, and instead stood staring at her over the top of the vehicle, waiting with an expression she couldn't read.

"I'm afraid you're going to kill yourself at this rate," she risked.

"What's that supposed to mean?"

"You're pushing yourself to the edge. I'm afraid it's going to make you sick—getting so worked up over this."

His jaw tensed. "And you think a little picnic is going to fix that?"

She shook her head and climbed in the car, wishing Mitch would pick one mood and stick with it. After a few seconds, he eased behind the wheel.

"I'm sorry." She stared out the windshield. "I never should have said anything."

He didn't respond.

"No . . . You know what?" Anger boiled up in

her and she angled her body in the seat to face him. "Maybe I should have said something a long time ago. Not that you'd have listened to me any more then than you are now."

He stared back at her.

"Mitch, it has been *months* and the authorities have done—"

"Barely five months and I feel like my hands have been tied most of that time!" He pulled out of the parking lot, consulted the GPS on his phone, and headed south out of town.

"The authorities have done *everything* possible to find Jill. What you're doing now—" She swept her hand across the vista of the road they were traveling. "Will it be enough? When you've driven every road in the state, will you be ready to admit it's over then?" She found the tenderness she'd wanted to have toward him. "Mitch . . . How long can you wait before you join the living again? Until it kills you? Until you've cheated your kids out of their dad? Until you've let your friends drop away? I can't—"

"Do you honestly think I can just sit back and do nothing? Just accept that she's gone? What if it was you out there? Do you think Jill would just shrug and say, 'Oh, well, guess we'll never find her'? You know she wouldn't. You know she'd be doing exactly what I'm doing right now. And she wouldn't stop until we found you."

Sobered, she stared back at him. There was

really nothing she could say. He was right. Jill would never have rested until they had answers.

How had they wound up in this same argument again? The very one that had driven them apart for *weeks* before? Why couldn't she let him search to the ends of the earth if that's what he wanted to do? She looked away, her thoughts churning.

She cared about him. She saw what this grief—this *not knowing*—was doing to him. Choosing her words carefully, she tried to explain. "Doesn't there come a point where you put this in God's hands? Where you just have to trust that He knows what He's doing?"

"Maybe." He sounded so wounded. So defeated. "Maybe that time will come. But it hasn't yet. And I couldn't live with myself if I stopped searching one day too soon."

"I understand. And that has to be between you and the Lord. I should have kept my mouth shut."

"You said . . . I've cheated my kids." He swallowed hard. "Do you think I've done that? Have the kids said something to you?"

"No. Oh, of course not, Mitch. You misunderstood." She reached across the console and put a hand over his. "I know you've been there for your kids through every day of this. It's just—It scares me, what I see happening to you. Seeing you so . . . tortured. It's become an obsession—"

He tensed, and she moved her hand away from his, too aware of the feel of his skin against hers.

She rushed to explain. "I know, because it's *her*, it can't really be anything else for you. But at some point—Mitch, you might have to accept that she's gone, and that you may never find out what happened. You might have to let her go."

"I can't. I can't let her go."

"Then this limbo you're living in . . . this grief will *kill* you."

He sagged in his seat. "Sometimes I think it already has."

The resignation in his voice weighed on her. "Then you need to get help. Hire a private investigator to do all this running around"—she motioned to the highway before them—"to do all these interviews."

"I thought that's what you were here for . . ." He smiled, trying, she knew, to lighten the moment. But just as quickly, he turned serious. "No one else could recognize if something Jill said to a teacher had significance or not. I'm the only one who could figure that out—or you. That's why I was so relieved when you offered to come with me. It was an answer to a prayer I hadn't even thought to pray."

"And I'm happy to be here with you—*for* you. But what worries me is *after*. If we come back to Sylvia Sunday night and we haven't turned up anything . . . If we come home without Jill, without even a clue about Jill, then what? What will you do then?"

The sigh he expelled wrenched her heart. But how could he really think they would find something that numerous police forces and detectives and law enforcement agencies had missed?

"I don't know, Shelley." He turned away from her and pulled the rumpled list of names from the visor overhead. "I can't think that far ahead. Right now I have to concentrate on what I *can* do."

"Okay. I can understand that. I can accept that. I'll help you in any way I can. But Sunday night, if we haven't—"

Mitch reached to put a hand on her arm. "I need you to think positively for me. I need you to believe she's out there. And that we *will* find her."

She opened her mouth to lie to him, to say that she would think *positively*. But even if she'd uttered all the right words, he would have read the truth in her eyes in a heartbeat.

21

Friday, January 14

"Why don't we stay together to talk to this teacher? The other school is just down the road." Mitch felt bad for jumping down Shelley's throat yesterday and had been trying to make it up to her on the road today.

She lifted a shoulder in a half-shrug. "Whatever you want to do."

Shelley wasn't the type to hold a grudge, but she wasn't exactly warming up to him either. He didn't blame her. He'd been a jerk. She was only worried about him—that he was working himself into exhaustion. And she was probably right. Jill would have done exactly the same thing in Shelley's shoes, and he would have loved her for it.

Shelley consulted her iPhone and directed him through the small town of Sedalia, to the elementary school. They were back on the Missouri side and had taken Highway 50, stopping to talk to a teacher in Warrensburg.

They were slowly working their way back toward Sylvia, but were still a good three hours from home. It was taking longer than Mitch had figured. He'd sat in the principal's office for twenty minutes at the previous school, waiting for a teacher to finish a class. At this rate, they'd still be interviewing the people on his list next spring.

He felt pressure on his arm and looked down to see Shelley holding out the bag of oatmeal cookies. "Last one. You want it?"

"Thanks, but I'm good. It's yours."

"How about we split it?" She broke the cookie in half before he could protest.

"Thanks." He took a bite, happy for what he

220

hoped was a peace offering. "South Warren should be coming right up. Turn left there."

The school was in a residential area and he parked in the shade across the street. "It would be nice to have you with me," he risked. "TP will be fine in the car. But you're welcome to wait here, too, if you'd rather."

Shelley unbuckled her seatbelt. "No, I'll come with you."

He cracked the windows for TP and they crossed the parking lot side by side. They checked in at the front office, and strolled down a corridor that still bore a few tattered Christmas decorations. At each of the schools they'd visited, he'd been interested to see another principal's turf, and to look at the notices on bulletin boards and displays in the cases along the walls. Looking down the hallways, he could almost imagine Jill stepping through one of the class-room doorways, herding a passel of third-graders out to the playground for recess.

He wondered if Shelley's imagination had played the same games with her. He started to ask her, but she pointed to a sign on a door to their right.

"Right there. Grade four, right? Mrs. Marnivot?"

Nodding, and trying not to get his hopes up, Mitch took in a breath and let Shelley enter the room first. He rapped softly on the doorjamb before stepping in behind her.

The gray-haired woman at the whiteboard looked over her shoulder, then put down the eraser she'd been using and approached them. She wore an expression of curiosity they'd become familiar with. "May I help you?"

Mitch introduced himself, and Shelley and explained why they were here. If it hadn't been so very real, it was starting to be almost comical to see the universal response to his story. One hand went to Mrs. Marvinot's crepey throat and she gave a little gasp. "Oh, my! Yes, we heard about your wife."

"I wondered if I could ask you a few questions. About the professional development conference you attended in Kansas City this past September."

"Of course. I didn't know your wife personally, but like I told Mrs. Waverly"—she motioned to the classroom across the hall—"after seeing the photographs on the TV, I realized she was in one of my breakout groups that first night of the conference."

"Really?"

"I sent a card to your house after I heard. I hope you got it. I was just sick when I heard that she'd passed away."

Beside him, Shelley gave a little gasp, and Mitch knew his face must have reflected his shock. "No. That's wrong." A horrifying thought nearly strangled him. "You don't mean . . . recently? You didn't just hear that news, did you?" He glanced briefly at Shelley, and wished there were something sturdy nearby to steady him.

"Oh, no," the teacher said quickly. "We heard about it right after the whole thing happened. Or shortly after anyway. Maybe a week or two. It was all over the news."

Relief flooded over him. "No, you're mistaken. Jill didn't die. She's not dead. But she's still missing."

Her eyes went wide. "I didn't know. Well . . . That's wonderful! I mean—" The woman sputtered and flushed twenty shades of red. "Not wonderful that she's still missing, of course, but . . . We heard she'd died." Her brow crinkled. "But—how do they know she's alive?"

"The search is ongoing." Shelley stepped forward and answered before he could. And she said it with a conviction Mitch hadn't heard in her voice in their private conversations. "That's why we're here."

He could have hugged her.

"I'm so sorry for the misunderstanding," the woman said. "I'll be sure to correct that rumor wherever I can. And of course, I'll do my best to help in any way possible."

"Do you remember any conversations you might have had with my wife during the conference?" He slipped the small notepad he'd been jotting notes in from his pocket and poised his pen over it.

"I wish I could remember more, but I didn't really speak privately with your wife. She seemed like such a sweet woman. And so pretty. I felt like I got to know her *so* well just sitting in that workshop with her and discussing our mutual passion for children and for teaching."

"Did Jill seem upset or . . . preoccupied?"

"Not when I was around her. She was very friendly and animated. Very insightful, too. She added a lot to the discussion."

People sometimes thought Jill was shy, but that was only because they hadn't seen her in her element. This woman was right. Jill was passionate about teaching and about kids. He asked a few more questions, and when it became clear that the teacher really didn't know anything helpful, he excused himself and walked with Shelley back to the office.

"Did you notice how that woman wanted to be Jill's new best friend?" he said when they were out of earshot.

"What do you mean?"

"It just seems like as soon as Jill went missing, suddenly anyone who'd had any relationship at all with her tried to magnify that connection— make it more than it really was in a lot of cases."

She shook her head. "You'd think, if anything, they'd want to distance themselves from the tragedy of it—like it might rub off on them or something."

"I know, but it's actually the opposite. Teachers Jill barely knew claim she was like a sister to them. And people we're only mildly acquainted with—from church and around Sylvia—suddenly want to claim her as their dearest friend . . . It just strikes me as very strange."

"It is kind of weird. And you're right— Remember that article in the *Sentinel* where your mail carrier claimed he talked to Jill almost every day?"

Mitch gave a little snort. "Interesting, since she rarely got home till long after the mail was delivered.

Shelley looked sheepish. "I guess I've probably done the same thing though."

"What do you mean? You *are* like a sister to her. And her best friend."

"And I *did* talk to her every day."

He smiled. "Sometimes twice a day."

"Man, I miss her."

"Yeah . . . Me too." A deep sadness washed over him. *I miss her.* Such inadequate words to express the hole in his heart. In his life.

As they passed the office on the way to the exit, a man in a dress shirt and tie stuck his head out the door. "You found Mrs. Marvinot okay?"

"Yes. Thank you."

The man stuck out a hand. "I'm Kenton Rosemond, principal here."

"Nice to meet you."

"Mrs. Hitchcock told me why you were here. My condolences."

"Thank you." He curbed a smile. Grapevines apparently worked the same at this school as they did in Sylvia.

Mitch introduced Shelley, and Rosemond shook her hand, holding it a few seconds too long, Mitch thought, and looking her up and down appreciatively. As many men did, he'd begun to notice.

Jill had often commented about how beautiful Shelley was. In fact, Jill had been intimidated by Shelley's beauty at first. More than once he'd reassured his wife that their neighbor had nothing on her. He hadn't been exaggerating either. Jill was lovely. Exactly his type. She was what most people—men anyway—probably thought of as "cute" or "pretty." Her blond hair, freckled skin, and wide blue eyes gave her a wholesome girl-next-door look.

Shelley fell more into the drop-dead gorgeous category. Her dark eyes and thick lashes, full lips and creamy skin gave her a mysterious, almost exotic, aura . . .

He pushed away the comparison. How had his thoughts even taken this trail? It wasn't that he'd never noticed Shelley's looks until now, but he'd put up certain walls.

But during these hours they'd spent on the road, their conversations were no longer only about Jill. They'd begun to talk about other things—their kids and their jobs. Dreams and disappointments. Mitch was disturbed to realize that Shelley had taken Jill's place as his confidante and sounding board.

And now, when he dared to think about what it would be like if Jill was ever found, he couldn't imagine how he and Shelley could go back to the way things were before Jill went missing. He'd come to treasure the close friendship that had grown between them. Yet, when he tried to imagine Jill in the picture, it left him feeling decidedly uncomfortable.

Because Shelley is becoming more than a friend.

The thought was disturbing and exhilarating at the same time. Spending so much time together over these past five months, going through everything they had surrounding Jill's situation, being so . . . vulnerable with each other . . . All those things had begun to chip away at the walls he'd once erected.

He needed to build those walls back up again. And quickly.

22

"Do you want to stop and get something to eat?"

"I'm fine." Shelley shifted in the seat beside Mitch. He looked as weary as she felt after a full day on the road. "I am kind of thirsty though. Maybe a Coke would be nice. If you don't mind stopping."

"I don't mind." He eased into the right lane and trained his gaze on the signs littering the exit ramp. "There's a Dairy Queen up ahead. That okay with you? I could go for a milkshake."

"Oooh, me too, now that you mention it."

He laughed and guided the car to the exit. It was good to hear him laugh. He'd been pensive most of the day, and especially so since the last school where the stupid teacher had told Mitch she'd heard Jill had died.

At least he wasn't snapping at her as he sometimes had when his hopes were being dashed. If anything, he'd been extra sweet to her, thanking her for coming in with him at the last couple of schools. She didn't tell him she would have been happy to go inside with him all along if he hadn't been so insistent that she wait in the car.

There were three cars ahead of them in the drive-through and they waited in line, not talking, the radio turned low, playing some classical piece she didn't recognize. Over the few days they'd been traveling together, they'd grown past feeling awkward at the silence between them. She felt comfortable with Mitch. Safe. In dangerous ways.

The idling car purred and Shelley's eyelids grew heavy. Her phone rang and she jumped. Mitch picked up her phone from the console between them and handed it to her.

She mouthed a thank-you and answered the call.

"Hey, Shel, sorry to bother you." Besides Jill, Jaclyn was the only one who called her Shel.

"Hi, boss." She suddenly ached with longing to see Jill, to tell her friend everything that had been happening.

"I hope I'm not calling at a bad time?"

"Not at all. What's up?"

"I hate to impose, but is there any way you could close tomorrow?"

She glanced at Mitch who stared out the window in a vain effort to give her some privacy, she knew.

"I . . . really have another commitment, Jaclyn. Cindy can't do it?" She wished Mitch didn't have to hear this conversation. He already felt bad enough about taking her away from work.

"No, Cindy's dad was rushed to the ER this morning. They think he had a stroke."

"Oh! I'm so sorry. I hadn't heard. Yes . . . I guess I could come in. Will they be okay if I just come in at six and stay to close?"

"Yes, sure. And thank you." Relief was thick in Jaclyn's voice. "I'll take whatever hours you can give me."

Shelley finished the call, then tucked her phone in the side pocket of her purse so she wouldn't forget it when Mitch dropped her off at home tonight.

"Everything okay?"

"One of the girls can't come in for her shift." She explained the situation.

"Well, don't turn down the extra hours on my account." The car ahead of him exited the drive-through, and he pulled up to the window and paid for their milkshakes. He handed her the chocolate one and a handful of napkins.

"I'm doing fine, Mitch. I won't short myself on hours I need. If you could have me back in time tomorrow to get to the store by six or so I could still come with you during the day. Jaclyn needs me to close."

"Of course. There won't be anyone in school to talk to tomorrow, so we'll just be driving the roads. Won't do any good to stay out once the sun starts going down anyway."

"Okay. Thanks, Mitch."

He gave her a sidewise glance. "Hey, don't thank me. You're the one who's doing me a huge favor."

She waved him off.

But he turned and held her gaze. "Listen . . . Are

you getting along okay? Financially, I mean." He held up a hand. "Not that it's any of my business. I don't mean to pry, but I don't have any way of knowing, and I'd feel bad if keeping you away from work is causing a hardship. Jill usually keeps me up to date on how you're doing and—" He winced. "That makes it sound like Jill blabs everything you two talk about. I promise she never—"

She put a hand on his arm, wanting to put him at ease, but a little charmed by his discomfiture, too. "Jill always made it clear that you two were one, and that if there was something I didn't want you to know, I'd better not tell her, because you guys didn't keep secrets from each other." Shelley cringed inwardly, remembering the secrets Jill *had* kept from Mitch.

She felt sure from the faraway look that came to Mitch's eyes that he was remembering too. She cleared her throat and mentally kicked herself for broaching the subject.

But to her surprise, Mitch didn't press the issue. "Well, rest assured, Jill never told me anything about you that I'd consider a deep, dark secret. Unless you count that night you spent in jail." He looked at her over his straw, an ornery glimmer lighting his eyes.

"I did not spend the night in jail!" She switched the cold styrofoam cup to her other hand long enough to smack his arm.

"Hmm . . . That's not how Jill told it." He took another sip of his shake.

"It was only a couple of hours, and I have the canceled traffic ticket to prove it."

He shook his head, the glimmer spreading to his whole face. "That's not at all how Jill told it."

"Cut it out."

He chuckled and turned to study the traffic signs.

It did her heart good to see him lighthearted and playful. And to talk about Jill this way. Shelley hadn't realized till now how much the tragedy had changed him. It was good to see a hint of the old Mitch returning.

When they were on the main road again, sucking thick milkshakes through too-thin straws, his mood turned solemn. "I'm serious about Jill not sharing too much. I don't want you to think she came home and gossiped every time you guys hung out. I didn't mean to—"

"I know that, Mitch. I trusted Jill—and I trust you. I admit I wasn't crazy about the whole concept when she first warned me that I couldn't confide anything that she couldn't share with you, but I've come to realize it's a good policy for marriage. Maybe if Tom and I had kept fewer secrets from each other things would have turned out differently."

He was quiet behind the wheel. But after a few

minutes he turned to her. "Hey, I just want to say how much I appreciate you coming with me. And . . . I know you probably wouldn't tell me anyway, but I just hope you're not losing too many hours at work. If I can . . . help make up some of that I'd be glad to pay you—"

"Don't even think about it." She gave him a smile she hoped was reassuring. "Really . . . I'm fine. Things are a little tight. I'm sure Jill's told you that much. But hey, after fifteen years, I'm used to it." She laughed.

"Well, if I can help, please let me know. I feel responsible for you losing the income."

She shook her head. "I need to learn to live one day at a time. And not worry so much about how I'll pay for a wedding some day, about whether Jaclyn will close the shop—"

"Oh? Is she thinking about it?" Concern creased his brow.

She rolled her eyes. "Well, she *threatens* to shut down twice a week. I don't honestly think she would, but it's scary to think about."

"Have you ever thought about buying the store?"

"Are you kidding?" She formed a cross with her index fingers and held it out as though she were warding off a vampire.

He laughed. "I'll take that as a no."

"I've seen the kind of hours Jaclyn works. And the headache of the paperwork. And I have a feeling her paycheck is smaller than mine. I'd be crazy to even entertain such a thought."

He cocked his head and studied her. "If you could do anything you wanted, what would it be? Or maybe you're already doing that?"

She shook her head. "No. I don't mind my job, but it's not my dream."

"So what is your dream?"

Sharing my life with someone like you. For one horrifying second she was afraid she'd spoken the words aloud.

But Mitch's gaze remained merely curious.

Yet, replaying her thought, she made a correction. It wasn't just someone *like* him. It *was* him. And admitting it, even just to herself, both terrified—and freed—her.

The monotonous whir of tires on the road emphasized the silence between them and she knew he was waiting for an answer and would press her until she gave one that satisfied him.

Outside the windows the wooded landscape rolled by, slate-barked trees standing like an army of Confederate soldiers against a dimming powder blue sky. Here and there an outbuilding sat nestled among the brown hills, and more rarely a humble house appeared around a bend, chimney puffing a steady plume of smoke. Even the air inside the car smelled of wood smoke. It gave a cozy feel to the day, and weary as she was, Shelley wished they had even farther to drive.

"My dream?" she said finally, sighing. "I really don't know. I guess—The last few years have taken so much energy just keeping up with the bills and trying to be both mother and father to Audrey I don't think I've dared to dream."

"So dare right now."

She smiled, realizing that she was completely unafraid to take his challenge. To voice what Tom had once laughed at her for. "I'd love to open a bed and breakfast."

"Really? So what's stopping you?"

She gave a dry laugh. "Reality. I'll be lucky if my savings covers Audrey's wedding."

"Won't Tom help with that?"

She shook her head. "He's getting college. The wedding bills will be mine. I'm just praying she doesn't meet anyone for a few years yet." Too late, she realized her comment might sound like she'd been glad when Evan and Audrey broke up.

But he didn't react, and simply said, "I'm sorry."

She shrugged. "Nothing to be sorry about. I'm just grateful Tom is taking some responsibility."

Mitch's mouth twisted. "If you want to call it that." He shifted in his seat and brightened. "So what part of opening a B and B appeals to you?"

"Everything but the bookkeeping."

His open expression said he was waiting for more, hanging on her every word. It was one of the things she loved most about him, and she wanted nothing more than to share her dream with this amazing man. But she could hardly do that when the dream of her heart—one she'd willingly allowed to grow over the last few weeks—included him. "I know it would be a lot of work," she said, choosing her words carefully, "but I think I'd love the challenge."

"You'd make a great innkeeper. I'd just hate to lose a good neighbor. I'm assuming you'd live at the inn. Maybe not . . ."

She gave an embarrassed laugh. "I don't know why I'm even talking about it. It's not going to happen."

"Don't be so sure. If you really want that, Shelley, why don't you make it happen?"

She tilted her head, intrigued. "What do you mean?"

"Have you even looked into it?"

She shook her head. "I can barely pay the bills for the house I live in now, and I don't know if there's enough equity in it . . . Besides, I don't even know if there's anything available in Sylvia that could be turned into a B and B."

He shrugged, but the look he leveled at her held challenge. "You'll never know if you don't look."

"Whatever."

He blew out a breath. "Now you sound like Katie."

She laughed, glad the subject had been defused. She slipped her phone from her purse and pressed the icon for the GPS app. "Which way are we going home?"

"Oh, no you don't." Mitch shook a finger at her. "Don't think you can shrug me off that easily. I want to hear more about this idea of yours."

She gave a sheepish laugh. "It's not even an idea, Mitch. It's . . . barely a dream."

"So dream a little with me. What about that old Victorian on the south end of Elm? You know the one I mean? Or are you picturing something more modern?"

She nodded. And blinked back tears. Did the man have any idea how much she longed to "dream a little" with him? She wished she could tell him to be careful . . . with her dream *and* with her heart.

23

Sunday, January 16

The worship team was already onstage singing when Mitch and Shelley entered the sanctuary. She'd been surprised when he suggested they attend church before heading out on another search trip this morning. But not as surprised as having him lead the way down the center aisle to seats in the fifth row from the front. She didn't think she was imagining more than a few heads turning to watch them slide into the row. But maybe she was just being paranoid. *Or feeling guilty?*

She was glad they were here, though. It seemed right. And even as the thought came, she whispered a prayer that they would learn something today—anything—that might provide a clue about what had happened to Jill.

They'd spent four full days on the road together, driving from dawn till after dusk each evening. Searching for what seemed like the proverbial needle in a haystack. They had this final day of combing the back roads before they both had to return to work.

If this day didn't produce some answers, she wasn't sure how Mitch would handle it. Whether he could go on without some hint of hope.

Pastor Radley, the worship leader, strummed his guitar and segued into a slower, deeply worshipful song. She blended her voice with Mitch's, struggling to focus on the lyrics, struggling against the urge to imagine what it would be like to sit beside Mitchell Brannon every Sunday —as more than just his friend. *Jill's friend.*

"Forgive me, God." How could she entertain such traitorous thoughts—and in church? The words of the song convicted . . . *Create in me a clean heart, oh, God.*

And still she warred with her thoughts.

She was glad when the last note died away and the worship team left the stage.

An hour later, amid the buzz of fellowship, she felt Mitch's hand at her back, guiding her through knots of animated conversation. Again, she felt eyes on them.

Most people smiled and nodded. A few stopped Mitch and gave masked condolences, telling him they were thinking of him, praying for him. But no one asked if there was news about Jill. Mitch received their words graciously, but Shelley knew he was sick to death of their sympathy—or perhaps he was sick to death of not having any news of Jill week after week.

"Shelley, how are you?"

She turned to see Trudy Beason eyeing her with curiosity. Trudy looked at Mitch, then pointedly back at Shelley. The former teacher was a friend of Jill's who'd quit her job a couple of years ago to stay home with her children. But Shelley knew Trudy and Jill had gotten together for lunch occasionally. "I'm fine. How are you, Trudy?"

"As well as can be under the circumstances." She looked past Shelley again. "Hello, Mitch."

He greeted her cheerfully, as if he hadn't heard the melancholy in her voice. "I hear Micah had a great game the other night."

Trudy was off and running, giving Mitch a play-by-play of the middle school game. It was a technique Shelley had seen him use before to divert unwanted sympathy—focus on the other person, get them talking about themselves. She admired him for it and wished she'd thought to use it herself just now.

"Well, we probably ought to get on the road," he said quietly to Shelley when Trudy had finished with her play-by-play.

"Are you back at work yet? I heard you'd taken more time off." Trudy put on her solemn mask again, and looked to Shelley as if she might answer the question for Mitch.

Shelley looked away, waiting for Mitch.

"I'll be back in the office tomorrow," he said. "I just had some things I needed to take care of this past week . . ." He let the sentence hang unfinished between them.

For the first time, Shelley wondered what he'd told people about where he'd been all week. She was thankful she hadn't said anything to Jaclyn about why she needed the days off.

Mitch took a step toward the door, and Shelley followed his lead.

But Trudy reached past her to grip Mitch's forearm. "Is there any news at all?"

He shook his head, frowning, but he left it at that. Before this week she might not have picked up that he was being evasive, but she read his silent cues differently since they'd spent so much time together. For whatever reason, he didn't want Trudy Beason to know what they were up to.

She gave Trudy a nod and moved forward. Again, she felt Mitch's hand at her back. The foyer had cleared and Shelley pushed through the door into the airlock entry.

"Let me know, Mitch," Trudy called after them, "if there's anything I can do. Anything at all."

"Thank you," he said.

The door closed, muffling her reply.

"Let's go," Mitch said, close to her ear, his voice tense. He practically pushed her along across the parking lot and started the car almost before Shelley was inside.

Fastening her seatbelt, she looked out her window to the door they'd just exited. Trudy stood just outside the door watching them, when her eyes met Shelley's, she looked away, but Shelley saw her turn animatedly to another woman —someone Shelley didn't know—and say something, gesturing toward Mitch's car.

She knew from the way Mitch winced that he'd seen the exchange too.

Well, let them talk. They'd done nothing wrong. If those women wanted to gossip right there on the church grounds, there was nothing she could do to stop them.

The curvy road was dotted with cars out for a Sunday drive, no doubt people taking advantage of sunshine and warmer temperatures than eastern Missouri had enjoyed in a while. Mitch had stopped by the house to get TP after church, and the dog lounged behind them on the backseat of the Saturn.

Shelley had run home and changed into jeans, but she looked extra beautiful this morning, with her hair flirting with her shoulders and tiny dangly earrings bobbing up and down when she nodded, attentive to every word. Jill had done that too, never taking her eyes off him when they talked. He'd taken it for granted. Why had he taken so many things for granted?

Mitch relaxed his grip on the wheel and looked over at Shelley in the seat beside him. They'd driven through these woods by another route yesterday, and he'd had to remind himself again that he was on a mission, not a weekend getaway. Though fall's beauty was long past, the woods held a different kind of magic in winter, especially with a sky as blue and cloudless as today's.

This was the last day they could search before they both had to go back to work, but the truth was, after yesterday, their time together had begun to feel more like the picnic outing he'd chided Shelley about that first day of this search. Or maybe more accurately, it felt like . . . a date.

He had to work not to shudder at the word. But it was true. He'd already felt like he knew Shelley better than he actually did because of her and Jill's close friendship. But traveling with her every day this week, sharing their hearts, he'd come to know her apart from Jill.

And it was easy to understand Jill's deep affection for Shelley Austin. She was thoughtful and interesting and fun. And it terrified him because at times his brain seemed to fog over and Shelley and Jill fused into one person in his mind. He loved the musical sound of Shelley's laughter far too much. He was far too fascinated with the way the corners of her eyes crinkled when she smiled. The way her auburn hair—so different from Jill's—shone in the afternoon sun.

His thoughts dragged him places he didn't want to go, and he tried to ignore them. When that didn't work he looked for something else to focus on. He reached over his seat to the backseat where TP was sprawled. "How you doing back there, boy?" He patted the thick neck and TP's collar jingled. "Did we wear you out yesterday?"

Shelley reached to pat the dog just as Mitch eased his arm back over the seat. Their elbows collided. Mitch tapped the brakes. "You okay? Sorry about that." He patted her elbow as if she were a child. Then, feeling awkward, he looked over the backseat again.

TP raised his head, cut his eyes between Shelley and Mitch, and gave Mitch a look that was the closest he'd ever come to seeing a dog roll its eyes. *You're no help at all, pup.*

Shelley winced and rubbed her elbow absently.

"Are you okay?"

She laughed. "I'm fine. It got my crazy bone is all. Haven't done that in forever. I forgot how much that stings." She opened her mouth again as if to ask him something, then closed it.

"What?" he said.

"I just wondered . . ." She worried the hem of her jacket with her thumb and forefinger. "Did you think people looked at us a little funny in church this morning?"

"What do you mean?" He knew exactly what she meant, but he'd hoped she hadn't noticed.

"It just seemed like maybe people thought we were . . ." She stared at her lap.

"An item?"

She smiled. "That's a good way to put it. You apparently noticed it too?"

He nodded, keeping his eyes on the road, feeling strangely exhilarated to be discussing their relationship. "I guess it probably wasn't the smartest thing in the world for us to show up at church together." Since Jill's disappearance, his church attendance had been patchy, and when he did go, he usually sat in the back for a quick getaway.

Shelley shifted, angling her body toward him in the passenger seat. "Why would you say that? I used to sit on the other side of Jill almost every Sunday. Was there . . . *Is* there anything inappropriate about you and me going to church together?"

"No. *No,*" he said too quickly. Too emphatically. "Just the whole 'appearance of evil' thing, I guess."

"It's not our problem if people interpret things wrong."

"Well . . . it shouldn't be. I'd say Trudy Beason was doing some big-time misinterpreting."

"Do you think?" She laughed.

He didn't need to look at her to know the impish gleam that was in her eyes. It made him smile. "You could solve this issue, you know."

"How's that?"

"Start dating someone."

"What?"

He did look at her now.

The impish gleam had turned fierce. "What are you talking about?" she said.

"I'm just saying that if you had a boyfriend, no one would mistake us for an 'item.' " He was surprised at the way his gut twisted at the thought of her with another man.

"Well, don't hold your breath," she muttered.

"So, how come you've never dated? Or . . . maybe I shouldn't assume. But Jill was always trying to think of a guy to set you up with and—"

"Yeah, and that ticked me off sometimes, if you want to know the truth." She rolled her eyes. "We had the biggest fight of our entire friendship over her trying to hook me up with that stupid Realtor friend of yours."

"Glenn?"

She nodded and gave a little laugh. "She just couldn't get that I was not interested. Not in him or anybody else."

"Is that because Tom . . . soured you on marriage? Or you just don't like men in general?" He said it lightly, but sobered when her expression hinted at an alternative he hadn't considered. "Or do you hope you and Tom might get back together?"

"Oh, heavens, no. He's had a dozen 'serious' girlfriends in the fifteen years we've been separated. That's not going to happen."

They were both silent for a minute, the hum of tires on the highway suddenly overloud.

"I have nothing against men," she said finally. "But I'm plenty leery of the whole idea of marriage."

"Hey, don't let one bad apple spoil—"

"You know . . ." She blew out a sigh and furrowed her forehead. "You people don't get that—"

"Whoa, whoa . . . What's this 'you people' business? Who are you referring to?"

She held up a hand. "People like you. If you've only known a great marriage, it's easy to go on about what a wonderful institution marriage is. Well, sorry, but it pretty much stunk for me. The only thing I don't regret about my relationship with Tom is Audrey. And for her, I'd go through a hundred years of the hell Tom put me through."

"I'm sorry, Shel." He put a hand on her arm—something he'd found himself doing too often the last two days. "I didn't mean to make light of it. I guess . . . I didn't realize how bad things were with you and Tom."

"I told you he cheated on me. Does it get worse than that?" Immediately she looked like she wished she could take the words back.

How had a perfectly good conversation deteriorated to this? He nodded. "I'm sorry. That didn't come out right. I guess I just thought—that was a long time ago. As long as I've known you it's seemed like you were doing okay. Like that was all in the past. But . . . I shouldn't have assumed. I'm sure something like that doesn't just go away."

"No. It doesn't. Ever. But I am doing okay. I've forgiven. I really have. And time does heal a lot of wounds. It's just that . . . In case you haven't noticed, not very many people have what you and Jill had, Mitch."

He acknowledged the truth of that statement with a nod. "But a few *do,* Shelley. It's not so rare that you should totally give up."

"I haven't. Not totally. I would love to have what Jill had—What you and Jill have," she corrected, too quickly. "I really would. But . . ."

"Then don't give up. God has someone out there for you." It felt like the right thing to say, and yet he felt awkward saying it.

She didn't seem to notice. "Do you really think so? It's easy to feel like a failure, comparing my marriage to your and Jill's."

"Don't blame yourself for what was Tom's fault. I know you know better than that. The past is the past. Didn't the pastor just read that verse this morning? Forgetting what lies behind and pressing on, and all that . . . Right?"

"Yes, sir." She gave a little salute, looking appropriately chastened. "I could tell you the same, you know."

He chose to ignore that. "I just know you have a tendency to blame yourself for things that aren't your fault. It's one of the little things Jill did tell me about. Back when we were trying to figure out who to set you up with next." He winked.

She glared at him. "Not funny." But a smile crept through the sternness.

They drove on toward Sylvia, and after they turned off on the designated back road—a long shot, he had to admit—they rode in silence, each watching out the window on their respective side of the car, looking into the ditches and beyond into the dense woods that grew on either side of the road.

In the backseat, TP sat up and watched out the back window on Mitch's side. But the dog didn't seem to take any interest beyond what he usually did on a Sunday drive.

The late afternoon sun filtered through naked tree branches, working its magic on the browning hillsides, shadowing them in myriad shades of blue and purple. He had to keep reminding himself of their mission.

Rounding a curve in the road, they came upon a narrow turnoff, and he slowed the car. "I'm going to stop and let TP out for a few minutes."

He got out and opened the back door. TP bounded from the car, sniffing the ground before making a beeline for the nearest tree. Shelley got out, too, and came around to lean on the driver's side of the vehicle, looking up into the treetops. "I bet it will be gorgeous here in the spring."

He leaned beside her against the car and followed her line of vision. "It's pretty close to gorgeous right now."

"It is. I'm just not a big fan of winter. I hate being cold."

He pushed away a disturbing image. Jill, alone somewhere in these vast woods, blanketed in snow. It had been a while since he'd had one of these waking nightmares. He fought to ignore it and shot up a prayer.

Shelley's presence helped. She cupped a hand over her eyes like a visor and peered through the woods where TP had disappeared. "I've never thought of myself as a country girl, but I can see why someone would want to build a cabin up in these woods."

"Yeah, me too. You've never been to our cabin, have you?"

"No. I've seen pictures, though. Jill was always trying to get me to take Audrey and go down sometime, but it just never worked out."

"It wouldn't be too far out of your way when you go down to Springfield to bring her home for the summer. Maybe you could stay there for a few days on your way back—or even when you take Audrey to school this spring. We won't be using it."

He'd grown comfortable enough with her that he'd quit trying to weigh every sentence before it left his mouth. It was one of the things he liked about spending time with Shelley. But now she looked at him like she was trying to decode his words.

He frowned. "No matter what happens, I doubt we'll be going to the lake this year."

"I'm sorry, Mitch. I'm truly sorry." She reached for his hand and entwined her fingers with his.

Only for a brief moment. And then she untangled her fingers and dropped her hand to her side. But the warmth of it remained. If he stood here in the shadows with her, if he inhaled one more breath of her delicate perfume . . .

He turned away, pretending to go check on TP again.

"Mitch—Wait."

He pivoted to face her again.

250

She looked at the ground before meeting his gaze again. "I feel like I should say I'm sorry. For . . . what just happened."

She'd felt it too. He wanted to pretend like he didn't know what she referred to, but she would have seen right through him.

"The truth is, I'm *not* sorry." She dropped her head and wrapped her arms around herself, as if seeking protection from his response.

But he was speechless. How could he possibly respond to that?

After a few seconds she looked up, a sort of resolve in her demeanor. "Mitch? What are you going to do now?"

He cocked his head, fairly sure what she meant, but not wanting to borrow trouble. "Do now?"

"Now that we . . . didn't find Jill. What's next?"

"I don't know." He kicked at a pile of soggy, decaying leaves. "I just don't know."

24

"It's been almost five months now, Mitch." Shelley looked at Mitch's profile in the waning light. "Don't you think it's time to accept . . . and move on?"

"Accept?"

"A person can't live in this kind of limbo, Mitch. You've got to give yourself a break."

He stared off into the woods. "I can't just . . . give up."

"You've done everything humanly possible, Mitch. With no leads at all . . . isn't it time to let it go? Let the authorities handle it. No one is asking you to give up hope, but you can't keep pushing yourself, searching like this when you have *nothing* to go on."

"How is that not giving up hope?" He turned to her with a look of anguish. "How do I just let her go? What if she's out there somewhere? Waiting? Counting on me?"

"Mitch. I know how hard it must be to face this, but . . . What scenario could that be true for? Think about it. Either Jill is . . . gone. Or she's chosen not to be found. And I can't imagine *any* reason whatsoever the latter could be true," she added quickly. "She never would have left you of her own free will."

He started to answer, but seemed to decide better of it.

"You know . . ." Shelly turned toward him, leaning her right side against the car. "A wise man once—not that long ago, actually—told me, 'The past is the past. Forgetting what lies behind and pressing on . . . and all that.' "

Surprisingly, a smile tipped the corners of his mouth. "Yes, ma'am." He mimicked the brief salute she'd given him moments ago and the glint in his eyes filled her with relief.

He shook his head. "What is the deal with this talent women have for throwing men's own words back at them like weapons?"

She laughed. "You don't really think I'm going to betray womankind and reveal that age-old secret, do you?"

He shook his head and grinned at her, looking like a little boy. "I guess I temporarily lost my mind."

"Just temporarily, huh?"

Again, that grin. The one that did funny things to her insides.

How, in the space of half a dozen sentences, had they moved from such sober talk to this . . . *flirting?* That was all she could label it. But it didn't matter how. She preferred this a thousand times over.

The sun was low, but still it warmed them against the chill that hung in the evening air. The tree branches cast dappled shadows over the road. It would be dark soon.

Shelley turned and pressed her back against the car again. She closed her eyes, stifling a yawn.

"Am I boring you, Ms. Austin?" He scooted close enough to nudge her arm with his elbow, teasing.

"Hey, be nice to me. I closed the store last night," she pouted. "It was after midnight before I finally got to sleep. And then somebody dragged me out of bed at the crack of dawn—"

"Oh, I forgot you had to work." He pushed off the car, stretching his arms over his head. "We'd better get you home." He gave a low whistle, and called TP.

"No, I'm fine." She made her voice bright. "Don't hurry . . . on my account. I don't have to go in until ten tomorrow. We can stay a while if you want. . . ."

"Whatever you want," he said, his voice raspy. He leaned back against the car again, close enough that the sleeves of their jackets touched. Without speaking, he looked over at her, and she recognized in his eyes the same longing that dwelled inside her.

Whatever you want. They were skating on treacherously thin ice. Surely he could hear her heart pounding. The sky had grown dusky, but could he read in her eyes that it was *him* she wanted? She tried desperately to look away. And when she couldn't, she tried to make her eyes say something else. To lie. It would destroy their friendship if he guessed her thoughts. She knew him well enough to know that. She had to keep her thoughts in check at all costs. She had to—

And then, somehow, he was holding her, kissing her, as if her thoughts had meshed with his and spilled over into this amazing moment that she'd barely dared to dream.

She let him kiss her, reached up to cradle the back of his head, and wove her fingers through his hair. He smelled like wood smoke and peppermint. He smelled like heaven.

No. Not *heaven. Create in me a clean heart . . . Oh, God . . .*

Against everything she longed for, she pushed him away, gasping for air as if she'd just surfaced from the depths of some lake. "Don't, Mitch. No . . ." It was so hard to say no when her heart was shouting *yes.*

Mitch groaned and covered his mouth with his hand, looking as stunned as she felt by what had just happened. "Oh, dear God. I'm sorry. Shelley, I'm sorry. I—I don't know what I was thinking."

She wanted desperately to reach for him. Instead she took another step backward. "It's okay," she crooned. "It . . . wasn't just you. It was me just as much . . . It's okay, Mitch. I think we've both wanted—"

"No, it's *not* okay." He pushed off the car, stumbling backward. His foot slid on the gravel, but he quickly righted himself and kept walking. He paced at the edge of the road, stopping to double over, looking like he might be sick.

Finally he came back to the car, looking like a man in shock. He kept his distance, his voice so strangled she had to strain to hear his words.

"Please forgive me. Oh, God . . . I am so sorry, Shelley. I'm sorry, God." He ran trembling hands through his hair, leaving it spiked and unruly. "Please, please forgive me."

She wasn't sure if he was talking to her or to God. "It wasn't just you, Mitch. Do you hear what I'm saying? It wasn't only you. I'm as much to blame as—"

"I don't know why I did that. I am so sorry."

"Mitch! Stop it."

"Shelley . . . I think the world of you . . . Absolutely the world." He closed his eyes. "You've made these months bearable for me. I truly don't know how I would have survived without all your help, but I'm afraid we're . . . slipping into something that isn't right. And . . . oh, God"—he buried his face in the bowl of his palms—"now I've just proven everything you said."

"What? What are you talking about?"

"About men who aren't faithful to their wives . . . About marriages that—I've just proven it all."

"No you haven't, Mitch. Stop it. How can you be unfaithful to a wife who's *gone*."

"We don't know that, Shelley. We don't!"

"Mitch . . . please . . ." His anguish broke her heart and she struggled to offer him relief. An endearment was on her lips and she bit it back, caressing him with his name instead. "Oh, Mitch, do you really think Jill is ever coming back? Deep in your heart, do you really think so?" She reached up to put a hand on his cheek, savoring the warmth of it, wanting so desperately to be in his arms again. And knowing that she couldn't be. Not now.

He pushed her hand away roughly and walked out to the middle of the narrow gravel road. He gave a sharp, high whistle, calling for TP.

The dog came running, and Mitch made a wide berth around where Shelley stood, still with her spine against the driver's side door. He opened the back door and TP bounded into the car, panting and slobbering.

"We need to get on the road," he said, not looking at her.

She trudged around to the passenger side, neither of them speaking. The leaves and twigs crunching underfoot compensated for their silence.

Mitch drove with his head bent, never taking his eyes off the road, still looking like he might be sick at any moment.

Her heart ached so deeply—physically ached—that had she not known the source of her pain, she would have feared she was having a heart attack.

But she knew the source. And she knew what she had to do about it.

MARCH

25

Monday, March 7

Shelley rounded the curve and punched the garage door opener on the car's visor, but it wasn't her own house she was focused on. As she had every day for the past seven weeks, she pulled slowly into her driveway and stopped, looking over at the Brannons' front yard, hoping she'd catch a glimpse of Mitch.

Over the past weeks—almost two months now —she had searched her heart and been chagrined by what she discovered. She'd let her desires for things that did not belong to her, things she had no claim to, cause her to act in ways she was ashamed of. They were subtle things, but they'd crept into her life and made her behave in ways she knew were wrong. She'd asked God to forgive her, and she'd prayed that she and Mitch could somehow find their way back to . . . friendship. That was all she dared ask for right now—of Mitch.

Or of God. But she was learning to be more honest in her prayers. "God, I don't know if I can ever be satisfied with mere friendship with Mitch. Please give me pure desires. Please show me your truth. Don't let me long for something that I can't have. Something that isn't Your will for me."

What had happened between them that last day on the road had provoked her imagination and kindled daydreams about what it would be like to be married to Mitch Brannon. What it would be like to know his love the way her friend had known it.

The very words of her thoughts brought instant shame. Could she not even think Jill's *name* anymore? No. Because after all that had happened between her and Mitch, if by some miracle Jill did come back, their friendship would be over.

She thought she'd mastered the monster of envy. She thought she'd finally learned to be content with her life. And to rejoice for all her friend had. How had one kiss undone everything she'd once asked God to accomplish in her?

And Mitch's apology—as if kissing her had been the most unpleasant experience of his life—made her feel awful. Crushed and rejected. Disgraced. And yet, she deserved it. If she was honest, she had to admit that in subtle—and sometimes not so subtle—ways, she'd been coming on to Mitch. And deep inside she'd known what she was doing. And all when Mitch was most vulnerable. *Oh, Lord, what was I thinking? Please forgive me.*

But was it fair that their lives be put on hold like this? If Jill *was* gone—and somehow, she

262

felt so certain that she was—then there was nothing keeping her and Mitch apart. Was it only wishful thinking that gave her such certainty?

She aimed her car into the garage, but glancing over at Mitch's house again, her breath caught. What in the world . . . ?

There was a Realtor's FOR SALE sign planted in his front yard.

Mitch hadn't spoken two words to her since that night on the way back to Sylvia when he'd kissed her. He'd apologized again, practically in tears, when he dropped her off at her house that night. He'd sworn to her that it would never happen again. That he didn't know what had come over him.

And she'd tried again and again to own the blame for that kiss, for what happened between them. But he wouldn't hear her. Wouldn't even let her finish explaining.

And since that night she would have sworn he'd planned his schedule around hers, so that their paths would never cross.

Now, apparently even that wasn't enough, because a large, red-and-white sign announced to the whole neighborhood that he was selling his home. The way gossip spread in Sylvia, she was surprised she hadn't heard about it at the store today.

She put her car in Park and turned off the engine. She tossed her keys beside her purse on the passenger seat. This was ridiculous. She should have insisted that he talk to her, that they talk things out, long ago.

She crossed her driveway and the alleyway that separated their properties. Her breath hung in the air in front of her, and she broke into a trot across the brown lawn. Her low heels sank into dead grass that was still soggy from this morning's dusting of snow. She rang the doorbell, then pounded on his door.

A few seconds later the door opened, and Mitch appeared, still in his suit jacket and tie from work. He seemed surprised to see her. "Shelley—"

"What is going on?" She looked back briefly toward the lawn and the offending sign.

"What do you mean?"

"You're selling your house? Moving?"

"Yes."

"Where? Where are you going?"

"I don't know yet. I have to sell the house first. That could take a while."

"But . . . What about the kids? It's . . . so soon. Where will they come home to for the summer? This is their home. Oh, Mitch. Please. They've already lost so much."

He studied her as if he couldn't believe she had the gall to ask such questions. "I think it's best for everyone this way."

She pressed her lips together and closed her eyes. He was still watching her when she opened them again. "Mitch, please don't do this. Please.

What about Jill? What if she tries to come home. What if—"

"I didn't think you expect her to come home." The hardness in his voice was like a physical blow.

And she deserved it. It was cruel to have played that card. The Jill card. Was she that desperate? "Have you told your kids?"

"Told them what? About—what I did?"

"No! That's not what I meant, Mitch. I wouldn't expect you to say anything to them." He was still wallowing in guilt. "I meant about the house. That you're selling."

"Not yet."

"This is my fault, Mitch." Her voice came out in a whisper. "Please don't do this. If . . . if anyone should move, it should be me."

"No. I would not do that to you, Shelley. I hope you know that."

"Why do either of us need to move? If you want me out of your life, I promise I won't bother you. We're both adults. We can figure out how to stay out of each other's hair."

"You shouldn't have to do that. You should be free to come and go from your own home without having to try to avoid me."

"I haven't been trying to avoid you." That wasn't exactly true, but he was the one who'd made her feel like she should stay away.

"No, but I've tried to avoid you."

So he admitted it. "Okay. So, we've done that

for weeks. We can keep doing it. Indefinitely. Come on, Mitch. This isn't fair to your kids. They'll be devastated. This is where they grew up. It's where their memories of Jill are. Where will they come home to this summer? Where will they spend next Christmas?"

He stared at her, his demeanor unyielding.

She pointed at the neighbors' house on the other side of hers. "I see the Rohrmeiers maybe four times a year. I can ignore you, too."

He shook his head. "That's just it, Shelley. I *can't* ignore you."

The realization of what he was saying left her speechless for a moment. But then her anger—and hurt—resurfaced. "I'd say you've done a pretty good job of it."

"I'm sorry."

"Why, Mitch? Is it because you're afraid . . . what happened that night will happen again? Is it—"

"Why?" He stepped out onto the porch and looked past her, panning the street, as if he was afraid they might be overheard. "I'll tell you why. Because I lost my wife and I should be consumed with finding her. But instead—no matter how hard I try to stay away from you—I'm drawn to you—more every day. That's why! Are you happy now?"

Her next breath wouldn't come, and she stared at him, in shock, not sure she'd even heard him right. "Then . . . then why don't we do something about that? Because I feel the same way about

266

you, Mitch. I have—for a long time." She couldn't tell him that she'd loved him long before Jill disappeared.

"No. *Shhh.*" He hung his head. "No, Shelley. I wasn't . . . trying to come up with reasons. I'm saying it can't happen. At all. I'm sorry."

"Mitch . . . Please. Why can't you let yourself move on? Go forward? Why can't you let yourself fall in love again? Are you going to be hanging on to Jill's memory three years from now? Five? Six? Feeling guilty because you *think* she might still be out there?"

"But that's just it. It hasn't *been* six years. It's barely been six *months.* Shelley . . . I care for you a great deal. You've been amazing—an amazing friend—through this whole ordeal. And I appreciate that. But—" He stopped, swallowed hard. She could see he was struggling for composure. "Even if Jill . . . died—even if I knew for sure she was gone—it would be too soon for me to be making decisions about . . . going on. I'm still in love with my wife. I can't forget that."

She dropped her head. "I know you are. I know that, Mitch. You'll always love her. Of course you will. That's why I love *you.* All I've ever wanted is someone who would love me the way you love Jill. I don't expect you to fall in love with me overnight. I know that will take time. I can live with that. I can live on hope—that you'll grow to love me the way you loved—the way you *love* her. Just please, give me a chance to—"

He closed the gap between them and took her hands in his. For one beautiful moment she thought he might kiss her again, the way he had that night in the woods.

Instead, he grasped her hands between his and held them tight. Too tight—the way he might have held a child in the throes of a temper tantrum. "Shelley, look at me." His gaze bored through her, his voice rough. "I don't want to lead you on, or offer hope where there isn't any. There can be nothing between us. Do you understand? There's *nothing* between us."

She didn't miss the subtle change in the tense of his words.

"There's something I need to tell you." The expression on his face made her heart pitch. "There's . . . something more you need to know."

"What is it? What's wrong, Mitch."

"I don't know if I can even explain this, but I just . . . I *know.* Somehow I know in my heart that I'm supposed to wait. I don't know if it's because Jill is still out there somewhere . . . I don't know. More and more I'm afraid she's not. That something . . . terrible happened to her. Maybe we'll never know. But I can't shake this feeling that God hasn't released me yet from my commitment to Jill. From my vows. And that He's asking me to wait."

"Why would God do that, Mitch? It makes no sense. Especially if Jill is gone."

"I don't know. I wish He *would* release me."
He stopped and put a balled fist to his mouth, as
if he wished he hadn't spoken those words.
When he spoke again, his voice was whisper soft.
"But He hasn't. And I can't ignore that. No matter
how much I might wish I could."

She studied him, willing him to soften. To
somehow change his mind. Even as she knew she
was wrong to do so.

But his resolve only shone brighter in his eyes.
"Don't you understand? This is no different
than if Jill had some sort of dementia and was
gone from me emotionally. Even if I knew she
would never be the same, would that give me the
right to . . . see other women? If that's true, what
good are vows? Why would two people ever
promise each other 'for better or for worse'?"

"That's different, Mitch. That's not even a fair
comparison."

"Why is it different?"

"For all you know, Jill is dead."

"And for all you know, she's alive."

She closed her eyes. How could she possibly
answer that?

"Can't you understand?" The kindness in his
voice hurt more than if he'd struck her.

"No. I can't. I *don't* understand."

"Then I'm sorry. But I have to honor what I
promised before God."

Her heart sank. Even if Mitch was wrong, if

he was basing his decision on some kind of misplaced guilt or loyalty, how could she argue with him? How could she compete with God? Or with an absent, beloved wife?

She put a hand over her mouth, overwhelmed with sadness. He was telling her there was no hope for them. None. *God said.* She hadn't felt this alone in the world since the night she'd discovered that Tom was cheating on her. "Please don't make me wait forever, Mitch. I can't wait forever."

"I can't make *any* promises. I don't know if this is just for a while, or if this is forever. I just know I can't ignore it."

"And I won't ask you to. I don't understand it, but I . . . I can't compete with God."

"Please don't put it that way. I'm not asking you to compete with God."

"Well . . . How else should I put it?"

He shrugged. "I don't know. I just . . . I need to ask you to stay away—I don't want to hurt you. But I need some space between us—some physical space."

"So . . . just stay out of your life? Is that what you're saying? Just pretend that we've never been friends. *Just* friends. All that means nothing to you?" She glared at him, anger welling up inside her.

"That's a little harsh. And that's not what I said."

"But it's what you mean."

"I'm sorry. I *don't* mean to be harsh, Shelley. But yes. For now, I think it would be best if we . . . didn't spend so much time together. If we didn't spend *any* time together."

She tried unsuccessfully to swallow the lump in her throat. "I won't interfere, Mitch. I'll leave you alone. But please don't move away. Don't do that to your kids. Especially not on my account. I couldn't live with myself if I caused you to sell your kids' home at a time when they've already lost their mother. I promise . . . I'll stay out of your life. You won't even know I'm here."

He raked a hand through his hair. "I'm not asking you to go into hiding. Please don't make it sound like that. And . . . I don't know what I'm going to do about the house. I don't know much about anything right now." He sighed, then reached behind him for the doorknob. "I just . . . I need to go now. I'm sorry."

He went into the house, leaving her standing alone on his front porch. Feeling like a fool. She stood there, staring into the encroaching darkness for a full minute before she descended the steps.

Finally she walked across the lawn and returned to the emptiness of her house.

Mitch watched her walk across the grass and disappear into her house, his heart heavy for her, yet knowing he'd done the only thing he could. It startled him to realize that the emotion eating him up was grief. Grief not unlike what he'd felt when he lost Jill.

Somehow, over the weeks and months, it seemed that Jill and Shelley had morphed into one, and sometimes he wasn't even sure which woman he was grieving anymore.

But he knew one thing. He could not betray Jill. She was his wife. He'd committed to love her until death parted them. And until he knew she was truly lost to him—through death or through some unfathomable decision of hers—he belonged to her. How could he be free to test the waters of love again when he didn't know what happened to Jill?

He couldn't. It was that simple. Why had he made the decision so difficult before?

But he knew the answer to his own question. It was because he'd *let* himself fall in love with Shelley. Maybe he was fooling himself. But he knew what love was, and he loved Shelley Austin. Perhaps not in the same way he loved Jill. But his feelings for her weren't some pubescent, hormonal thing either. He'd known Shelley nearly as long as he and Jill had been married—though certainly not as intimately.

But through these most difficult months of his life Shelley had been at his side. Her own love for Jill had helped him heal. And his feelings for her had grown into something deep and abiding.

Yet, somewhere along the way, things had been tainted, and he'd let his emotions run the show. Self-contempt boiled up in him when he remembered that night he'd taken Shelley in his arms. *Kissed her.* Never in all the years of his marriage had he considered being unfaithful to Jill. Not once. He hadn't dreamed he was even capable of such a thing.

And yet, it had happened. And worse, in his indiscretion, he'd hurt Shelley deeply. But there was nothing he could do to make that up to her now. Whatever feelings he had for her didn't matter now. He had to quit wavering on this. Either he was committed to Jill or he wasn't.

And he was. *Lord, I am! I want to do what's right. Please, God, I want to do the right thing. Help me. Please. Make my heart right.*

MAY

26

Friday, May 6

The bell on the door jangled and Shelley looked up from the back of the store where she was stacking leftover Easter merchandise on the clearance table. "Welcome to Serendipity," she called out, peeking around a display shelf to catch the customer's eye. "Let me know if there's anything I can help you with."

"Just browsing," the woman said. "Thank you."

Shelley went back to arranging pastel egg-shaped candles and a few dented boxes of chocolate bunnies on the clearance table. Thankfully, it was a small table. Serendipity had enjoyed brisk sales all year, and, thanks in part to an ad campaign that had been her idea, they'd done record sales so far this spring.

Since Tom left her—just before their fifth anniversary in May—the season that had once been her favorite had become one that was full of reminders. Outside, the pear trees on Main Street were in full bloom, and a fat robin splashed in a puddle from the recent rains. But she struggled to find joy in the advent of spring.

Cheer up, Austin. Enough of the pity party already. She hated the blanket of melancholy that had settled over her the night Mitch asked her to stay out of his life. Okay, maybe she was being a tad overdramatic to think of it that way, but in essence, that's what he'd asked for.

And that's what she'd tried to give him. She timed her comings and goings so she wouldn't be outside when he was, and on the few occasions when they'd seen each other across their adjacent driveways, she pretended she didn't see him and quickly drove inside.

Most days she felt like a prisoner in her own home. She'd told Mitch that day that she rarely saw her neighbors on the other side, and that was true. It wasn't quite as easy to ignore the man she'd once been friends with, the man her best friend loved.

Her cell phone vibrated in the pocket of her work apron. Audrey. She hadn't talked to her daughter for more than a week. She hurried to the opposite corner from where the only shopper browsed and pasted on a smile before she answered the phone. "Hello there, stranger."

"Hi, Mom. You sound like you're at work. Do you want me to call back later?"

"No, it's okay. We're not busy right now."

"Uh-oh. Is that bad?"

"No, actually things have been hopping for the last few weeks."

"Well, hey, that's good. Listen, the reason I called—"

"Wait—let me guess . . . you need money." She smiled genuinely, her spirits already lifting.

"Why do you always say that?" An exasperated sigh. Then a pregnant pause. "Well, okay . . . don't answer that. I know that's usually why I call, but not this time. And you're gonna like this."

"Oh?"

"I'm going to come home for the weekend—not this coming weekend, but the next one."

"Well, that'd be great, but . . . You'll be home for the entire summer just two weeks after that. I'd love to see you, honey—you know that—but that's a lot of gas money to make two trips." She hated that money ruled her life the way it sometimes did. She would have loved nothing more than to have her daughter home, but it cost well over a hundred dollars in gas every time she made the trip, and that simply wasn't in her budget right now. And Audrey didn't have the cash. She swallowed hard and put on her best teasing voice. "It'll be extremely tough, but think I can survive without you a couple more weeks," she teased. "Why do you want to come home now anyway?"

"No reason really." Something in her voice hinted otherwise.

Audrey had come home more often her first year of college, but this year, besides having a weekend job, she had good friends in the dorm. Since school started last fall, she'd come home for two weeks at Christmas and that was it. Shelley nudged away a pang of loneliness. "No reason, huh? Just want to spend some time with your ol' mom?"

"Mom, if I tell you why you'll just freak out and then I—"

"I promise I won't freak out." So there *was* a reason. She held her breath, waiting, and trying *not* to "freak out."

"Well—Swear you won't jump to conclusions?"

"You know I don't swear."

"Mom! You know what I mean."

"I promise I will remain calm and rational."

"And reasonable?"

"And reasonable."

"And civil?"

"Out with it, you crazy girl!" She laughed, relaxing a little and suspecting whatever Audrey's news was, it wasn't going to rock her world as much as she'd first feared. It probably had something to do with a boy if she read her daughter's nervous giggles correctly.

"Okay, but remember, you promised."

"Audrey . . ."

"Okay, okay . . . Here's the deal. Evan is going to be home this weekend and I want to see him."

"Evan? Evan *Brannon?*"

"Duh, Mom. What other Evan would it be?"

"Okay. So why do you suddenly want to see Evan?"

"We've been talking—mostly e-mail and texting, but he called me last night, too, and we talked for a long time. He wanted to let me know he was coming home for that weekend. I think he's pretty worried about his dad, so he and Katie are going to try to come home more often."

Shelley tucked away the news that Evan was worried about Mitch. She tried to fit the pieces together, cautious to keep her voice calm lest Audrey clam up, and accuse her of breaking her promise already. "Is there something—going on between you and Evan? Again?"

"I don't know, Mom. Maybe." She got that shy, little girl squeak in her voice. "We just kind of started talking about what we had together—before—and, I don't know . . . We don't want to rush into anything, but we just want to see if there's still . . . anything there."

"Wow." She didn't know what else to say. Did Mitch know this was going on? Jill was the one the Brannon kids usually confided in. But hopefully, with Jill gone, they'd started confiding in Mitch now.

If that was true . . . Her heart lurched. Did this have anything to do with Mitch's insistence that they keep their distance from each other? At least he'd come to his senses enough that the Realtor's sign had disappeared from his yard the morning after she'd confronted him.

She tried to breathe and barely succeeded. If

Audrey and Evan started dating again . . . She couldn't process the ramifications of how that would affect her hopes for the future.

Before the thought was even complete, she scolded herself for entertaining thoughts about a future with Mitch. But this news of Audrey's shook her. It could change every—

"Mom? Are you there?"

"Oh . . ." She started up the main aisle of the store, forcing herself to focus, looking down each corridor for her lone customer. "Hang on a second, honey." Finding the woman thumbing through a rack of greeting cards, she cupped the phone in her palm and approached the customer. "Are you finding everything okay?"

"Just fine."

She smiled. "Let me know if I can help." Making her way to the back of the store again, she put the phone back to her ear. "Sorry, honey. I have a customer. I really need to go, but you know you're always welcome to come home. You can let me know the details sometime next week. I'll be praying about the whole thing— with you and Evan. That's . . . Well, just—wow."

Audrey's laughter told her that her reaction hadn't made her daughter suspicious. But she needed to talk to Mitch. What on earth she would say to him, though, she didn't know.

How could things have gotten so crazy? It was bad enough that she was barely on speaking terms

282

with Mitch, but if there was something brewing between Audrey and Evan . . . Audrey had told her that first year of college that she thought Evan was doing some partying at school. Shelley had never told Jill. She probably should have, but she hadn't wanted to betray Audrey's confidence. And from what Audrey said, it didn't seem like anything beyond a freshman's experimentation. But if Evan was still drinking, if he might be driving Audrey places . . . She shuddered. She would have to have a serious talk with her daughter.

Maybe she should say something to Mitch. But that would be about as welcome as a fur coat in July. She'd wait till after she'd talked to Audrey about it.

She sighed, feeling a little queasy. Life was getting too complicated. At least she had her job for a distraction. And Jaclyn was giving her as many hours as she wanted to work—a bittersweet benefit when she would have given every extra dime for a chance to have her friendship with Mitch back.

But it could never go back to the way it had been before that kiss. She knew that. They'd crossed a line. And deep inside, she knew Mitch was right about needing to put some space between them.

She would honor his wishes, but she hated that what had happened between them had ruined their friendship. She hated it, even as she dreamed about that kiss. About his arms around her and his breath warm on her face.

The bells on the door jangled again and she took in a deep breath and forced her thoughts back to her work and away from all the "what ifs" swirling inside her.

27

Sunday, May 8

"Mitch? Hello?"

He jumped at the voice behind him, and whirled, wielding the oversized spatula he'd been flipping burgers with.

Shelley stood on the bottom step of the deck, looking like Queen Esther waiting for him to raise his scepter and grant her entrance. He laughed self-consciously and closed the lid on the burgers, realizing how ridiculous he must have appeared.

"I'm sorry I startled you," she said. "I hollered when I came through the gate . . ." She motioned over her shoulder toward the fence that separated their lawns.

"I guess I didn't hear." He opened the lid of the grill again, just for something to do.

"I'm sorry to bother you, Mitch. I know I said I would make myself scarce, but—" She came up two steps, but no farther. She looked pale—almost scared. "I need to talk to you. Just for a minute."

He put down the spatula and went to the edge of the steps. "Is everything okay?"

"Audrey said Evan was coming home next weekend?"

He nodded. "Yes. He and Katie both are." Odd she'd only mentioned Evan. "I was a little surprised when Katie called and said they were coming back again since it's so close to school being out. Katie will be home for the summer in three weeks. Not that I'm complaining."

"Audrey's coming home next weekend, too."

"Really?" He went to close the lid on the grill and turn down the heat. He motioned to the lawn chairs. "Come on up and have a seat."

She shook her head. "No. I'm not staying.

He sat down on the top step. "Is there something . . . going on?"

"That's what I wanted to ask you. Did you know Evan and Audrey have been—talking?"

"Talking? What do you mean?"

"Audrey said they want to"—she chalked quotation marks in the air—"see if there's still something between them."

He knew his jaw must be hanging open, but he couldn't seem to close it. "Really?"

She nodded. "Evan hasn't said anything?"

He shook his head. "Wow. Are you . . . okay with that?" She didn't look okay with it. Not at all.

"I don't know. It seems like those two fought a lot when they were dating before and—"

"Yes, but that was back in high school. They've both grown up a lot since then. I know Evan has."

She nodded, but she still didn't look too thrilled with the whole prospect.

"I wasn't implying that Audrey hasn't grown up, too," he said, suddenly realizing Shelley might have misunderstood. He was still too stunned to decide how he felt about it. He'd never dreamed those two would get back together. He'd actually been relieved when they broke up. Evan had enough trouble concentrating on school without the distraction of a girlfriend. And living next door to the girl had presented all kinds of challenges for him and Jill—and Shelley, too, he was sure.

"No, no . . . I didn't think you were saying that. I'm just—I'm having trouble adjusting to the idea."

He motioned between them. "Is it because of us? Because you think it means we'll have to see each other more?" May as well let loose the elephant in the yard.

Her smoky eyes narrowed. "I'm not the one who wanted to pretend we don't know each other." She said it so quietly it took a minute for her words to register.

But when they did—*ouch*. Well, he had that coming. "I told you why I needed for us to—keep our distance. I'd rather not have to say it again."

"I'm not asking you to say it again. I just

wanted—This is going to complicate things, Mitch. I don't want our kids to know that we're not on speaking terms. I—" Her voice broke.

He hated it when Jill cried. Katie, too. He was a goner the minute either of those women he loved shed tears. Jill had taken to crying in secret "so you won't think I'm just trying to manipulate you." But he'd never felt manipulated by her tears. They simply moved him. Jill had accused him of being an old softy. And, maybe he was, but he couldn't afford to let Shelley "manipulate" him—whether that was her aim or not. He looked away briefly, steeling himself.

She wiped away a tear and took a deep breath. "Evan and Katie don't need anything else to worry about. And I don't want Audrey worrying about me. And—maybe I'm flattering myself, but your kids are special to me, Mitch. I know things are different now that they're grown, but I'd like to see them whenever they're home. Like before. I can wait until you're at work or . . . maybe they could come over here sometime and you could" —she shrugged—"find something else to do." She looked at him again with pleading eyes.

"Shelley—" He'd been such an idiot. "Of course I want my kids to see you. They love you. And you've been—so good for them through everything that's happened this year. I'd feel terrible if my own stupid lack of self-control kept you and Katie and Evan from seeing each other. That was never my intent when I said we needed to avoid seeing each other. I'm so sorry if I ever made it seem that way." He swallowed hard, threatening to choke up himself.

The way her countenance brightened only made it worse.

"Please forgive me, Shelley. If I could take back what I've done . . . What I did . . . I would do it in a heartbeat. Will you forgive me?"

She gave him a tight smile. "I forgive you. I haven't exactly been innocent though . . ." She seemed to think better of finishing that sentence.

He was grateful.

"I'm just glad I can see the kids," she said. "Maybe you guys can all come over for spaghetti some night."

After his big, dramatic apology, he couldn't bring himself to ask her to put the brakes on. But he hoped she didn't think things could ever go back to the way they'd been when—when she'd begun to consume his thoughts and take the place in his heart that should have belonged to Jill.

He had to guard his heart, and the only way he knew to guard it from Shelley was to keep some distance between them.

Saturday, May 14

The house smelled like Little Italy and the smiles around her dining room table did more to lift

Shelley's spirits than anything had in a very long while. It did her heart good to see Audrey and Evan and Katie laughing like children, playing a new board game Evan had brought from college.

She and Mitch bowed out after the practice round. It was one of those convoluted role-playing card games where the rules seemed to change just when she was getting the hang of it, and she'd been relieved when Mitch pled too-dumb-to-get-this.

She was afraid he'd view her following suit as a ploy to spend time with him alone, so she excused herself to the kitchen to clean up while the kids played their game. She rinsed dishes and loaded the dishwasher, and she couldn't help but smile hearing the raucous laughter coming from the family room.

"Kind of reminds you of the good ol' days, doesn't it?"

Mitch's voice behind her reminded her of the good ol' days, too—or at least better days. But of course, she couldn't tell him that.

He picked up a soggy dish towel. "Can I dry?"

"No, it's okay. I think I can fit everything in the dishwasher. But thanks."

"The spaghetti and meatballs were great. Thanks for doing this." He folded the towel in quarters and leaned his back against the counter, bracing the heels of his hands on the countertop.

He looked relaxed and handsome—and exactly how she'd imagined him looking in her kitchen. *Stop it, Austin!*

"It was fun having the kids all together," he said. "It's good to see they haven't outgrown each other."

She frowned. "Do you mean Evan and Audrey?"

"Oh, no. That's not what I meant. I just meant it's good to see our kids enjoying each other— all three of them—like they used to when they were little." He picked at an invisible thread on his sleeve before looking up at her. "It's been good being neighbors, Shelley. Over the years, I mean . . ."

She stopped short and glanced at him. "You make it sound like that's coming to an end. Did— did you sell your house?"

"Oh. No. I'm sorry. I didn't think how you'd take that. In fact, I took the house off the market. You were right. That wouldn't be fair to the kids. And besides, I didn't have a clue where I'd go." He shot her a sheepish grin.

She tried not to let him see the relief she felt. And it took everything she had not to say, *I told you so.*

"I just meant . . . We've been blessed to raise our kids in this town. Next door to each other. They've been good years. And I've missed it these last few weeks—being neighbors. I'm sorry, Shelley. I overreacted and overcorrected and over-just-about-everything I could 'over.' I'm so sorry."

She shook her head and offered a cautious smile, surprised at another apology from him. "Forget about it. I understand. I probably did some overreacting myself."

"It's been a strange time for all of us." He circled a hand toward the dining room, including the kids. "But I'd like to get back to normal—to the way things used to be."

She got the feeling he was choosing his words very carefully, and she was quick to put him at ease. "I understand. I know you're not suggesting anything more than neighborly friendship. I promise I won't abuse the privilege."

"I feel bad for making you feel like you even had to say that."

She shrugged, grateful that he was calling off the ridiculous impasse between them. And for that she was so happy she could have cried. "I'd like to be neighbors again, Mitch. And friends. I'd like that a lot."

He bobbed his head as if that fixed everything between them.

She knew better, but she was grateful for a truce. They could figure out the rules of engagement as they went along.

"Do you think there's anything between Evan and Audrey? Has she said anything?"

"No. Has Evan?"

He shook his head. "They seem to be enjoying each other."

"Yes, but if there's anything romantic going on, they're hiding it well."

He shrugged. "Who can tell? I never have been any good at this romance stuff."

Shelley ignored that comment and pretended not to notice Mitch squirm when it hit him how she might take that. "Do you want some ice cream?"

"Um, sure. Sounds good. I'll go see if the kids want any." He smiled, trying, she knew, to put her at ease.

"Thanks." She went to the deep freeze in the laundry room and opened the lid. Tears pushed at her throat, taking her aback. But they were tears of gratitude. For with just a few words, Mitchell Brannon had made everything right with her world again.

No, it wasn't her daydreams come true, but she could live with this. She had her friend back. And she would somehow make that be enough. "Thank you, Lord," she whispered.

She waited a long minute, fighting to get her emotions in check before she retrieved cartons of chocolate and vanilla ice cream and carried them back to the kitchen.

28

"Mr. Brannon?"

Mitch looked up to see Jennae Wilcox, a student office aide, standing in his doorway. "Hi, Jennae. Can I help you?"

"Mrs. Janssen said I have to ask you about using the library for our Pet Awareness Training meeting this summer."

"You're not going to bring a bunch of horses and potbellied pigs to the meetings, are you?"

Her bright eyes went wide. "Oh, no. Definitely not. We don't even bring our pets to the meetings. It's just about raising aware—"

"Um . . . Jennae? I'm teasing." He winked.

"Oh." She giggled.

"If community ed doesn't have the meeting room scheduled, I think that would be fine for your group to meet there this summer. As long as you have a sponsor, right?"

"Yep, Brandy Fishbern's mom is going to be our sponsor." She flashed a smile that made him miss his Katie. "Thanks, Mr. Brannon."

Jennae gave a little wave and dashed down the silent hall toward the front door.

Graduation was over and the halls were quiet

with only underclassmen in the building for the last week of school. He was looking forward to the quiet of his office during the upcoming summer months. There would still be plenty to do, but a lot fewer distractions.

Except that next week Katie would be home from college for the summer. It would be tough on her being there without Jill. He wished Evan would come home, too, and thought he might if there was anything going on between him and Audrey. But coming back to Sylvia would've meant giving up the summer job he'd already lined up. Besides, it was too late to try to find work here in town when he'd be going back to Lawrence in the fall.

Mitch went back to his computer and pulled up his calendar, flipping through meeting dates for the upcoming school year. Another year. Jill had disappeared at the beginning of a school year, and now that year was ending. And plans were under way for a new year that, right now, didn't look like it would include Jill.

Slowly, things had returned to normal at work. Teachers and students had quit looking at him with those doleful, pitying eyes. He could finally walk into a room without everyone turning silent. He was glad and relieved—and guilty at the same time. Because those very things meant that people had forgotten Jill, or at least gotten used to the idea of a world without her in it. Maybe they were just giving him permission to carry on with his life without her. But he still had trouble fathoming a life that would never again include Jill.

He'd gotten the renewal statement for the insurance on Jill's Camry last week and he hadn't yet dealt with that. He wasn't sure he would ever grow accustomed to receiving mail addressed to Jill, or seeing her photo on a poster at the post office.

Sometimes he contemplated moving to a town where no one knew his tragic story. Just starting over. But if he did that, he would always feel like he had a secret he was keeping from every new person he met. At least in Sylvia, people already knew his story. He was the man whose wife had disappeared off the face of the earth. He would probably always be whispered about behind his back as those who knew about Jill explained the sordid details to those who hadn't yet heard. It made a good story. He got that.

But that didn't make it easy.

He rose from his desk and took some papers to the file cabinet in the corner. It was Cyndi's job to file these, and come Monday she would give him a hard time about trying to put her out of a job. It was too late in the day to start a new project, though, and besides, he needed a distraction. He didn't want to feel sad today. He'd had enough sad to last a lifetime.

Pulling out of the high school parking lot an hour later took him back to that Friday last September when he'd driven home with such hope for the beginning of a new season of life with Jill. Nine months ago now. The length of time Jill had carried their babies.

How different everything had turned out than *his* plans. He didn't think he would ever understand how God's plans for his life could be so very different from his own. How could Jill's disappearance—his children losing their mother—possibly be a part of a loving God's plan?

He didn't know. All he knew was that he was learning—in spite of himself—to huddle in closer to God, to live one day at a time, trusting that he didn't need to have answers to those questions any more than his children had needed answers when he'd told them not to play in the street, or not to run with scissors.

No, he didn't need answers to live. But that didn't stop him from wanting them.

Sitting at the stop light at Washington and Main, a spot of color caught his eye and he looked down at the median. A bright red poppy had sprouted through the asphalt. He had to admire its pluck. Jill would have made him stop the car and get out to look and snap a photo with her cell phone. Shelley would have done the same.

He smiled, and it felt good to feel happy over a memory of Jill. That he could smile about Jill one minute and about Shelley Austin the next bothered him a little. He prayed he would never overstep his boundaries with Shelley again.

He acknowledged the reminder, but pushed the thought aside. He didn't want to dwell on the past right now. He only wanted to nurture the feeling of promise he had for this weekend. The temps were only in the midsixties today, but spring was giving way to summer. A new season—in the world, and in his life—and he wanted to find a way to go on living. He'd done everything he knew to do in order to find Jill. And now, he felt God was asking him to simply take each day as it came. *Easier said than done, Lord.*

He drove into the cul-de-sac and checked Shelley's lawn as he turned onto his driveway. She'd reseeded her lawn last week and had asked him to help her get the sprinkler system reprogrammed. She'd plied him with the promise of dinner, and he happily accepted. Since that night when the kids were home, ever so gradually, things between them had gone from civil to friendly, and now to . . . something more—he wasn't sure how to define it yet. He was just glad their friendship was one he could enjoy without guilt. Well, most of the time anyway.

He retrieved the mail from the box at the end of the driveway and went inside to change clothes and grab a Coke from the fridge in the garage before heading over to Shelley's.

She was waiting for him in her backyard, sporting a Cardinals T-shirt, her hair tied up in a ponytail. "Hey, there!" she said when she spotted him. "We picked a perfect day to do this, huh? It's almost chilly."

He shaded his eyes and looked up into a cloudless, blue Missouri sky. "I don't know about chilly, but I'll take this weather any day."

"Come on around." She motioned toward the garage. "The controller is in there and I hunted up the manual, too, in case you need it."

"Ha! Real men never refer to the manual."

"Oh, sorry. My bad. How could I have forgotten."

"We'll let it go this one time."

Her laughter set the tone for the evening and he felt the cares of the week—maybe the cares of the last nine months—begin to slip off his shoulders. At least for tonight.

He opened the control box and inspected the settings. "Hmmm. This is a little different from ours. Different brand."

"I do have the manual. . . ." She snickered behind him.

He turned and glared at her. "You know, don't you, that you're only making it increasingly unlikely that I would even consider reading the manual now?"

She held up her hands, palms out, and backed away. "How about I go finish clipping the rose-bushes and let you handle this?"

"I'd say that's an excellent plan."

He caught her grin as she pulled pruning shears from a pegboard near the door and ducked into the backyard.

He worked at the control box for a full ten minutes, afraid he might have to eat crow and take a peek at the instruction manual after all, but he finally figured it out and got the thing set up like she wanted it, to run on odd-numbered days of the month. He set the timer for a test run and went to the backyard to find Shelley.

She was at the far corner of the yard near the wrought iron arbor, on a garden kneeler with her back to him. A pile of thorny branches collected at her side.

He hollered her name, not wanting to startle her.

She turned expectantly.

"I've got the sprinklers set to run for a test. I'm not sure where your different zones are, so you might want to get out of the way of the sprink—"

A muffled pop was followed by a *chicka chicka chicka* noise and then, whichever zone it was that Shelley was sitting in chose that exact moment to kick on. Mitch watched the spray erupt and could see that with one more *chicka* it was going to make Shelley the target. But it was too late to do anything about it.

The sprinkler head pivoted and its spray hit her full in the face. Pruning shears went flying. She squealed and scrambled to her feet—and ran directly into another chilly stream of water from an adjacent sprinkler head.

Mitch watched it all with mouth agape, and when he could finally get his feet to obey, he trotted across the lawn to rescue her. He had to brave a spray of water himself, but when he saw she was okay, it was all he could do not to laugh at the comical sight they must be.

Biting the insides of his cheeks to curb a smile, he placed his hands on her shoulders and met her soggy gaze. "Are you okay?"

"Are you *laughing?*" Her attempt at looking incredulous failed, and he could tell she was on the verge of laughter herself. But she sputtered and flipped her ponytail at him, spraying him with a much milder dose of water than she'd received.

"Hey!" The water was *cold.*

His laughter escaping now, he put an arm around her and gave her a quick hug. "I am so sorry, Shelley. I swear to you, I did *not* do that on purpose!"

"Oh, yeah, sure you didn't." She wiped her face with the sleeve of her sweatshirt. "Is that retaliation for my suggestion that you consult the owner's manual?"

"No! I promise!" He laughed harder.

She joined in. "Well, at least we know they work."

"Yes, and for the record, I did not refer to the owner's manual once."

"And maybe you should have." She shook her ponytail again and headed for the house. "I need to go check on dinner."

"Hey," he called after her. "Do you think it's warm enough to eat outside?" Somehow it felt safer out here.

"Definitely." She grinned. "But not until I change clothes and dry my hair."

"I truly am sorry," he said again, doing his best to look contrite.

"Don't worry about it. It . . . was actually kind of fun."

"You have a strange idea of fun. Do I look as bedraggled as you do?" He shook his head, sending a few more drops of water flying. "All I can say is, thank goodness for tall fences."

That cracked her up, a feat he considered worthy.

"Can I do anything in the kitchen while you change?"

"No. Everything's ready. You can grab a couple of Cokes from the fridge if you like. Or I've got some iced tea made if you'd rather. Get me a Coke, will you?" She shook her head to one side as if she'd just emerged from a swimming pool and had water in her ear.

Chuckling again, he went for drinks and brought them outside. The sun was low in the sky and felt warm on his back, but the evening air had a nip to it. He remembered seeing a portable fire pit in the garage and went to get it. He located matches on a nearby shelf and carried a few logs from the woodpile at the side of the garage. He moved two lawn chairs and a side table down onto the flagstone patio near the fire pit, and by the time Shelley reappeared he had a nice little fire going. "I hope you don't mind. It's going to be a little chilly once the sun goes down."

"It's lovely." She came down the three steps of the deck balancing a platter of something steaming —and delicious smelling. She was bundled up in a flannel shirt and denim jacket. Her hair was dry, and the ponytail gone in favor of soft auburn waves that touched her shoulders. He looked away. Maybe this hadn't been such a good idea after all.

29

The sun set quickly, but the fire pit provided enough light to eat by, and a delightful warmth. Mitch relaxed and determined to enjoy the evening—and a rare home-cooked meal.

Shelley had fixed an old-fashioned pot roast in the crockpot with carrots and potatoes, and onions that had caramelized into a buttery sauce. He'd almost forgotten what a good, home-cooked meal tasted like.

He looked up into a clear, fathomless sky and

would have gasped—or prayed—if he'd been alone. Unlike in his own backyard, the streetlights on their cul-de-sac didn't encroach on the starlight in Shelley's yard. The night sky was peppered with a trail of stars that twinkled and winked at them as if the heavens possessed a secret they couldn't reveal.

Beside him, Shelley leaned her head back, following his line of vision. "It's beautiful, isn't it?"

"Amazing. How can anyone not believe in God when they look at something like this?"

She murmured her agreement. "Oh, there's the Big Dipper . . . See it?"

He looked where she was pointing, and after a few seconds he found the constellation's pattern. They stared into the dome of the night together, no words necessary. He couldn't remember the last time he'd felt so comfortable and at ease—and he didn't want to try to remember. He felt happy being right where he was. Not letting himself think about the past—or even the future. Just this moment of complete contentment. Of *ordinary life*—something he hadn't known for too long. And would never again take for granted.

The fire pit crackled and hissed, making pleasant background music while they talked quietly about their jobs, and local politics, and about their plans for spring gardening. Simple subjects that held no hidden land mines. They talked about their kids, and he discovered that Shelley had sent several e-mails to Katie "just to encourage her."

"That was really thoughtful of you, Shelley."

"It was no big deal." She shrugged. "I just remember how hard that first year of college was—under ordinary circumstances. I figured she could use a little encouragement."

"Well, thank you." It choked him up just a little. When he was sure he could trust his voice, he tiptoed around the subject of Evan and Audrey's renewed friendship. "Audrey hasn't said anything to you, has she? I can't get a word out of Evan on the subject," he told her. "Not that it's any of my business."

"She still just says they're friends—and 'seeing where things lead.' That's about all I get. I guess we should be glad they're just taking it one day at a time."

"That's a good way to live," he agreed, not wanting to ruin the evening by bringing up subjects that had the potential to hugely complicate his friendship with Shelley. She seemed more than willing to leave the subject alone, too, and they moved on to books they were reading and movies they wanted to see.

The one thing they didn't talk about was Jill. And that was a relief. Not that Jill was an unpleasant subject. Ever so gradually he'd been growing into a tentative peace about what had happened. With the knowledge that he'd done everything in his power to find her, to discover what had happened, he had no choice but to be willing to accept that he might never know the answers.

He looked at his watch, thinking it must be getting late, but was surprised to find it was only nine o'clock. He shifted in his chair.

Shelley must have thought he was making a move to leave. She scooted forward in her lawn chair and touched his arm briefly. "Hey, I picked up a DVD on my way home from work." The eagerness in her voice betrayed her loneliness. "I can't even remember the name of it, but Audrey and her roommates watched it and recommended it. Would you want to watch it with me?"

He feigned a suspicious look. "It's not some chick flick, is it?" He was buying time, not sure if this was a good idea.

"Not a chick flick. Well, at least I don't think so. I'll have to check, but I think it's more of a Western. Or something historical. You're welcome to watch."

He hesitated for a second too long.

"It's fine if you'd rather not." She rose and gathered their supper dishes. "You won't hurt my feelings if you don't stay. I promise I'm not trying to make you feel uncomfortable—and I'm sorry if I already did."

Her words went a long way toward easing his wariness. "No. It's okay, Shelley. I just . . . I'm still feeling like I need to be careful. Guard my . . . heart." Once the words were out he realized he wished he hadn't put it that way. He debated whether it would make things worse to try to explain himself. But it wasn't fair to Shelley for him to reveal how much he still struggled with his attraction to her. Especially when he knew that—at least at one time—she'd reciprocated his feelings.

But she seemed calm, willing to let his comment stand without further explanation. And truly fine whether he stayed or left.

That helped and he let himself relax again. "I'll watch a movie with you. At least for a little while. Till I make sure you're not tricking me into watching a chick flick."

She reached over and delivered a playful slug. "I told you, it's *not* a chick flick."

He put the grate over the fire pit and made sure it was safe, then helped her carry in their supper dishes.

She made popcorn that filled the house with a smell that caused a wave of—it felt like home-sickness—to roll over him. He suddenly ached for things he'd taken for granted. Having someone to watch a movie with. Sharing a meal. He doubted Shelley knew what a gift she'd offered him tonight.

In the family room off the kitchen, she got the movie playing and turned out the lights, leaving only a table lamp burning, and the dim strand of light that shone from under the kitchen cabinets behind them.

He started to plop on one end of the long sofa, then caught himself in time to gracefully make a different choice. The leather club chair near the window felt—safer.

As the movie theme music crescendoed, he was transported to the rare Friday nights not so long ago, when the kids were both out with friends and he and Jill would declare a date night. Tonight had that same "treat" feel to it. He quickly checked the thought. Because he and Shelley were certainly not dating.

Still, he was thankful for this comfortable friendship they'd grown into. Shelley had helped him feel moments of true happiness again. She'd helped him deal with the kids—especially Katie, filling the gap for a girl who still needed her mother so much.

She'd meant the world to him in these days since he'd lost Jill. And more and more he'd started wondering if there could be something more between them. Something his thoughts welcomed a little too eagerly. Because he hadn't yet felt the Lord release him from Jill—from his wife. And he was certain of that. Because he'd been asking.

•••

Shelley jerked awake. The light from the TV cast a gray glow over the room, the image set on the menu for the movie. Groggy and disoriented, she threw off the afghan she'd covered up with and eased off the sofa. She had to work tomorrow. She needed to get to bed and get some real sleep.

Fumbling with the remote, she looked up and her heart nearly stopped seeing the tall form sprawled in the leather club chair.

Mitch. The movie must have bored them both to sleep. With his feet up on the coffee table, one arm behind his head, and his mouth slack in sleep, he looked boyish and sweet.

She checked the clock on the DVD player. Almost one a.m. She considered tucking the afghan around him and going on to bed, but she knew he wouldn't be happy about that when he woke up in the morning.

She nudged his foot. "Mitch?"

He stirred and closed his mouth, but settled back to sleep.

"Mitch?" she said louder, nudging harder. "It's one o'clock."

"What?" He swung his feet off the coffee table and slipped on his shoes. He stretched, then rubbed his eyes. "What time is it?"

"One o'clock," she repeated.

"In the morning?" He seemed fully awake now.

She laughed softly. "Well, it's not afternoon. Look outside."

He glanced toward the darkened windows. "Holy cow. I'm so sorry. I must have dozed off."

"It's okay. I did too. But I'm going to bed now. You can stay if you want—on the sofa, I mean. In here. I just didn't want you to wonder . . . when you woke up." She was rambling, trying to get her foot out of her mouth. Mostly unsuccessfully.

"Thanks, but . . . I'll let myself out." He rose and straightened the cushions on the chair "Thanks again for dinner. It was great."

"Any time. Good night," she whispered. She let him out the back door and locked it behind him. It had felt strange having Mitch here all evening—in the middle of the night. Strange, and just a little wonderful.

Wide awake now, she carried their popcorn bowls to the kitchen and put the rest of the supper dishes in the dishwasher and started it running. She felt a little like she had as a fifteen-year-old babysitter, playing house in somebody else's home, dreaming about what it would be like to have her own family someday. Only now the imaginary hero in her pretend world had a face. A real face.

She tried to sober herself by imagining what it would be like if someday Jill knocked on her door, returned from wherever she'd been all this time. The thought brought tears to her eyes. She missed her friend desperately. But if Jill came back she would assuredly lose her as a friend. And lose another friend—one who'd become every bit as dear to her.

Oh, Jill . . . What have I done? I love him. I love your husband.

JUNE

30

Mitch started a pot of coffee and took his ritual morning walk through the house. Feeding TP, checking on the weather from two different windows, watering the houseplants, which weren't looking so hot without Jill's deft touch.

He almost tripped over a pair of flip-flops and smiled to himself. A year ago it would have driven him nuts to have Katie's things strewn around the house. Now it warmed his heart. She'd only been home for a week, but already her presence had brought some life back to this lonely house.

He headed for the shower, rapping twice on her door as he went by. "Up and at 'em, Katiebug."

She groaned in response, but her iPod speakers blared, and he heard her feet hit the floor. They'd already fallen into an easy schedule. She was working as a lifeguard and teaching swimming lessons at the city pool again this summer, as she had all through high school. Her two best friends from high school had remained in Springfield over the summer, but Katie had become close with a couple of girls she worked with at the pool.

Mostly she was her sweet, cheerful self, but when she was home she spent more time in her room than she had even in those angst-filled early teen years. He knew, for her, the house didn't even seem like home without Jill here, and she was struggling. He'd heard her crying—sobbing—one night and it nearly tore him apart. But when he'd knocked on her door and asked if she was okay, she pretended everything was fine. He wished he'd called her on the deception, but he didn't have a clue what he would say, how he could help, if she admitted how much she was hurting.

Twice, Shelley had invited Katie to go shopping with her and Audrey, who was home for the summer too. But each time Katie had come up with an excuse. Mitch wasn't sure what was going on. Jill would have known exactly what to say—or whether to say anything—but he didn't have a clue how to start that conversation.

When he came back to the kitchen twenty minutes later, his hair still slightly damp from the shower, the aromas of coffee and toast mingled enticingly.

Katie sat at the bar counter in her bathing suit and cover-up, buttering toast over the morning newspaper. She looked up briefly. "Hey, Dad."

"Morning. You work till eight again tonight?"

She nodded and went back to the op-ed page.

The TV in the family room blared the weather, and after starting a bagel toasting, he went to find the remote and turned the volume down.

"Hey! I was listening to that . . ."

He turned it back up two notches. "How can you read the paper and watch TV at the same time?"

"It takes special talent," she deadpanned, eyes still on the paper, "which you obviously do not possess."

Trolling his brain for a snappy comeback, he came up empty, but her droll humor made him smile. He pulled his favorite travel mug from the dishwasher and poured coffee, leaving room for milk. "You want some?" He held up the carafe.

She looked up from the newspaper, glanced behind him at the clock on the microwave, and gave a little gasp. "No, I've gotta run. See you tonight." She gathered her gear and started out the door, but turned back to him, one foot still in the garage. "Did you get Shelley's message? About the cookout?"

"Oh? No, I didn't see it. Where? Answering machine?"

"No. She left a note in the mailbox. I put it—" She hiked her bag up on her shoulder, and went to the bar counter and lifted the newspaper. A small sheet of notepaper fluttered off the counter. Katie gracefully caught it just before it hit the floor.

She handed it to him and he skimmed it quickly. *I'm making BBQ chicken tomorrow night. You guys are invited if you can come. 7:00 unless we need to go later for Katie.*

"Tonight or tomorrow?" he said. "When did you find this?"

"It was in with yesterday's mail. She means tonight."

"Oh, good. I wasn't sure what I was going to do for supper. Can you come?"

Katie started to say something, then seemed to change her mind.

"What?" he said.

She studied him. "Dad, do you think Shelley is trying to . . . I don't know"—she lifted one shoulder—"*catch* you?"

"Catch me?" He gave a laugh that sounded every bit as false as it was. "What do you mean?"

She shrugged again. "It just seems like she's awfully friendly to us. *You* especially. I think she likes you." Her tone said she didn't think that was such a good thing.

He weighed his words carefully. "I think Shelley just knows how hard things have been for us since Mom's been gone. She just wants to help. I think she's . . . trying to make things easier for us. You know how close she and Mom were. Maybe spending time with us helps her not to miss Mom so much."

"Whatever." She shot him a look that made him squirm a little.

"What brought all this up?" He wasn't sure he wanted to know.

She cocked her head and eyed him. "Would you ever—get married again?" The words rushed out as if she was afraid she'd lose her courage if she didn't say it now.

"Oh, honey . . . I don't know. I haven't really—" He'd started to say he hadn't really thought about it. But that would have been a flat-out lie. He thought about it all right. Every single day.

He desperately missed the little things about marriage—well, and the big things, too. If he thought too long about the possibility that he might live alone the rest of his days—especially after Evan and Katie were truly on their own—it was easy to sink into a depression he wasn't sure he could crawl out of.

What he couldn't—wouldn't—tell Katie was that not only did he think every day about remarrying, he thought about marrying Shelley Austin.

As if she'd read his mind, she made a funny face. " 'Cause if this thing with Evan and Audrey goes anywhere, it would be *really* awkward if you and Shelley started, like, going out." She grimaced and gave a little shudder as if the very thought grossed her out.

"I don't think you have to worr—"

"Never mind, Dad." She hitched her bag up again and headed for the door. "I really have to go. I'm late as it is."

She was out the door before he could ask her

again about supper with Shelley. Still, he breathed a sigh of relief that he'd gotten out of addressing her question.

But knowing his Katie, she'd find a way to ask it again.

He didn't know the answer, but for his sake, as well as Katie's, he'd better come up with something. And soon.

Shelley put another piece of chicken on Mitch's paper plate and sat down across from him at the picnic table in a shady corner of her backyard. She rarely used the table in June, when the massive cottonwood tree that formed a canopy over them was shedding its "cotton." But temps had hit almost ninety today and it was too warm to sit on the deck.

She swatted away another of the fluffy white tufts and filled her own plate. She would have preferred to eat in the air-conditioned kitchen, but Mitch seemed more comfortable staying outdoors when it was just the two of them.

"I'm sorry the girls couldn't be here," she said.

"I'm not," Mitch said, taking another bite.

She shot him a questioning look, hoping for a split second that he wanted to talk to her about — No . . . She didn't dare to hope.

"There's more for me this way," he said, holding up a forkful of chicken like a trophy. "And rumor has it there's homemade ice cream for dessert."

"Audrey told you?"

He nodded.

"That little snitch. I told her it was a surprise." But she laughed.

"You didn't happen to make any of that amazing chocolate sauce you make, did you?"

"Okay, now you're pushing it."

He gave her a look that reminded her of TP when the Lab knew he was in trouble.

"Yes, I made chocolate sauce. Your wish is my command."

"Oh, man. I must be doing something right."

As much as she loved bantering with him like this, part of her wished he wouldn't be so . . . *flirtatious*. And yet when she reciprocated in kind —which just seemed to come naturally with him —Mitch pulled away. And sometimes grew sullen.

She knew why. He still hadn't felt God "release" him from his marriage to Jill. Then why did he torture her with these little tastes of what it would be like to share a life with him?

She went in the house and fixed bowls of ice cream, then carried them out to the picnic table. He took a bite and made soft, appreciative sounds that caused her thoughts go to places they had no business going.

"So where's Audrey tonight?" He stretched his back and leaned forward to scoop another spoonful of ice cream.

"She and some friends went to the movie. That

new Robert Downey Jr. film finally made it to Sylvia."

"Oh, hey, I've heard that's good. Evan saw it and really liked it." He took another bite of ice cream and spoke over it. "You wouldn't want to go, would you?"

She eyed him, not sure she'd heard him right. "To the movie?"

He nodded and shaded his eyes, looking up at the sun. "The night's still young, right?"

"I'd love to, but—" She gave a little wince. "I'd rather not run into Audrey and her friends . . ."

"Good point. I think that show is still playing in Cape though . . ." He checked his watch. "We could still make it. I'm game if you are."

His smile made her feel like she'd just won the lottery. "I'd love that, Mitch. Let me go check the newspaper and see what time it starts."

"Um . . . maybe we should go to a late show. If you don't mind," he added quickly. "I just don't feel like running into anyone we know."

"Yes. Good idea. We both know what people could do with that."

He cocked his head. "With us being . . . *out* together, you mean?"

She nodded.

"I don't want to make you feel uncomfortable, Shelley. If you'd rather not . . ." He looked like he was having second thoughts and she wanted to kick herself for being hesitant.

"I'm fine with it. Mitch . . . You're the one who's been so hesitant about our friendship being misunderstood. I just want you to know that this"—she motioned between them—"is just two friends going to a movie together. Nothing more. I know where you stand on this."

"I know you do. And thank you for that. I've felt very . . . *safe* with you. And I appreciate that."

"Well, can I just say that I'm really glad to see you finally be able to enjoy life a little bit again."

"Yeah, well, maybe I shouldn't be." He dipped his head before meeting her eyes again.

But she threw him a stern look. "You just stop that. You'll crash and burn if you don't give yourself a break, Mitch. Nobody could have done more."

"I would have crashed and burned a long time ago if it wasn't for you."

She waved him off, and wished again that he wouldn't be so terribly sweet to her. It did not help her resolve one bit.

"No, I mean it, Shel." Jill's nickname for her rolled off Mitch's tongue as if they'd always been so familiar. Shelley tried to pretend she didn't notice, but she could tell he felt self-conscious about his slip.

"This whole . . . *thing* has been so insane," he said. "I haven't ever really stopped to tell you how much that's meant to me. And the kids, too. You've gone way beyond what most friends would do."

"I haven't done anything Jill wouldn't have done for me if the tables were turned." Now that she'd put it out there, the comparison gave her pause. She knew it wasn't an apt analogy— because she had no husband for Jill to fall in love with.

But Mitch didn't call her on it. Instead, he reached across the table and touched her hand briefly. "Well, I appreciate it more than I'll ever be able to express." He untangled his legs from under the picnic table and rose, gathering their soiled paper plates and bowls as he did. "Now, if we're going to make the movie, we'd better get moving."

"Let me just go do something with my hair real quick."

"Okay. I'll go get my car and meet you in your driveway."

Gathering up their drinks and watching him walk across the lawn to his backyard, she scolded herself for hoping. But she couldn't help it. She pushed away the twinge of guilt that tried to ruin her mood.

Another puff of cotton from the cottonwood tree sailed above her on the evening breeze, and feeling every bit as buoyant, she practically floated across the grass to the house.

31

They'd made it to an eight thirty showing of the film, but just barely. Shelley stood at the sink in the women's restroom, washing her hands, eager to get to the auditorium and locate Mitch before the lights were dimmed. Movie tunes played softly over the speakers, and each time the door opened, the excited murmur of moviegoers filtered into the large tiled restroom.

In the mirror's reflection she saw two women enter, deep in conversation, not paying attention to her. She thought she recognized the older woman—an occasional customer at Serendipity.

Great. She lowered her head and reached for the paper towels, ready for a quick exit if they looked her way.

But the women went into side-by-side restroom stalls carrying on their conversation, loud enough for Shelley to hear. She only half listened, checking her hair in the mirror and quickly slicking on lip gloss.

Seconds later, something made her focus on the conversation between the two restroom stalls, and she stilled to listen.

". . . I'm just sure that was them. She works at that gift shop in Sylvia—you know the one I told

323

you about that has those candles I like? I forget the name of it."

"How long ago was that? His wife was a teacher, right? I remember hearing about it on the news, but I never heard the end of the story."

"That's because there wasn't an end to it. They never found her. I think it's been almost a year since that happened."

"Seriously? That's just scary."

"It seems a little convenient . . . them living next door to each other like that."

Shelley's breath caught.

"Do you think there's really something going on between them? Where'd you hear that?"

"Oh, I've heard more than one person say that."

"You don't think they had something to do with his wife going miss—"

"Oh, surely not. The police would have figured that one out pretty quick. But it does look a little fishy, when you think about it."

Shelley stood there, listening, knowing she needed to get out of there, but paralyzed by their gossip.

"Well, it'd make a great movie of the week."

The younger woman giggled. "More like a reality show."

"Yeah, *Desperate Housewives* meets *The Biggest Loser*. Get it?"

"Lucy, you're terrible!" The two cackled at Lucy's bad joke.

At the sound of a toilet flushing, Shelley tossed her lip gloss in her purse and dashed out into the lobby.

She hurried around the corner and made her way down the corridor to the theater where their movie was playing. Replaying the conversation in her mind, a wave of nausea washed over her. Was this what people were saying behind their backs?

Except for that Sunday she and Mitch went to church together, they hadn't gone anywhere in public together. How could people make such harsh judgments about them? Turn the whole thing into a joke.

She took a deep breath and ducked into the theater, grateful for the relative darkness.

From his seat near the top of the stadium-style theater, Mitch watched for Shelley. He'd saved them seats, but she'd been gone so long he was starting to worry something was wrong.

He checked his watch, afraid the lights would dim and the previews would start rolling before she could find where he was sitting. Jill always knew where to look for him—three or four rows from the top, right smack in the middle of the theater. Best seat in the house. But Shelley didn't know that, and he hadn't thought to tell her.

Just when he was about to text her and ask if everything was okay, he saw her enter the theater.

She stood at the bottom of the wide stairs searching the crowd for him, her expression serious. He rose halfway from his seat and waved, and the smile that bloomed on her face when she spotted him said everything was fine.

Following her graceful gait as she came up the stairs, he wondered if she was aware of the heads she turned as she passed by. If she was, she didn't show it. It was one of the things he appreciated about her.

She settled into the seat beside him and slid her purse beside her in the seat—on his side—putting a bit of distance between them. Another thing he appreciated. She took a breath that came out in a sigh.

He leaned around and searched her face. "Is everything okay?"

She gave an odd half-smile and glanced surreptitiously around the area where they were sitting, before she leaned over and whispered, "We didn't go quite far enough away from home."

"What do you mean? Uh-oh . . . Did you see someone we know?"

The lights overhead dimmed and the music swelled. Slowly, the curtain parted.

"Yes, but nothing to worry about. Just gossip. It can wait." The way she rolled her eyes, he could guess what had happened.

He glanced over at her several times while the

previews were playing, and thought she seemed preoccupied, but once the movie started, she seemed to relax beside him and enjoy the film.

Things were just getting good with a chase scene through congested city streets when his cell phone vibrated in his pocket. Much as he wanted to, he hadn't been able to ignore his phone since everything had happened with Jill. He slipped it out of his pocket and checked the screen. Evan.

He leaned to whisper to Shelley. "It's Evan. I'd better take it."

He slid down the row, apologizing as he went. When he was in the lobby just outside the theater, he answered. His phone had already gone to voice mail. He called Evan back without checking the message.

"Dad. Thank goodness I got you." He couldn't tell if it was excitement or concern in his son's voice.

Turning away from the doors, he spoke softly into the phone. "What's going on?"

"Did you rent out the cabin for this weekend?"

"Our cabin? No. Why?" They hadn't rented out the lake cabin for at least five years. After a couple of bad experiences with renters who left the place a mess, they'd decided it wasn't worth the extra money it brought in.

"Somebody is staying here." Evan's voice sounded strained.

"Here? What do you mean? You're *at* the cabin? In Arkansas?"

"Um . . . yeah. And there's already somebody staying here—"

"Wait a minute! What are you doing at the cabin?"

"Dad, I'll explain later, but you've got to get down here. I'm telling you, the cabin is open. There's somebody's stuff in here. Woman's stuff. It's got to be Mom! Doesn't it? It's got to be her. You've got to get down here and—" Evan's voice cut to static, then a garble of words Mitch couldn't make out.

"Hang on, bud. Slow down. You're cutting out." He left the theater and walked ten feet down the plushly carpeted corridor, trying to get a better signal. "Can you hear me?"

"Yeah, I'm here."

"Why are you at the lake, Evan?"

"I brought some friends down for the weekend. But that's not impor—"

"Are you kidding me? You didn't have permission to do that, Evan." He shook his head. That Evan would have taken the liberty of using the cabin without permission . . . Not to mention it was probably a six-hour drive from Lawrence. "What are you doing there?"

"Dad, cool it. We were just gonna hang out. Mess around at the lake. Just for the weekend. We're all going stir-crazy with our jobs . . . We couldn't afford to go anywhere. But Dad! Did you hear what I said? I think Mom's here!"

Mitch walked quickly down the corridor that led to a side exit. He opened the door and felt the warm evening air rush over him. Holding the door open with his knee, he felt his chest pocket for his ticket stub so he could get back in if he got locked out of the theater. He stepped into the night air and paced the narrow sidewalk that ran in the alley along the side of the building. The streetlights painted patches of light on the side of the building, but it was dark in the alley.

"Why do you think it's Mom? Is there a vehicle there?" He was skeptical, but something must have made Evan think it could be Jill. "Have you seen anyone? Was the house broken into?"

"No. Nobody. No car. And the back door was unlocked. Nothing's broken. But it's obvious somebody is staying here. You're sure you didn't rent it out?"

"I'm sure. I haven't rented it in years." The Missouri Highway Patrol had checked the cabin in the early hours after Jill first went missing, and as Mitch expected, found the cabin empty. But was it possible . . . had she hidden out somewhere else until they stopped looking, and then returned to the cabin?

"Well, somebody didn't get the memo, Dad, because there's shampoo and lotion and stuff open on the bathroom counters, and dirty dishes in the sink. And clothes—underwear and stuff—women's stuff . . . And you guys' bed has been slept in."

Mitch tried to process it all, and failed.

"Dad . . . This might sound crazy, but . . . it *smells* like Mom in here."

His gut clenched. "Where are you right now, Evan?"

"We're in Jason's car out in the driveway."

"Okay. Listen . . . call 911 and tell them what you told—No, wait . . . On second thought, let me make that call. I need to let Missing Persons know about this, and they may not want the local police to go in yet. You guys go over to the Marleys' and see if they're home. Stay there until you hear from me, do you understand? Don't go back inside and don't touch anything."

"Okay. But . . . What if it's Mom?"

"Evan, is there anything besides the women's toiletries that makes you think it's her?"

"I don't know. It just seems . . . like it might be. What if it is, Dad?"

He closed his eyes, struggling to sort out his thoughts and emotions. "If it is . . . we'll have our miracle, buddy."

32

Shelley held tight to the armrest in the passenger side of Mitch's Saturn. He drove at least ten miles over the speed limit, racing toward Lake Norfork and the Brannons' cabin—a good four-hour drive past Cape Girardeau.

Shelley felt lightheaded and numb. The movie had barely started when Mitch came back from a phone call with Evan and told her they needed to leave. The look on his face had scared her sick. She'd been certain something must have happened to Evan or one of the girls.

But when he'd explained about Evan finding their cabin open—and someone staying there—her thoughts had spun out of control. They'd been spinning ever since. What would it mean if it *was* Jill at the cabin, as Evan believed.

It didn't seem like the gravity of it all had quite soaked in for Mitch. For the first ten minutes of their trip, he railed about Evan taking his friends to the lake without permission. "What was that bonehead thinking? All he had to do was ask. . . . We might have been able to work something out. But the fact that he didn't tell me makes me wonder if this isn't the first time. And so help me, if I find out this was going to be some big beer bash, that kid is in so much trouble he can't even begin to—" His breath caught as if he'd just thought of something.

He fished his phone from his pocket and handed it to Shelley, keeping his eyes on the night highway and his foot on the accelerator. "Would you dial Evan for me, please?"

She found the number in speed dial and gave the phone back to Mitch.

He held it to his ear, expertly navigating the curvy two-lane road. "If they've gone down to the lake before and no one was there, then she hasn't been there all along. If it's even Jill—" He held up a hand. "Evan? Hey, have you guys been to the lake before this? Since September?"

Shelley tried to follow Mitch's side of the conversation but soon gave up. She couldn't remember ever seeing him so angry. Not even that night when Evan and Audrey had stayed out till the wee hours of the morning, scaring them all out of their minds.

When he hung up, he blew out a sigh. "He swears this is the first time they've done this."

"So, are you thinking she could have been there all this time?"

He shook his head. "I don't know. I can't imagine why she would go there. Knowing we were all worried sick about her. And I still go back to that last message she left." He tightened his grip on the steering wheel and glanced her way. "You heard it, Shelley. She sounded happy. Didn't she?"

"Yes. She sounded happy. She *was* happy, Mitch. She . . . had a wonderful life with you." He didn't need to know that her words were for her as much as they were for Mitch. And that she spoke them with less resolve than she might've hoped to muster. "Wouldn't your neighbors have noticed if someone was staying at the cabin?"

He nodded. "Probably. They live almost a mile in the other direction from the highway, so they can't see our place. But they check on it once a week or so—just drive by. They don't go inside. No reason to. We close the place down and lock it up whenever we leave.

"If someone has been there with the gas and water turned on, I would have noticed that on the utility bills. And . . . Jill could have figured out how to turn on the utilities, but that's not something she ever did. That's always been my job. I just don't think there's any way she could have been there all this time without someone knowing."

He drove in silence for a minute, then continued his train of thought, as if he'd never stopped talking. "Unless she's lived without power or water all these months. And I can't imagine that. Not through the winter." He shook his head, obviously as mystified as Shelley was. "Even if the neighbors saw a car with Missouri tags at the cabin, they'd just assume it was me—that everything was on the up-and-up."

"*Did* Evan see a car? Jill's car?"

"No. But he said there was a woman's stuff in the house. Clothes . . . underwear . . . and shampoo and lotions in the bathroom and bedroom."

That brought an image of Jill's bathroom at home. She always had many lotions and potions from her favorite bath and body store lined up on her vanity counter. The first time she'd seen the display in Jill's bathroom she accused her friend of plotting to open a gift store in competition with Serendipity. "Good grief, woman!" she'd teased. "How many lotions can one woman use?"

Jill had laughed, explaining that most were gifts from special third-graders. "I don't want to have to lie when one of my kids asks me if I liked what they gave me for Christmas."

The memory brought a lump to her throat. "But . . . no one was there?"

Mitch shook his head, then turned to her, agony etched in the lines of his face. "Do you think she . . . had a breakdown? Did she think she had to get away from—everything?"

He was starting to believe they would find Jill at the cabin. *Oh, dear Lord.* "Mitch, Jill would never have done that to you. Or your kids. Or to her students. She didn't have it in her to do something like that. You know that."

"Do you think God has a reason for this?"

"Mitch . . ." Shelley looked over at him. He gripped the steering wheel as if it were a lifeboat. She didn't like the gray pallor his complexion had taken on, or the way his clothes had begun to hang on a frame that had once been muscular. "I don't know anymore, Mitch. I—I'm sure He does, but . . . I have a hard time imagining what it is."

He nodded, and she felt guilty that she'd given

him such a hopeless thought with which to agree.

"It feels like we gave up."

She raised a questioning eyebrow.

"Like we gave up on Jill. Too soon. If she's there . . . how can she ever forgive us?"

"Oh, Mitch. You couldn't just keep living in this *limbo* you've been in. No one is going to think you gave up."

"And what if I have?" His gaze challenged her.

"Given up? Oh, Mitch . . ." She'd long ago lost fresh words to comfort him with. She prayed for just a few to come now, but came up empty.

Shelley had called Audrey, and Mitch had called Katie as soon as they left Cape Girardeau, telling them only that there was a problem with the cabin and they were driving down to check on it . . . just enough to keep them from worrying. And—in light of Katie's suspicions about her and Mitch—hopefully enough to make it clear that they weren't just running off to spend the night together at the lake. But they probably wouldn't arrive at the cabin until well after midnight. And depending on what they found when they got there, she assumed they'd be staying the night.

Another hour passed in silence, the dull grind of tires on the highway the only soundtrack to her scattered thoughts. And with every mile, the full import of what they might face when they got to the cabin became even clearer.

She could almost read Mitch's thoughts in the

set of his jaw. Within a few short hours, he might be holding Jill in his arms.

And I might be facing my friend. The dearest friend I ever had. The friend she'd never had a secret from—and from whom she now had a whole lifetime of secrets to keep.

When they drove through Poplar Bluff, it crossed her mind that she could ask Mitch to drop her off at her aunt's house. But it was late. Aunt Mona would already be in bed for the night, and Shelley wouldn't have a way back to Sylvia tomorrow. And besides, Mitch wouldn't want to take the time to stop. But if Jill *was* at the cabin . . .

Shelley closed her eyes and leaned her head against the passenger side window. The glass was cool despite the sultry evening, and the vibrations of the road echoed the chaos of her thoughts. When she thought about the reunion that might be imminent, she could hardly contain all the emotions warring inside her. Maybe she was a coward, but if by some unbelievable chance Jill was there—Shelley flinched—she didn't want to be present when Mitch saw her for the first time.

And when Jill looked into *her* eyes, she would know the truth.

Shelley gripped the armrest tighter and her heart stuttered. There were things she needed to say to Mitch. Things that must be said before he saw Jill again. Things she knew God was asking her to do—and had been for a while now.

And they were going to be the hardest words she'd ever spoken. But the miles were melting away and she knew she could never live with herself if she didn't obey what her heart now compelled her to do.

When they stopped for gas in Doniphan, Mitch called Evan again to see what was going on. "Where are you guys? Did the sheriff show up yet?"

"We're at the cabin. And yeah. They just left. They went through the house and looked around outside, but they didn't see anybody."

"Has the detective from Missing Persons arrived?"

"Not that we've seen, but we were at the Marleys' for quite a while. The deputies said we could stay at the cabin tonight though."

If it was truly Jill staying at the lake, she might be—had to be—unstable. *Or if she was with someone . . .* The thought took the breath from him.

"I don't want you staying there, Evan. Not until I get there."

"What? They said they'd keep an eye on the place. If Mom's here, we need to be here."

"I want you to wait until I get there before you go back inside. Do you understand? We don't know for sure it's Mom."

A long pause. Mitch could almost feel Evan's

frustration. "Fine. So what are we supposed to do for two hours?"

"What were you going to do if the cabin had been empty?"

"Just hang out."

"I just hope you weren't planning anything stupid." If the boys had brought a bunch of beer with them—or bought it after they got to the lake—Mitch hoped to goodness none of them were underage. Lakes and booze could be a deadly combination, and the sheriff's department in Baxter County didn't take kindly to minors in possession of alcohol.

"Dad, we're not idiots."

He wanted to say, "Then stop acting like it," but decided to save that argument for another day. And if by some miracle Jill was at the lake, there would be no argument. He would simply thank God for the mysterious ways He sometimes worked.

He looked over at Shelley, who was watching him anxiously. He couldn't let himself think about what it would mean—for her, for them—if they'd found Jill. If after all these months, it was really her.

He collected his thoughts, trying to think what to tell Evan. "You guys can go down to that convenience store on the highway, on 412. I think they're open all night. I'll call you when we're almost there." He looked at his watch. "We're probably still a good two hours away . . . Shelley's with me."

"Where's Katie?"

"She's at home. You haven't talked to her, have you?"

"No."

"I didn't tell her that we think Mom might be there. I didn't want her to worry, since she'll be home alone tonight. And—I didn't want to get her hopes up. So don't say anything if she calls you, okay? About Mom."

"I won't. How come Shelley's with you?"

"Hey, bud, I need to go. I'll call you again when we get close. Should be there by twelve thirty or so. You be careful, okay?"

"I will."

He felt cowardly skirting Evan's question, but he didn't want to try to explain in front of Shelley.

"Everything okay?" She shifted in her seat and looked up at him. And in that moment, he saw in her eyes that she knew this one night could change . . . *everything.*

"It's fine," he said. "The guys are going to hang out at a convenience store. They didn't find anything at the cabin but—" He paused. "Are you okay?"

In the greenish glow from the dashboard, her face was hard to read, but her eyes brimmed with tears. "Mitch . . . I need to talk to you."

"What's wrong?"

"If Jill is there . . . at the cabin—" Her voice broke and she took a deep breath before starting again. "I want you to know that I understand the way things have to be. I don't expect anything from you. And . . . I won't say anything to Jill about—us."

"Shelley." Her agony was *his* fault. He rummaged in a brain full of pathetic excuses for something that would ease the pain he'd caused. "If it's Jill . . . if it's really her at the cabin, I won't keep anything from her. We'll have to see how she is—why she left in the first place. But I don't want to add secrets to the list of hard things we'll be dealing with."

"I think—"

"Please." He reached to put a hand briefly on her arm. "Shelley, I hope you know me well enough to know that I don't blame you. For any of this. You were only trying to be a friend to me. You were only . . ." *You were only responding to my advances.* He felt sick to his stomach.

"How could I ever face Jill now?"

"Shelley, all those years, when you were Jill's friend . . . you never once acted inappropriately toward me. Maybe I'm just too dumb to read those things, but I never guessed what your feelings were. I'm sure Jill didn't. And after she disappeared, you believed she was gone. You—" He stopped himself and dipped his head briefly before turning to face her. "This isn't your fault. Do you hear me?"

The whir of tires on pavement echoed the tension between them.

"No. That's not true, Mitch." Her voice held resolve. "I love you. And I'm not telling you that to complicate things. I'm telling you that because you're trying to take the blame for something that—maybe I'm more guilty than you know. It —it doesn't matter anymore. I've . . . made some decisions." She closed her eyes, and he knew she was struggling to get her emotions under control.

When she finally looked up, her eyes were clear. She straightened in the passenger seat. "I think maybe God has been preparing me for this all along. So, please, Mitch. Don't argue with me. I'm ready to step away from our friendship. I know it would be best for everyone."

"No, Shelley. You don't have to do that. I'm not asking you to do that." The headlights cast a long beam in front of the car, illuminating the road before them. But the car barreled into the engulfing darkness faster than the beam could pierce its mysteries. Shelley drew in another hard breath. Watching her, his heart broke. *He loved this woman.*

"Mitch . . ." Her voice was barely a whisper above the noise of the road. "We both know it can't be any other way." She turned to stare out the side window. "You know," she said after a moment, a false bright note coming to her voice, "Aunt Mona has been trying to talk me into moving to Poplar Bluff for years. Maybe I'll take her up on it. I'd be closer to Audrey and . . ." She shrugged and gave a him a quivery smile. "Who knows? Maybe I'll open up that bed and breakfast I've always dreamed about."

33

Saturday, June 18

Evan and his friends were waiting beside his car at the cabin when Mitch and Shelley pulled onto the long, curving lane to the cabin at twelve forty in the morning. Shelley climbed out of the car, her stomach in knots—and not just because they'd traveled for four hours on winding roads.

Even though she knew Evan would have called if Jill had appeared at the cabin, her nerves were taut, thinking about what might lie ahead.

A light shone from a small back porch, but Shelley could barely make out the outline of the cabin against the dark backdrop of pines.

Evan introduced the three friends who'd come with him. They were clean-cut and seemed nice enough, but Mitch was uncharacteristically curt. He barely nodded in acknowledgment, then turned to Evan. "Have you been back inside since the sheriff was here?"

"Just now." Evan motioned toward the cabin. "There's no one here. I unlocked the back door and turned on the electricity and water."

Mitch gripped Evan's shoulder, his eyes narrowing. "I want your key to the cabin. Before you leave." Without waiting for a response, he swept past his son to the back door. Evan and his friends followed, and Shelley fell in line behind them, feeling awkward and out of place.

Mitch switched on lights as they went through the cabin, looking the place up and down. The cozy house felt strangely familiar as Shelley recognized things Jill had talked about—the rolling library ladder on a wall that was ceiling-to-floor bookshelves, an end table Shelley had helped Jill refinish with the infamous crackled paint, the stone fireplace where the Brannons made s'mores on rainy days. She remembered the birthday gift of s'more makers she'd ordered and wondered if she'd ever have a chance to give them to Jill. She recognized several decorative items Jill had bought for the cabin when the two of them had traveled fifty miles of the famous Hundred Mile Yard Sale one May.

She breathed in the scent of a recent fire, and something like burned toast. Overhead she could see the rail to the loft where the kids slept—dark now.

Mitch poked his head into a bathroom off the kitchen and flipped on a light. Leaving it on, he exited and went down a narrow hallway. When he disappeared through a doorway at the end of the hall, Shelley stepped into the bathroom.

Like Jill's bathroom at home, bottles of scented lotions and soaps were clustered on the counter. Jill's teacher gifts. Some of the bottles and tubes were open and lying on their sides, as if someone had been interrupted while sampling them. And Evan was right. It *did* smell like her in here. A variety of scents, and nothing that "matched," but they all had a single undertone, mingling to form one familiar scent—the way it smelled in the bath and body store. *Oh, Jill.* She had to brace herself against the counter for a moment to catch her breath.

Jill had no doubt brought the bath products from home. But they'd been used recently. Was she here? She wondered if Mitch had noticed the scent.

Bath towels and clothes lay heaped in a corner by the walk-in shower. Gingerly, she picked up a T-shirt. It was turned inside out, but even so, she could read the raunchy slogan printed on it. She picked through the rest of the laundry, and knew immediately that these weren't Jill's clothes. They were too small, and too . . . sleazy.

She didn't want to analyze—much less admit—the hope that grew inside her. "Mitch?" She stepped out into the kitchen. Evan's friends had gathered around the oak table, one of them asleep with his head on the table, the other two talking in hushed tones, obviously intimidated by Evan's dad. She gave a little wave and went to look for Mitch.

She found him in what must be the master bedroom. His and Jill's room. The light was on. He was rifling through a pile of newspapers on top of a dresser.

"Have you found anything?"

He shook his head, seeming preoccupied.

"The clothes in the bathroom aren't Jill's."

For the first time since they'd arrived, he met her gaze. "You're right. I—I don't think she's here."

She gave him a questioning look.

He met her gaze and shook his head, his eyes saying the words before his lips even moved. "I don't think she's ever been here. Not since—" He didn't have to finish the sentence. "I'm not sure how I know. But I know."

"I'm sorry."

He took a deep breath and pressed his lips together like he was trying to keep it together.

Everything in her wanted to go to him, put her arms around him and comfort him. And yet, somewhere in the recesses of her subconscious, she was bargaining with God. *Maybe now he'll realize that she's never coming back. Maybe now . . .*

He gathered up the pile of papers in front of him and wadded them into a ball.

"Don't you think they might need those? The sheriff?"

He stuffed it all in a small wastebasket beside the dresser. "It's just newspapers . . . grocery ads. There's nothing here."

"The dates might be important, Mitch."

He halted, then pulled the wad of papers out and tried to smooth the wrinkles.

She'd never seen him look so haggard. Like he carried the weight of the last year on his shoulders. And it was more than he could carry.

"Let's get some sleep. We'll deal with this in the morning." He reached for a pillow on the unmade bed and stripped off the pillowcase. "There should be clean sheets in the closet there." He motioned toward an armoire on the wall at the end of the bed.

She went to open it and found a stack of clean sheets and pillowcases.

"You can sleep in here. The boys will all fit in the loft."

"What about you? Is there another bedroom?" She knew Evan and Katie always slept in the loft, and she hadn't seen another room on her brief tour of the cabin.

"I happen to know the couch is very comfortable." He stripped off the contour sheet and wadded it up with the rest of the bedding.

"Besides, I'm so beat I think I could sleep on a rock pile." He went to the window and drew heavy drapes over a wall of dark windows.

"I don't mind sleeping on the couch, Mitch. You should have your own bed—"

"Shelley . . . I'm too tired to argue. Just please, help me make up your bed. I'll lock the doors."

She did as he asked.

Sun streamed in the window, and Mitch covered his eyes against it and rolled over on the narrow couch. He'd told Shelley the couch was comfortable—and it was, for Sunday afternoon naps. Overnight, not so much.

In the loft above him someone—maybe two someones—snored loudly. Squinting at the clock over the fireplace, he felt suddenly disoriented. The clock must have stopped. It wasn't two a.m. and it sure wasn't two p.m.

He heard the sound of the shower in the bedroom. Jill must be up too, and—He stopped breathing. *Shelley.* Not Jill. All the events of yesterday rolled over him, pressed in on him. The movie with Shelley, Evan's phone call, the drive to the cabin with Shelley—and her insistence that she bow out of his life now . . . Then coming to the cabin and realizing Jill wasn't here. Likely never had been. Likely never would be again.

Would a loving God ask him to accept that he may never know the truth about what happened?

And yet, God had brought him this far. And through it all, he was learning to seek the Lord more closely. He'd made mistakes. He hadn't come through unscathed, and yet God's presence had been so very real to him. And eternity seemed closer than it ever had.

Last night he'd felt as heavy, as utterly overwhelmed as he had that first night after Jill went missing. But now, with the sun lighting the room and a renewed sense of God's very presence with him, he felt a quiet peace descend over him like a cool breeze.

He didn't have answers about Jill. Maybe he never would. He'd lived with that blackness for nearly a year and at times it had felt like a living hell. But here he was. Faith tattered, but intact. He folded his hands on his chest—the nearest posture of prayer he could manage without risk of discovery—and in the space of one breath, he relinquished the remnants of his life to the One who'd held them all along.

"I give up, Lord," he whispered. His prayer was a surrender of all the things he'd held so tightly to, had not been willing to let go of until this moment in time. The right to know what happened to Jill. The right to be bitter about the way his life had gone. The right to explore his relationship with Shelley.

Could it be this simple? Could a person go to sleep one night feeling crushed and defeated and confused, and wake up only a few hours later to sun in his face and a heart filled with peace?

So peaceful. The words to a song they sometimes sang in church wove itself through his thoughts. *Let not your heart be troubled. My peace I give to you. I'll turn your mourning into dancing and clothe you with joy.*

Maybe not joy. Yet. But . . . peace. *And hope.*

Those, he could live with.

34

Shelley awoke early and showered and dressed, wishing desperately for a fresh change of clothes. She pulled her hair into a ponytail and did the best she could with what little makeup she had in her purse.

The sunrise revealed a door behind the draperies Mitch had closed last night. She stepped outside to discover a deck that ran the length of the cabin and afforded a stunning view of the lake. A morning breeze whipped up frothy whitecaps on the dark surface of the water, and a pair of gulls took turns diving for breakfast. At the edge of the deck, a stand of cottonwoods whispered in a language all their own.

Under different circumstances, it would have been a little taste of heaven. She stood at the rail, mesmerized by the lake, thinking and praying, waiting for Mitch and the boys to wake up. Dreading the drive back.

When she heard them rumbling around in the living room half an hour later, she went inside to the kitchen to make coffee.

"Good morning," Mitch said, coming to stand beside her at the counter. "I see you found the coffee."

She nodded. "I hope you don't mind that I rummaged around in your cupboards. It's a beautiful place you have here. I enjoyed being out on the deck this morning. The lake is so peaceful."

He gave her an odd look, as if she'd said something surprising. Or maybe he'd just expected her to be more upset about everything that had happened.

But he shook his head and she didn't press him. There would be plenty of time to talk on the drive home today.

"There's nothing to eat here," he said, "but I'll send the boys into town to get us some break-fast. Did you sleep okay?"

"I did." For a few hours anyway.

"Listen, I need go make some phone calls . . . let Detective Fredriks know there's no need for him to come down. And I need to talk to the sheriff and the Marleys before we leave. Oh . . . and I also need to get someone to change the locks this week." He tapped out notes on his phone, then looked up and caught her eye. "I'm really sorry you got dragged along on this joyride. I'm hoping we can be on the road in an hour or two."

She waved him off. "Don't worry about it. Do whatever you need to do. I need to call Audrey. But maybe not this early . . ."

"What time is it?" He checked his watch. "Katie has to work. She'll be up. I'll call her first."

He roused the boys with a shout up to the loft and they straggled down, not looking too happy about the way this weekend had turned out. But Mitch gave instructions about breakfast and the guys headed to town in Evan's car. Mitch went out to the deck with his phone.

Shelley watched him from the kitchen window, rehearsing the things she wanted to tell him on their drive home. Nothing had really changed. Maybe all this had happened to spur her to tell him what she should have told him long ago.

Maybe she'd needed something to help her understand that even if Jill was never found, Mitch would always be looking over his shoulder thinking that tomorrow's phone call, tomorrow's new clue, really might be Jill. No, unless Mitch got some answers about Jill, nothing would change for a very long time. Maybe ever.

So, she would do what she'd promised and move on. Because she couldn't live next door, loving him as she did, and pretend it was otherwise.

But—for both their sakes—she would pray every day for answers about Jill.

Mitch heard the back door open and looked up to see Shelley bringing two steaming mugs out to the deck.

He took the one she offered and cupped his hands around it. "Thanks." The warmth was welcome, even though the sun was already promising another scorcher.

She tested a sip from her cup. "I know you prefer it with cream, but unless Evan picks up some half-and-half, your choices today are black, black, or black."

He smiled. "I'll take black."

At the sound of tires on the gravel drive, they both looked up. A sheriff's patrol car came around the curve and parked near the house.

"I'll be right back," he told Shelley, and went down the steps to meet the officer.

The deputy climbed out of the car. "Everything okay here now? Anybody ever show up?"

"No. But . . . it's not my wife. I'm sure of that. I'll have someone come out and change the locks this week, but what do we do with the stuff they left in the house?"

"What'd they leave?"

"Mostly clothes. I'm honestly not sure whether some of the stuff is ours or not—towels and such."

"I'll haul off anything you don't think is yours. Or you can just trash it."

"Good. I'd like to get back on the road as soon as I can. Let me get the stuff for you."

The officer followed him into the house and Mitch gathered the whole pile of clothes—towels and all—and brought them into the living room. He put them in a heap on the floor beside the sofa. "Let me get a bag to put these in."

Mitch heard voices outside, Shelley talking to someone. Probably the guys back with break-fast. But a minute later, a knock sounded on the kitchen door and Shelley came in with Wayne Marley.

"Hey, Wayne!" Mitch crossed the room and greeted the burly man warmly. "How's it going? Long time, no see."

Wayne Marley shook hands with the officer, then turned back to Mitch. "I hear you had a break-in last night? Your boy and his buddies came by."

"Yes. Thanks for putting up with them. I wouldn't call it a break-in exactly. No doors or windows were broken, but somebody's been camping out here. Don't know for how long, but it doesn't look like anything was stolen." He didn't want to imply that he blamed Wayne for not keeping a closer eye on the place. Anyone who left a lake home unattended knew break-ins were a risk.

"Sorry to hear it. Everything looked fine the last time I drove by. That was last Tuesday." Wayne looked past him, panning the room as if to check things out for himself. "You going to have the locks—Hey! What's that doing here?" He lumbered past Mitch to where the laundry was piled. He picked up the T-shirt with the offensive logo. "What the—" He looked from Mitch to the sheriff and back. "What's my daughter's shirt doing here?"

"That's Becky's shirt?"

"It was. That jerk of a boyfriend of hers gave it to her for her birthday, but her mother forbid her to wear it."

The sheriff took the shirt and looked at it, chuckling a little at the crude humor. "You're sure this is your daughter's?"

"She had one like it."

"Where is Becky now, Wayne?" Mitch asked, putting two and two together and coming up with a solid four.

"She's at work—at the café. At least that's where she's supposed to be."

The sheriff eyed him. "Any chance your daughter's the one who's been camping out here? Was she home last night?"

"She and her mom haven't been on the best of terms lately. Becky's been staying with a friend in town." Wayne's face drained of color. "Least, that's what she told us."

"Do you know where your key to my place is?" Mitch asked as gently as he could.

"I have a feeling I do know." Wayne gripped

his beard and hung his head. "Man, I'm sorry, Mitch. I should've wised up. We'll make this right. I swear we will. I feel like an idiot. . . ."

"No harm done. I just hope she's—"

"If it *was* her, we'll pay whatever it takes to get the place cleaned up, or the locks changed . . . whatever you need. You just let me know."

"Do you want to press charges, Mr. Brannon?" It was obvious in the way the officer asked he knew what Mitch's answer would be.

"No. Not if it turns out to be Becky. Definitely not." He stepped forward and put a hand on Wayne's shoulder. "If it was her, we'll work it out between the two of us."

"Okay, then." The sheriff moved toward the door. "You need anything else, you give us a call."

After the officer had gone, Marley apologized again.

Mitch caught Shelley's eye across the room and her soft smile buoyed him. He turned back to Wayne. "If it helps any, the whole reason I'm here today is because my son came down to stay in the cabin without permission. Sounds like we've both got some hard issues to deal with."

Marley shook his head. "I appreciate that, man. Good luck to you."

"Yeah. You too." Mitch thought of Evan and his buddies—and the beer that was no doubt either buried at the bottom of the lake or stashed in a ditch somewhere waiting to be retrieved on the drive home. He sighed. He would send Evan back to Lawrence today so he wouldn't miss any work. But he needed to clear his calendar and make a trip to Lawrence to have a tough talk with his son. And soon.

35

Shelley peered at the dreary sky through the windshield of Mitch's car. The wipers beat a hypnotic cadence as he navigated the winding roads back to Sylvia. They were an hour from home yet, and it had rained on them the entire way. It reminded her of those days last winter when she and Mitch had driven the crisscross of roads on the opposite end of the state. Searching for Jill. Searching for answers. And searching for a way to have a friendship with each other that they could both live with.

In two weeks it would be July, and she wasn't sure they were any closer to the latter than they'd been that day Mitch had kissed her.

Oh, they'd talked easily on the drive home—about Evan, and how Mitch should handle his son's trespassing at the cabin. And his drinking. Shelley wouldn't say anything yet—Mitch didn't need one more thing weighing on him—but she was deeply concerned about Evan, especially if he and Audrey were still exploring a renewed relationship. She needed to talk to Audrey and find out if her daughter knew that Evan was drinking and that he'd committed a crime by trespassing on private property to do so. It wasn't something to be taken lightly, even if the property was Mitch's.

It was something she and Mitch would have to talk about eventually. Certainly if Evan and Audrey were seeing each other again. Shelley hoped it wouldn't cause friction between her and Mitch, because there was already plenty of that. Both good and bad.

She and Mitch had skirted around the question of where their friendship should go from here. But they'd reached no conclusions on any of it. The "now what?" question still hung heavy in the air between them.

Still, Mitch seemed to have a new peace about him, and while the fact should have made her happy, it merely made her lonely. Because ever so subtly, as the miles disappeared behind them, she felt him pulling away from her.

It surprised her that she didn't feel more hurt by that fact. She'd even dared to hope—just for a moment—that this "false alarm" might jolt Mitch into realizing that Jill probably was not coming back.

At the same time she was encouraged that her heart had stood by the things she'd told Mitch: She had to let him go. She knew that now. And as much as it hurt to let the dream of him die, nobody got to have all their dreams come true.

It was almost three o'clock when they pulled into the Sylvia city limits. It felt like eons since Mitch and Shelley had left for an evening at the movies, and in one sense, he felt deflated that the whole trip to the lake had turned into nothing. And yet, the peace and . . . *resolve* he'd felt lying on that couch in the cabin this morning had stayed with him all the miles back to home.

Mitch passed by his own driveway and turned into Shelley's.

"You don't have to do that," she protested. "I think I can walk the thirty feet to my house."

But he ignored her and pulled the car up as close to her front door as he could.

"It's not like I have luggage to carry or anything." She fluffed her ponytail and gave him a wry smile.

He reciprocated, appreciating her upbeat mood. She opened the car door, but he put the Saturn in Park, causing her to pause and look expectantly at him.

"Thanks again for coming with me, Shelley. I know I didn't leave you much choice, but—" He chose his words carefully, still unsure of—*everything.* "It was good to have a friend along. I mean that."

"I'm glad I could be there. I'm . . . sorry things didn't turn out differently, Mitch."

He sensed the layers of meaning in her apology, but now wasn't the time to unravel them. "I want to ask you—" His sigh came out heavier than he intended. "The things you said . . . Please don't do anything rash, Shelley. I know you said those things thinking we might be bringing Jill home with us. But—I don't want you to feel like you made promises to me that you have to keep. I think we were doing okay before this all happened. Weren't we?"

"I don't know, Mitch. Sometimes I think we were, and other times . . ." She shrugged and worried the hem of her shirt.

"Can I just ask you—for now—don't let me come home someday and find a Realtor's sign in your front yard . . . without talking to me first. Okay?"

She shot him an are-you-kidding-me? look. "Oh, my goodness. *Look* who's talking!" But she was laughing too.

He grinned, his spirits already buoyed.

The door to Shelley's house flew open and Audrey jogged down the walk.

"I'll let you go," he said. "Thanks again."

"Take care, Mitch. Thanks for the curbside service."

She climbed from the car and greeted her daughter with a warm hug.

He watched them for a moment, feeling warmed. And yet feeling the deep ache of loneliness at the same time.

"Dad? Is that you?"

Mitch had been home all of ten minutes when TP's ears perked and he trotted out to the kitchen. The back door slammed and Mitch heard Katie baby-talking the dog and tossing her shoes and bag on the mudroom floor.

"In here, Katiebug." Mitch inhaled, steeling himself to answer Katie's questions about what had happened at the lake.

He met her in the kitchen and gave her a hug that filled in a nice corner of the pocket of loneliness he'd felt watching Shelley hug Audrey earlier.

"So what was the deal at the lake?" Her demeanor told him she suspected more than he'd told her.

"Have you talked to Evan?"

"No. What happened?"

"Your brother got the bright idea to take some of his friends down to the lake for the weekend without checking it out with me."

Katie gave a little gasp. "Are you kidding me? Oh, man, his butt is *so* grounded."

He rolled his eyes. "That it is. And for future reference . . ." He pulled Evan's keys to the cabin from his pocket. "These are mine now, and you can just turn yours in, too, if you have any idea of a similar trip in your future."

"You think I'm stupid?"

He reached to give her another hug. "No, I don't. I think you are my very bright and obedient fair-haired child."

"I bet you say that to all your daughters."

"As a matter of fact, I do."

"So you went down there just to get his keys?"

"No. We went down there because . . . there was someone staying in the cabin when Evan got there. Evan thought—" He swallowed hard. "He thought it might be Mom."

"What? What do you mean?" She looked stricken.

"There were some women's clothes and some of Mom's toiletries had been used." He hesitated, debating whether to tell her about Becky Marley. Katie and Becky had played together at the lake when they were little girls. But if he didn't tell her, Evan no doubt would. He leveled a stern I-mean-it look at her. "Don't say anything to anyone until we know for sure, but it looks like it might have been Becky Marley."

He told her about Wayne's discovery.

"Are you kidding?" Katie responded the same way she did when her friends shared a morsel of juicy gossip. But then she sobered and looked him in the eye. "They're not going to find her, are they, Dad? They're not going to find Mom."

She said it so matter-of-factly, it broke his heart.

"I don't know, honey. I just don't know."

"I don't want to not have faith that God could bring her back. But . . . I'm starting to think maybe He's—not going to. I'm starting to think maybe Mom's in Heaven." Her voice broke and she stood looking at him with those beautiful, so-like-Jill's blue eyes brimming.

Mitch scrubbed at the two-day beard he was sporting. If she was looking for him to build her faith back up, to tell her to hold out hope, and keep believing, he had nothing to offer.

But maybe, like him, she needed someone to give her permission to *abandon* hope. He took the plunge. "I'm starting to think the same thing, honey. I think . . . maybe we have to just leave it in God's hands now." He put an arm around her and squeezed her close. "And trust that He knows what He's doing, even when we can't begin to imagine how any of this could be part of God's plan."

Oh, Lord, be with this precious girl. And God . . . Help me to feel the conviction of my own words.

36

Tuesday, June 28

The phone was ringing when Mitch walked in the back door from work.

"I've got it!" Katie hollered from the family room where she was watching some reality show. Mitch fed TP and went to put his briefcase in the den.

A few seconds later Katie appeared in his doorway with the handset to the landline phone. "It's for you, Dad." Something about her expression gave him pause.

In the week and a half since he'd returned from the cabin, he and Katie had bonded—maybe because a door had been opened for them to talk more openly about Jill. He was sure their mutual concern about Evan was a factor too.

He and Shelley, by mutual agreement, had only seen each other briefly since they'd come home from the lake. They'd agreed to spend some time apart, reflecting and praying, asking God for direction in their lives before they talked again.

He hoped these days had been as full of peace for her as they had for him.

Katie handed him the phone with a shrug that said she didn't know who it was.

He answered and Katie gave a little wave and went back down the hall.

"Is this . . . Mitchell Brannon?" The female voice seemed hesitant.

"Yes, it is." The caller ID showed a name he wasn't familiar with. *Vernon Pritchell.* He'd become very cautious about answering the phone since getting some strange calls after Jill's story had hit the news. In those early days—especially after Katie had been on the receiving end of some weirdo's call—he'd considered changing his phone number. But Detective Simonides had advised against it on the chance that Jill might try to call home.

Thankfully, those calls had subsided significantly in recent months. Still, he was on his guard. "Who's calling, please?"

"My name is Marjorie Pritchell."

He checked the Caller ID again. The number had a Missouri prefix.

"This might sound a little strange, but I came across something today that I thought you would want to know about. I suppose I should be sure I have the right person first . . ." She cleared her throat. "This *is* the Mitchell Brannon who is married to Jill Brannon—that woman who went missing in September of last year?"

His guard edged up several notches. "Yes . . .

that's right. What's this about?" Mitch wasn't about to give out any information until he knew what she wanted.

"Well, I hope your wife has been found and everything is okay . . ."

His better judgment said to be suspicious, but his curiosity won over good judgment. "No, unfortunately, Jill has never been found."

"Oh, gracious! I'm so sorry to hear that. Well, I hope this isn't upsetting for you, but I was wrapping some glassware here in the shop this afternoon . . . I run Pritchell Antiques southeast of Camford. Are you familiar with us? You're from Sylvia, right? That's what the paper said."

He managed to slip a quick "Yes" in between her ramblings. Camford was a good three-hour drive.

"I'm sorry." Nervous laughter filled the line. "I have a dealer there in Sylvia that I get some of my antiques from. And I really will get to my point. I just wanted to be sure I had the right person before I launched into this whole story."

"Yes. I'm Jill's husband. Now what is this about, please?"

"You see, I was wrapping some glassware, and came across a picture of your wife in one of the old newspapers I was using for wrapping."

He had no idea what wrapping glassware had to do with Jill, but the woman certainly had his attention. "I'm sorry, I don't understand . . ."

"The photograph was with the article in the

paper . . . about her having gone missing. I looked online and tried to find anything about her ever being found, but when I didn't, I thought I should let you know."

"About finding her picture?" What was she getting at? Simonides had told him about several calls from psychics and mediums who claimed they could lead police to Jill. According to the detective that sort of "lead" came with the territory. He'd said they took every call seriously until they had reason to do otherwise. "Are you saying you have some information about Jill?" This woman didn't sound like a nut case, but he was still cautious.

She gave a muffled gasp. "Oh, dear . . . so you really haven't found her yet?"

"No, ma'am, we haven't."

"The thing is, I *saw* her the day she disappeared."

"You saw her? Where? Did you contact the police?" It was an effort to keep his voice steady. There was no steadying his heart.

"No. Like I said, I *just* now came across this today as I was wrapping some crystal to mail out some eBay purchases."

"Yes," he said. It took everything in him not to shout "Get to the point, lady!" into the phone. *What was this about?*

"Well," she said, "it's a wonder I even happened to see this article. It was in one of the Sunday papers."

"But how do you know you saw her? *Where* did you see her?"

"That's just it. I thought to myself, 'Where have I seen that woman before?' And of course, then I remembered it was right here at the store. She came in that day. I don't remember for sure what time it was, but I'm guessing it would have been afternoon because I worked in the stockroom most of that morning, so I wouldn't have seen her if she came in before two o'clock or so."

"You're sure . . . it was her?"

"Oh, I'm positive."

"And you're sure about the day she was there?" It seemed odd that the woman would recall so many details about something that had happened ten months ago.

"I didn't make the connection at first, but then when I remembered what she bought, I went looking for the receipt. It wasn't my booth she bought it from, but I keep receipts for all my dealers. Well! I checked the receipts for that day and that jogged my memory. I'm *certain* it was her. I can show you the receipts if you like."

"How late do you stay open today?"

"We close in half an hour."

He looked at his watch. "I don't think I could be there before eight."

"If you can come tonight, I'll be glad to meet you at the store."

37

Pulling into a parking space in front of Pritchell's Antiques, Mitch tried to steady his shaking hands. "We were so close, Jill," he whispered. "So close."

He and Shelley had been not two miles from this spot on one of their search trips last winter when they'd traveled the state talking to teachers. *Two miles.* And yet, if they'd tried to stop at every store, every school, every gas station, every park along the way, they would *still* be working their way back from Kansas City.

In some ways, it comforted him to realize that they'd taken on an exhausting, impossible task in trying to search for Jill. Still, they'd tried so hard. . . .

He took a deep breath and blew it out, then climbed out of the car. The CLOSED sign was hanging inside the door, but Mitch tried the latch and the door swung open to the musty, not unpleasant smell of ancient dust and mold and lemon polish.

An attractive woman with snow white hair looked up when they came in. She came out from behind the counter to greet them. "I'm Marjorie Pritchell. You must be Mr. Brannon."

He shook her hand. "Thank you for agreeing to meet me so late."

She greeted him warmly and went back behind a checkout counter that held an ornate antique cash register. "Let me show you what I have here." Smudged reading glasses hung from a chain around her neck and she slipped them on her nose before pressing a key on the register. The drawer popped open with a *ding*.

"The thing is, my husband and I left for Venice—a four a.m. flight—on the Saturday of Labor Day weekend." She launched into a more detailed version of the story she'd told Mitch on the phone. "But we didn't stop our subscription to the *Missourian* while we were gone. They like to read it here in the shop—and of course, it makes such good packing material, don't you know? So we just had the woman who manages the shop for us put the newspapers in the bin. Anyway, wouldn't you know, I came across that picture and one thing led to another and here you are!"

With manicured fingertips, she slipped a small stack of papers from under the cash tray and laid them on the counter. "Here's the receipt. I gave your wife the carbon copy." She handed it to him.

The receipt, handwritten in a feminine cursive, was for an "ornate 4-inch magnifying glass." It had cost eighteen dollars.

"Your wife was a delightful woman. We had a lovely visit." She pointed to the receipt. "I'm partial to magnifying glasses too. This was a nice piece. I remember because I'd considered buying it from my dealer. To be honest, I was a little hesitant to let it go. But your wife seemed so excited about finding it. And when she said it was for a friend who collected them, I was glad it was going to someone who would enjoy and appreciate it."

For a friend. Shelley. Jill had bought it for Shelley. He listened in awe, picturing it all, feeling like Jill had given him a gift as well—this glimpse into what may have been her final hours.

Mrs. Pritchell slipped her glasses on and looked at the receipt again. "You can see that she paid cash for the item, so there wasn't a name on the receipt, but I keep a sign-up sheet here on the counter"—she tapped a clipboard lying near the cash register—"for people who want to get my newsletter and information about special sales. So I looked through my old mailing lists. When I saw that story in the newspaper, I was just sure it had to be the same woman. And sure enough, she was on the list."

She pulled a folded sheet of paper from the pile the receipt had been in. "See there? Jill Brannon, Sylvia, Missouri. When I looked at the date the paper said she went missing, and then when I realized it was the same time we were away in Italy, I realized that's why I'd never seen it on the news. I asked the gals that work for me about

370

it, and they all remembered seeing the story on the news, but of course they didn't remember her coming in to the shop."

"Thank you so much for contacting me." He found it difficult to speak. "May I have these receipts and the list? Or at least copies of them?" The newsletter sign-up was in Jill's handwriting. He felt like he was holding a precious document.

"I've already made copies for myself. You may keep those. I thought you might like to have them."

"Thank you. This is the first real lead we've had." He turned to the proprietor, suddenly aware of the profound evidence he held in his hands. "I need to make some phone calls."

She nodded. Mitch thanked her again, and took a business card from the counter.

Back in the car, he sat for a long minute, stunned, barely able to imagine what the surreal discoveries of these past few days might have launched.

He quickly found his voice when Detective Cody Fredriks answered his phone.

Wednesday, June 29

Not only did Detective Fredriks show up at Pritchell Antiques the following day, but Marcus Simonides was with him, along with a small retinue of law enforcement officers and investigators. The case had been reopened and a new search ordered along the main routes between the antique store and Sylvia. It was still a broad area, with dozens of county roads and smaller rural capillaries to search, but the evidence that Jill had made it as far as Pritchell's had greatly reduced the square miles to be searched.

And it lent new strength to Greg Hamaker's alibi too. "If Jill made it that far," Simonides said, "if she was at that antique shop—alive and well—when the owner says she was, there's no way Hamaker could have been involved."

The antique store owner's discovery seemed to have lit a new fire under the Highway Patrol's Missing Persons Unit, and now, with the search area tightened, the possibilities for what could have happened to Jill were narrowed.

Simonides warned Mitch that the area was rife with washed-out county roads, meth labs, large deer populations—and at the height of summer, the wooded landscape was overgrown. The going would be slow.

Mitch and Shelley both took Thursday off from work—it was a wonder they both still had their jobs—and made the three-hour drive again to meet the detectives at the antique store.

It was around ten when they arrived and the searchers had already been at work for an hour.

Mitch apologized to Mrs. Pritchell for turning her shop into search headquarters. But the proprietor had been gracious and helpful, and even brought cookies and iced tea for the small search team—mostly local law enforcement—that had gathered.

Mitch and Shelley spent the day driving the web of county roads, trying to stay one step behind the searchers and thus out of their way, yet still available to help if they were needed. After the team had come in from a first—unsuccessful—day of combing the back roads, Simonides pulled Mitch aside. "I want to be frank with you . . ."

Mitch saved him the burden of having to speak the words. "You're not expecting to find her alive. I understand."

"Just so you don't hold out unrealistic hope."

Given how everything had happened, it was difficult *not* to hold out "unrealistic hope." And yet, it struck Mitch—and was painful to realize —that at this point any kind of closure, any- thing that would assure him that Jill had not suffered, any news that would offer his children and Jill's parents comfort, would be a small hope fulfilled.

He hadn't yet informed Miriam and Bert about the call from the antique store, or about the renewed search. Simonides assured him they wouldn't release information to the news media until they'd had a chance to investigate, and Mitch hadn't wanted to raise false hopes—

especially if Simonides was expecting, at best, to recover a body.

The detective put a hand briefly on Mitch's arm and a wave of appreciation for the difficult job this man did washed over him. "You and Ms. Austin may as well go on back to work. No sense waiting around."

Mitch's apprehension must have shown in his expression because Simonides gripped his shoulder in a fatherly fashion. "Don't worry, we'll let you know the minute we find anything at all. I know where to find you if we need you."

JULY

38

Saturday, July 2

Shelley sprayed water from the garden hose over a pot of begonias that had seen better days. Eight a.m. and already the thermometer was headed toward triple digits. The summer heat had taken its toll on the flowerpots on her front porch—and on her—but she was determined to revive the flowers. With everything else that had happened, it was too depressing to watch them wither away.

Through the screen door, she heard the faint *ting ting* of a text coming through on her cell phone. The special tone she'd set for Audrey. She turned off the water and hurried inside, drying her hands on the back of her shorts as she went.

Audrey had driven down to Springfield for the weekend to spend a weekend with her roommates. Sliding the arrow to power on her phone, Shelley frowned. She hoped Audrey hadn't had car trouble. Her old beater had been acting up.

Can u call when u have time to talk?

That sounded like an emergency to a mom. And not a car emergency. Trying not to imagine the worst, she dialed the number and Audrey answered on the first ring.

"Hey, sweetie." She tried to keep her voice casual. "Is everything okay?"

Silence on Audrey's end, and then sniffles.

"Honey? What's wrong?"

"I think . . . it's over with Evan. For good."

"Over?"

"We just talked for an hour and—I think we broke up."

"You think?"

"No . . . we did. We decided . . . we make better friends than boyfriend and girlfriend."

"Are you okay with that?" She couldn't read her daughter's voice, but it wasn't like her to be so calm under such circumstances.

Audrey sighed into the phone. "I really am. I mean, I'm kind of sad, I guess." Her voice broke, but when she spoke again, she sounded steady and strong. "Evan's a great guy. He really is. But I don't think he's anywhere near ready to settle down."

"Guys usually take longer to get there than girls."

"Yeah, I know . . ."

"And he's been preoccupied with everything happening with his mom."

"I know. But . . . I think it's more than that. We just weren't—quite right together. When I meet the right guy, I think I'll know it. Won't I? At least I hope so. I don't think I'll be as uncertain of things as I always have been with Evan. From Day One."

"I think that's very wise coming from some-body who, just yesterday, was a little freckle-faced girl in pigtails."

Audrey laughed that patronizing daughter's laugh, but then her tone turned serious. "Thanks, Mom. I'm glad I can talk to you about stuff like this."

"Me, too, honey." *Don't let me cry, Lord . . . please don't let me cry.*

Audrey asked her about how work was going, and they talked and laughed for another twenty minutes. And when Shelley hung up the phone —after she'd whispered a prayer of thanks for the news about Evan—it struck her that Audrey was slowly growing from daughter into friend.

Thoughts of Jill made the tears come. She missed her friend so desperately. Ever since Mitch had told her about the call from the antique store where Jill had stopped on her way home that fateful day, she'd missed Jill as though her disappearance were fresh.

How she longed for someone who would let her pour out all her confused thoughts and emotions, someone who could be her sounding board and help her see things more clearly, the way Jill always had. Of course she could never talk to Jill about the things that troubled her heart in recent days.

Did she dare share these things with her daughter? Could Audrey understand how Shelley had grown to love Mitch more deeply every day? That she still longed for Mitch—someday—to be more than a friend?

No. That wasn't something she could explain to herself, let alone her daughter. She couldn't burden Audrey with that part of her life. Not yet. Maybe not ever. Even the best of friends had to grow into trust before such tender confidences were shared. And no matter how much Audrey might want her to be happy, the childhood romance she and Evan had shared couldn't help but complicate Audrey's opinions about such a revelation.

No, for now anyway, Shelley's feelings for Mitch would remain something she explored quietly in the privacy of her own heart.

Still, having her daughter become her friend was a lovely transition.

And an answer to prayer. The thought startled her. And yet, how true it was. It was not so long ago that she'd begun to ask God to put someone in her life to fill the empty place Jill's loss had created in her life. *Send me a friend, Lord. Just one friend.* How like Him to fill that need with the daughter who'd been there all along—and who, God willing, would always be there—but only needed to grow into the role of friend.

She went back out to finish watering and had just turned on the spigot when she heard a car coming into their quiet cul-de-sac. She glanced up to see a Highway Patrol vehicle roll slowly up the street. It turned onto the Brannons' driveway next door, and two officers in full dress uniform stepped out of the car and walked to Mitch's front door, their heads bowed.

She knew he was home and she watched as the door opened and the officers disappeared inside his house.

Trembling, she turned off the water, and stood like a statue in the shadows of the porch's eaves, the blood pounding in her ears. *Something had happened.*

It had been three days since Mitch received the call from the antique store and the searchers had found nothing new. Still, the fact that Jill had been at that shop on the day she disappeared was the evidence they'd craved so desperately from the beginning.

But it had come so late. So very late. Probably too late.

Mitch had gone with the searchers over the weekend and had kept her updated on their efforts over the last few days. But hopes were flagging. Not that any of them dared to hope too hard after all this time. Mitch told her that Simonides had warned him they didn't expect to find Jill alive.

She didn't think anyone really expected that any more, and yet, now that everything had been bumped up to the front burner again, none of them could help but have their hopes on the front burner, too. Shelley struggled to be grateful for this new lead. There was a time when she wouldn't have wanted to examine her reasons for feeling that way. But she wasn't afraid to do so now.

She loved Mitch, and it tore her up to see him hurting. Whether she would ever have the right to express her love for him didn't matter so much anymore. She only wanted him to be happy, to be able to move on with his life. She wasn't sure how much longer he could be ripped from hope to despair and back again—and not be changed by the torture of that tug-of-war.

She must have stood on the porch for twenty minutes, watching his house, praying for Mitch. She prayed desperately that God would give him strength for whatever news the officers had brought. That he would finally have closure on this tragic chapter of his life. That he would be strong for Evan and Katie.

Everything in her wanted to go over there and be with him. But something stopped her. This wasn't for her to bear. Not now. Some grief had to be carried in private.

She finally went inside and when she checked the driveway ten minute later, the patrol car was gone. "Oh, Lord," she whispered. "Be with him. Help him. Let him feel Your presence like he's never felt it before."

An urgency compelled her to her knees and she knelt in front of the sofa, head in her hands, praying for mercy for the man she loved. Praying, until there were no words left and she could only weep.

An hour later, the doorbell rang. Shelley hurried to answer it, praying again for the right words.

Mitch stood there looking haggard and distraught, wearing an odd half smile that crumbled the moment he spoke her name. "Shelley . . ."

"Oh, Mitch. What's happened? What is it?" She opened the door and beckoned him in.

"They found her, Shelley. They finally found her."

She led the way to the family room, to the sofa she'd just bathed in tears and prayers. He sat down, staring into the empty fireplace. For a full minute, he didn't speak. *Couldn't* speak, she suspected. She wanted so badly to put her arms around him, but she didn't dare, not knowing yet what "they found her" even meant.

He squinched his eyes shut and the words came—agonizing, halting. But they came. "They found her car in a ravine. Buried under water. She . . . she was still inside."

She couldn't help the gasp that escaped her throat. "Oh, Mitch. Oh, dear God. I'm so sorry." She began to weep. Her friend was really gone. "When?" she whispered.

Mitch reached for her hand. "They think probably that same day. The windshield was broken and they found . . . deer antlers broken off . . . caught in the steering wheel. Oh, Jill . . ." He released a sob and struggled for composure. "She—She must have swerved trying not to hit the deer. They said the car had to have been airborne for twenty feet to land in that ravine the way it did."

Oh, Jill. Jill . . .

"The car has been underwater, hidden by the underbrush, all this time. Two hours from home. So close, Shelley. She was almost home."

Morbid thoughts bombarded her. Her friend out there all this time. Eerie images of tree branches and deer antlers intertwined in her mind. A million questions that had no answers on this side of heaven.

"She was flesh of my flesh, bone of my bones. How could I not have known—in my heart"—he placed his palm over his chest—"that she was in trouble? That she was . . . gone? How could I not have known?"

"But don't you see, Mitch . . ." The words she'd prayed for came then. "She wasn't in trouble. At least not for long. All this time, Mitch, we've imagined the worst. And Jill wasn't lost at all. Or lonely or suffering. She was *home*. All along, she was already home."

By the glow that lit his eyes, she knew they were exactly the right words. And not her words at all.

He nodded. "They said she probably died . . . almost instantly."

Now Shelley was the one who could barely speak. "She's in heaven. God had His hand on her all along. She's probably been praying for *us!*" A strange excitement welled up in her. "Oh, Mitch! Almost before Jill could even realize that she was leaving this earth, she was being ushered into heaven. Straight into Jesus's arms."

He wept then. And she took him in her arms and held him. Not as the woman who loved him —though she did. *Oh, how she did.* But as a friend—the friend of the woman he loved. The woman he'd lost.

"How can I tell Katie . . . and Evan? How can I tell them she's gone?"

"They know, Mitch. I think in their hearts, they know. And just like it is for you, the worst is not knowing for sure. Your kids are strong. They'll get through it. You'll all get through it. It's over now. It's over . . ."

He nodded against her shoulder and she felt the tension go out of him.

It's over . . .

AUGUST

39

Saturday, August 27

A few of the slides were blurry and the music a little tinny-sounding, but it didn't matter to anyone in the room. A week short of the first anniversary of her death, the life of Jill Evangeline Brannon was being celebrated by those who loved her most.

Shelley laughed softly along with the others at some of the photos Jill's kids had chosen for the slide show. As the images scrolled by on the screen overhead—marshmallow-smeared faces at the cabin, two-year-old Evan spraying the garden hose at a bathing-suit clad Jill, Mitch and Jill in silly party hats and sillier Year 2000 eyeglasses celebrating the turn of the millennium —memories overwhelmed Shelley. And she wept openly at a photo of her and Jill, arm in arm at one of their impromptu backyard picnics a couple years ago. Warm, tender memories. Truly things to celebrate.

Tears flowed again seeing Katie's shoulders shake as photos of a much younger Jill flashed on the screen, pudgy baby Katie in arms, and more recently Jill and Katie, arm in arm at Katie's high school graduation.

A family's life reduced to a ten-minute slide show always seemed an apt and sobering metaphor for eternity. This life, in all its beauty and pain, was over in a flash, whether you lived to be forty-four or ninety-four.

Two weeks ago, Jill's remains had been buried in the church cemetery of her childhood home in southwest Missouri. And they had a date to inscribe on a grave marker. Given the alternative, it was a gift. Given the media circus they'd endured over the past year, Mitch had wanted to let that brief, private graveside service be enough. But Evan and Katie insisted on a memorial service. And as difficult as this day was, Shelley could already see what a healing time it had been for them all, even just in planning the program and putting together photos for the slide show.

It was a small, private event, with only family members and a few close friends from church present, plus Mitch's coworkers and Jill's friends and fellow teachers. Jill's father was in nursing care now, and hadn't been well enough to make the trip, but Shelley had enjoyed some wonderful talks with Jill's mom over the three days Miriam had been staying with Mitch and the kids. Jill had been so like her mother. It was a privilege to get the chance to tell Miriam so.

The music stilled and an expectant hush came over the sanctuary. Shelley glanced over at Mitch and saw him rise from his place and climb the shallow steps to the podium.

Give him strength, Lord.

Mitch breathed in a prayer and steadied himself on the podium.

He'd dreaded this moment, afraid he would fall apart in front of the people he cared about most. To his surprise, he felt strong—and privileged to have this time to honor Jill, to remember her life.

He looked out over the sanctuary, overwhelmed by the blessing of friends. He found Shelley—head bowed, lips moving—and knew she was praying for him. Mitch had asked her to sit with the family today, but she and Audrey had chosen seats a little apart, at the end of an aisle behind Jill's mother. And that seemed just right. Yet another thing he loved about Shelley Austin.

He looked down at the front row where his children sat. Katie gave him a watery smile. But she sat with her back straight, her eyes bright. She fingered the silver band she wore on her right hand—Jill's wedding ring. She would always be his little girl, his Katiebug, but she was turning into a lovely, gracious young woman and he could scarcely contain his pride in her.

Evan sat beside Katie, stone-faced. But Mitch liked the way he propped an arm on the pew behind his sister, protecting her, ready to offer a big-brother hug if she needed one. Evan would be all right. He would find his way. Only he might keep Mitch on his knees for a while first.

But he was learning that on his knees was a good place to be.

What a relief that they could finally erase from reality the nightmarish fears for Jill's well-being that they'd carried with them for all these months.

Mitch shuddered. Yes, there were new images in his mind, horrific ones, given how long it had taken them to find Jill. Simonides had gently recommended that Mitch not view her remains. The car was undeniably Jill's, and dental records positively identified the remains. He didn't need more proof than that.

But there was deep peace in knowing that on her final day on this earth, Jill had lectured an old boyfriend about what it took to have a happy marriage—a subject she knew well. She had called her husband to say she was on her way home and she couldn't wait to tell him about her week. And she had traveled back roads toward home and stopped at an antique store to buy a gift for her best friend. Had Jill made it home to Sylvia, she might have called it an *interesting* day—her highest compliment for any day. Given her new, eternal perspective, Mitch thought she might have even declared it a perfect day.

He was overwhelmed with gratitude for answers to his questions—answers he could live with. Or would learn to. Though none of them would ever understand why this tragedy had touched their lives, why God hadn't allowed them to find her sooner, the facts they did have were ones he—and his children—could find closure in.

He slipped his notes from his pocket and read the brief eulogy from the program. Then he put his notes aside and, speaking from the depths of his heart, he honored this woman he'd loved and gave thanks for the years God had given him with her.

"It's important for us to remember Jill's life," he said, after he'd spoken for fifteen minutes, "but I want us to also consider Jill's death. As a very dear friend of Jill's reminded my family"— he looked out over the sanctuary and caught Shelley's eye—"all those hours . . . All the days and weeks and months that we were sick with worry about Jill, searching for her, praying for her . . . She was—already home." His voice broke. He swallowed hard and took a long moment to regain his composure. "She was *home* in the most wonderful sense of the word possible. Already with Jesus—probably praying for *us,* if I know Jill. I don't expect to ever understand—on this side of heaven anyway—why we had to suffer through all those long months. Why we had to worry and wonder. Why God allowed this to happen to Jill. Why we had to *wait.*"

He looked up and found Shelley's eyes again, and what passed between them in that instant was so subtle he was sure no one else even noticed. And yet it was so profound it almost captured his breath.

They'd made it. They'd done the right thing. Yes, they'd slipped—he'd slipped, and almost fallen. But ultimately they'd done the right thing. They'd obeyed. They'd honored the vows he had spoken to Jill before God. They'd honored Jill and Shelley's friendship. And they'd discovered a friendship of their own that had not only sustained them both through the most difficult test of their lives, but a friendship that would carry them into the next season of their lives. *Jill would have been pleased.*

The thought made him smile. And he knew it was true. That infernal lump came back to his throat. All this grief and joy mixed together so thoroughly it was hard to sort it out, hard to tell one from the other. . . .

OCTOBER

Epilogue

It was jacket weather again—Shelley's favorite time of year—and though Mitch had instructed her to dress casually and wear comfortable shoes, she considered this their first official date, and she'd dressed up her favorite khaki jacket with an Audrey-approved scarf and tiny earrings.

But he wouldn't tell her where they were going. "We'll be doing a lot of walking" was all he'd said. And had they ever. All over Sylvia's charming streets, and in some of the most glorious weather God had every created. They'd had a wonderful day, growing in the new freedom their friendship now enjoyed.

But she was curious whether—suspected even —he had something else up his sleeve. At times, he'd seemed like he was weighing his words carefully, at others, even a little preoccupied.

They'd gotten coffees downtown and walked the ten blocks to her favorite park on the north side of town. Mitch led her across the playground toward an empty park bench. "Let's go sit for a little while."

They settled in a sunny spot, a canopy of autumn leaves shimmering overhead, and a view across the street into a neighborhood of

Victorian houses with white picket fences and porches full of mums and pumpkins and cats sunning themselves.

The minute she was settled on the bench, Mitch angled his body toward her, wearing an expression she couldn't interpret. "I have something to give you," he said.

For one breathtaking moment she was afraid he was going to drop to one knee and propose. That was a day she felt certain was coming, and one she looked forward to with joy—but it was too soon.

He must have read her mind, as he seemed wont to do. "Don't worry," he said. "It's not that." He winked and gave her that smile she loved more with every passing day. "Not today any-way." The spark his eyes held was that of a man she hadn't seen in a long time—the man he'd been before everything that had happened with Jill. She'd almost forgotten this laughing, jubilant side of him. How she'd loved it.

And now she had the right to love it in a whole new way. "You're being awfully mysterious," she said. "So, what are you giving me, besides a lovely day?"

"Two things, actually. But they both come with warnings. Oh, and . . ." He dug in the pocket of his jacket and produced a packet of tissues. "I brought these, just in case."

"Oh, please don't make me cry," she said,

warming to the playful mood he'd set. "We were having such a good time."

He reached into his other pocket and pulled out an oddly shaped package wrapped in brown paper. Looking almost smug, he handed it to her.

She laughed and began to undo the mishmash of Scotch tape. "I'm going to guess this did not come from Serendipity."

"What makes you say that?"

"We try to limit our Scotch tape consumption to three rolls per package."

He laughed. "Guilty as charged."

She started to unfold the layers of paper, but he put a hand over hers. "Maybe I should explain before you open this."

She waited, head tilted.

"I got Jill's things back—out of the car."

She nodded, remembering when he'd given Katie Jill's wedding rings.

He touched the brown wrapping paper. "Jill bought this. That day at the antique store. It's . . . in pretty bad shape, but I thought you'd like to have it. She bought it for you."

She finished unwrapping the package and lifted a beautiful silver-handled magnifying glass. "Oh . . . Mitch. Oh!" Tears sprang to her eyes.

She gently placed the gift in her lap and reached for a tissue, but Mitch beat her to it. She took it from him and dabbed at her eyes before picking up the magnifying glass again.

The ornate handle was badly tarnished and the ring around the glass itself had rusted in spots.

"We might be able to take it to someone and have it restored—maybe even replated or—"

"No. No, it's . . . perfect, just the way it is."

"I thought you might say that." He reached to squeeze her hand, looking pleased.

They sat that way, in silence, for a few minutes before Mitch reached into his pocket yet again. Grinning, he handed her a folded sheet of paper.

"What's this?"

"Do you see that house over there? The one with the black shutters on the windows?" He pointed across the street, ducking down to see under the autumn foliage that partially blocked the view.

"Yes? I see it . . ." *What on earth was this man up to?*

He handed her the paper and she unfolded it. It was a Realtor's brochure. She skimmed the brochure, seeing all the usual real estate details, for a house she would have adored living in. And the house pictured at the top of the page was the one across the street.

"What . . . ?"

"Just read." Again, that smug smile.

She laughed. "You did not buy me a house. At least you'd better not have. You haven't even proposed yet."

When he stopped laughing, he lifted the

magnifying glass from her lap. "You're going to need this to read the fine print." He wrapped her hand around the magnifying glass, and moved it to the bottom of the page where a block of tiny print had been added. "Read," he said.

She bent and squinted, trying to make out the words. "This certificate grants the holder permission to—" The tears came again, with a rush of love for this man. ". . . permission to dream . . ." Her voice betrayed her again, and she gave him a sidewise look.

His smile said he couldn't have been more pleased with her soppy reaction.

She read the rest to herself, through a curtain of tears.

This certificate grants the holder permission to dream—about owning a bed-and-breakfast someday (maybe even this one, who knows?), about men who can be trusted for a lifetime (well, except when it comes to dirty socks and taking out the garbage), and about happily-ever-afters. Remit certificate to Mitchell C. Brannon for further information.

Dear Reader,

In *The Face of the Earth*, I explore what it might be like to be that person for whom, suddenly — and forever after—you are defined as the wife of the suicide, the couple whose baby drowned, the parents of the school shooter, or the man whose wife disappeared off the face of the earth.

How can a person ever go on with life after being marked by such disaster? Can God truly redeem and redefine a tragic life? I believe He can, and in fact, I've seen it over and over again in the lives of friends and family who have experienced what most would think is more than their share of tragedy.

This novel also explores what it really means to commit to love someone "till death do us part." How far does God expect us to carry that devotion when the other person is unwilling or unable to give their commitment? The answer, I believe, lies in following God. In listening for His still, small voice leading us through His Word, and by His Holy Spirit. It's not an easy question, but there is peace and joy in knowing we are learning to listen for and heed His voice.

We rarely understand, on this side of heaven, why God allows tragedy in the lives of His children, but we can always trust that He is our Comforter and that above all, He is the Redeemer of lives. God's Word is true when it says in John 16:33, "In this world, you *will* have trouble," but when your life is built around a relationship with Jesus Christ, those troubles are ultimately redemptive, and meaningful.

In Christ there is always hope.

Deborah Raney
July 1, 2012

Discussion Questions

1. In *The Face of the Earth*, Mitch Brannon's wife of more than twenty years disappears, seemingly into thin air. How would losing someone in this manner be a different kind of grief than losing someone to death?

2. Shelley Austin has always been attracted to her best friend's husband, but as a Christian, she's never acted on those emotions. Do you believe it's possible to be close friends with a person you're physically and emotionally attracted to, but who is unavailable to you (or you to them)?

3. Shelley tells Mitch she "knows in her heart" that Jill is dead and not coming back. Would you trust a feeling like that, or would you need proof? Do you tend to think Shelley's "intuition" was from God/the Holy Spirit or do you tend to think it was her own desires coming into play?

4. What about Mitch? Why do you think God had not "released" him from his marriage commitment, even though it seemed there was no hope of them finding Jill after so much time had passed?

5. Mitch had to consider what the marriage vows, "for better or for worse . . . till death do us part" really mean, and how they apply in his situation. Have you ever known someone (or been yourself) in a situation where you weren't sure how to apply your wedding vows? Are there circumstances where "till death do us part" or "for better or for worse" may not apply?

6. Jill Brannon was invited to lunch by an old boyfriend. Her initial reaction was to accept the invitation. Why do you think she had second thoughts? Was there any reason that she shouldn't have met for an innocent lunch with Greg Hamaker? Why do you think she didn't tell Mitch about the lunch invitation?

7. Jill didn't tell her husband about reconnecting with her old boyfriend, but she did tell her best friend, Shelley. Do you confide things in your friends that you don't tell your spouse? Discuss the pros and cons of that. If you were Shelley, what kind of responsibility would you have felt knowing that information? Do you think Shelley waited too long to tell Mitch about Greg Hamaker?

8. How do you feel about Mitch going to see Greg Hamaker when the authorities had

asked him to let them handle the investigation? Would you have done the same thing in his shoes?

9. Did the novel end the way you expected it to? Were you disappointed in the ending? Or satisfied? Discuss happy endings. Does real life ever have happy endings?

10. How do you imagine these two families two years after the close of the novel? What do their lives look like, and how have the tragedy and struggles they've faced shaped their lives for the good? How have they been wounded by the events of the novel, and how might they struggle in the future because of it?

11. How has tragedy shaped your own life for better or worse? Where does God fit into the picture of that "better or worse"?

Author Q&A

1. What inspired you to write *The Face of the Earth*? Was it a struggle to keep the story from becoming too sad?

I knew from the beginning that I didn't want the sadness of the situation to be oppressive. And that was a challenge, especially from the perspective of Jill's children. But in real life, even in the midst of tragedies like this, life goes on, and there is beauty, and even joy, to be found in it. I hope the growing—though decidedly complicated—friendship between Mitch and Shelley, and the loving support of Mitch's children offered relief from the sad parts of the story.

2. What was the most difficult part of writing *The Face of the Earth*?

The research is always the hardest part for me. I always struggle with making the technical aspects of the plot fit with the story that's unfolding in my imagination. I'm blessed with writer friends who are lawyers, detectives, and authorities in the various other areas that came into play in this novel, but because of the specific setting of *The Face of the Earth*, sometimes I just had to quit writing and pick up the phone and call an authority and then hope and pray that what he or she told me didn't derail what I wanted to happen in the story. Most of the time things fit together nicely the way I wanted them to.

3.As a wife and mother, did you find yourself putting yourself in the place of your characters?

I think that's what writers do! One of the qualities that delineates writers from normal people (ha!) is that we have an ability to put ourselves in another person's shoes and vividly imagine what it would be like to be that person. Sometimes it takes us to uncomfortable, or even scary, places. But we can't write with compassion or empathy if we don't crawl into our characters' skins. I empathized with Shelley and Jill, but also with Jill's parents, and with her children— especially Katie. Maybe more than any of the characters, I empathized with Mitch. I'm a very girlie girl, but I often find the heroes of my books trying to take over the story. In truth, I enjoy writing the male point of view more than any other.

4. Mitchell was determined to keep his wedding vows, even when it seemed like Jill's disappearance would never be solved. Why was this so important to him, and to you as a writer?

It seems our society has all but discarded the value of loyalty in marriage. It breaks my heart to see the petty things people allow to destroy their marriages. I believe the wedding vows are sacred and precious, and it's been one of my goals as a writer to portray the kind of marriages I've seen modeled in my family—my parents and grand-parents, who all celebrated fifty-year anniversaries and well-beyond. My husband's grandparents lived to celebrate their 81st wedding anniversary! My own marriage has "toughed out" thirty-eight years now. It hasn't always been a breeze, but it has always been worth fighting for. I want to portray that truth in my novels.

5.Could you see this story ending any other way? Jill's safe return would have made her family happy, but other relationships would have been complicated.

I considered several possible endings (including an all too realistic one where we never find out what happened to Jill) but I knew readers would want to know, and I wanted to give Mitch and his family closure and as close to a happy ending as a book like this can have. After all, as much as I love exploring real-life situations in my novels, we read (and I write) fiction as entertainment and to find hope and a satisfying ending.

6.Would this story be different if the children were younger and still living at home? Why did you decide to have Mitchell and Shelley be empty nesters?

It would have been a very different story if Mitch and Shelley had both had children at home. And perhaps the answers to their questions of "how long must we wait" would have been less complicated if the needs of their children had taken precedence. But I didn't want to make it too easy for Mitch and Shelley. And I wanted their reasons for desiring to have a relationship to be selfish, which made their reasons for doing the right thing, self-sacrificing. Self sacrifice is so rare today. And yet it is the foundation on which our nation was built, and of every successful marriage and family. Self-sacrifice is the foundation of our faith. I'd love to see it come back in style.

7. Shelley and Jill had a close and beautiful friendship before Jill's disappearance. How important are good female friendships to you, and your writing?

I remember reading, early in my marriage, that I couldn't expect my husband to meet all my needs, and that God created women friends to fill in the gaps. I've been blessed with so many wonderful women friends throughout my life. Women of all ages who mentored me, struggled with me, helped me learn to be a good wife and mom, laughed and cried with me . . . I can't imagine my life without the precious friends God has granted me, and thinking of losing even one of those friends brings tears to my eyes.

8.How have your opinions on marriage and faith changed as you've gotten older? Would this story have been different if you were newly married yourself?

Perhaps I don't see many things quite as "black and white" as I did when I was younger. But on the topic of marriage, if anything, I see commitment in marriage as even more priceless and precious the longer I am married. I think as we grow older, we begin to understand "the two shall become one" of the Bible even more profoundly. Which is why Mitch's challenge was so great.

9.Several characters used social media in the novel. Has your writing changed at all to adapt to new technologies?

Definitely! I didn't even realize it until I was rewriting my first novel for reissue ten years after its first release in 1996. I'd thought I was only going to update the medical information and fix some of the writing mistakes I'd made as a first-time author. But what I discovered when I got into the rewrite was that my characters—professional Chicago suburbanites—did not own cell phones or computers! Quite realistic for the early nineties when my story was originally written, but not at all for this twenty-first century. So I ended up adding seven thousand words to my original manuscript and bringing my past characters into the future, which is now their present. (And if that confused you, join the club!) That process made me realize how much technology has changed our daily lives, and how well-connected we are now—sometimes to the chagrin of writers who don't want their characters to be connected in certain scenes!

10. For you, what is the most difficult part of starting a new novel? Is it hard to say good-bye to your characters after you've finished writing?

Starting a new novel is always exciting and fun. I begin by finding photos of my characters, making idea boards and brainstorming scenes. It's five chapters into the actual writing when I realize I have thirty-five or more chapters to go that things get difficult. I always hit a wall just a few chapters in, then once I get a dozen or so chapters down, it starts to feel like "I can do this!" I hit another wall closer to the end when I'm trying to tie everything up in a neat bow. And yes, it's difficult to say good-bye to my characters. I usually cry when it's time to type "the end."

11. How has your writing changed from your first book until now?

I hope I've grown in skill as a writer—learned some tricks that engage my readers more, make the actual writing recede in favor of the story. It's all about the story. I'm not as "flowery" of a writer as I was in the beginning. I've learned that adjectives and adverbs are not necessarily my friends, and that many times less truly is more. More than that, I hope I've grown in my faith and as a person, so that I can bring that depth of wisdom to my writing and endow my characters with some of the wisdom I've gained over the years. At the same time, I can't let all my characters be wise from the beginning. They must have room to learn and grow over the course of the story. And face it: some of my characters are just jerks. ;-) Ultimately, although I write primarily to entertain, I hope the underlying themes of my novels reflect my maturity as a Christian, and my growth as a writer.

About the Author

Deborah Raney dreamed of writing a book since the summer she read all of Laura Ingalls Wilder's Little House books and discovered that a little Kansas farm girl could, indeed, grow up to be a writer. After a happy twenty-year detour as a stay-at-home wife and mom, Deb began her writing career. Her first novel, *A Vow to Cherish*, was awarded a Silver Angel from Excellence in Media and inspired the acclaimed World Wide Pictures film of the same title. Since then she has won the RITA Award, the HOLT Medallion, and the National Readers' Choice Award and is a two-time Christy Award finalist. Deb enjoys speaking and teaching at writers' conferences across the country. She and her husband, Ken Raney, make their home in their native Kansas and love the small-town life that is the setting for many of Deb's novels. The Raneys enjoy gardening, antiquing, art museums, movies, and traveling to visit four grown children and a growing brood of small grandchildren, all of whom live much too far away.

Deborah loves hearing from her readers. To e-mail her or to learn more about her books, please visit www.deborahraney.com or write to Deborah in care of Howard Books, 216 Centerview Dr., Suite 303, Brentwood, TN 37027.

Center Point Large Print
600 Brooks Road / PO Box 1
Thorndike ME 04986-0001 USA

(207) 568-3717

US & Canada:
1 800 929-9108
www.centerpointlargeprint.com